THE YEAR'S BEST

MYSTERY AND SUSPENSE STORIES

1988

Other Books by Edward D. Hoch

The Shattered Raven
The Judges of Hades
The Transvection Machine
The Spy and the Thief
City of Brass
Dear Dead Days (editor)
The Fellowship of the Hand
The Frankenstein Factory
Best Detective Stories of the Year 1976 (editor)
Best Detective Stories of the Year 1977 (editor)
Best Detective Stories of the Year 1978 (editor)
The Thefts of Nick Velvet
The Monkey's Clue and The Stolen Sapphire (juvenile)
Best Detective Stories of the Year 1979 (editor)
Best Detective Stories of the Year 1980 (editor)
Best Detective Stories of the Year 1981 (editor)
All But Impossible! (editor)
The Year's Best Mystery and Suspense Stories 1982 (editor)
The Year's Best Mystery and Suspense Stories 1983 (editor)
The Year's Best Mystery and Suspense Stories 1984 (editor)
The Quests of Simon Ark
Leopold's Way
The Year's Best Mystery and Suspense Stories 1985 (editor)
The Year's Best Mystery and Suspense Stories 1986 (editor)
The Year's Best Mystery and Suspense Stories 1987 (editor)
Great British Detectives (co-editor)
Women Write Murder (co-editor)

THE YEAR'S BEST

MYSTERY AND SUSPENSE STORIES

1988

Edited by Edward D. Hoch

WALKER AND COMPANY
NEW YORK

First published in the United States of America in 1988 by the Walker Publishing Company, Inc.

Published simultaneously in Canada by Thomas Allen & Son Canada, Limited Markham, Ontario

Printed in the United States of America

10 9 8 7 6 5 4 3 2 1

The Library of Congress has cataloged this serial title as follows:

The Year's best mystery & suspense stories.—1982– —
    New York: Walker, 1982–
        v.; 22 cm.
    Annual.
    Editor: 1982–   E.D. Hoch
    Continues: Best detective stories of the year.

    1. Detective and mystery stories, American—
Periodicals.   2. Detective and mystery stories, English—
Periodicals.   I. Hoch, Edward D., 1930–   . II. Title: Year's best
mystery and suspense stories.
PZ1.B446588   83-646567   813'.0872'08—dc19
Library of Congress   [8406]   AACR2   MARC-S
ISBN 0-8027-1050-6

For Dave and Anne Warner

CONTENTS

Acknowledgments

"The Stamp" by Isaac Asimov. Copyright © 1987 by Nightfall, Inc. First published in *Ellery Queen's Mystery Magazine.*

"The Woman in the Wardrobe" by Robert Barnard. Copyright © 1987 by Robert Barnard. First published in *Ellery Queen's Mystery Magazine.*

"Stroke of Genius" by George Baxt. Copyright © 1987 by George Baxt. First published in *Ellery Queen's Mystery Magazine.*

"Final Marks, Final Secrets" by Brendan DuBois. Copyright © 1987 by Brendan DuBois. First published in *Alfred Hitchcock's Mystery Magazine.* Reprinted by permission of International Creative Management, Inc., New York.

"Soft Monkey" by Harlan Ellison. Copyright © 1987 by The Kilimanjaro Corporation. Reprinted by arrangement with, and permission of, the author and the author's agent, Richard Curtis Associates, Inc., New York. All rights reserved.

"King's X" by Brian Garfield. Copyright © 1987 by Brian Garfield. First published in *Murder California Style*, edited by Jon L. Breen & John Ball. New York: St. Martin's Press, 1987.

"Mr. Felix" by Paula Gosling. Copyright © 1986 by Paula Gosling.

"The Au Pair Girl" by Joyce Harrington. Copyright © 1987 by Joyce Harrington.

"Roger, Mr. Whilkie!" by Eric M. Heideman. Copyright © 1987 by Davis Publications, Inc. First published in *Alfred Hitchcock's Mystery Magazine.*

"Exit Line" by Reginald Hill. Copyright © 1979 by Reginald Hill.

1. INTRODUCTION

For both the mystery and mainstream fiction, 1987 was one of the best years ever for short story anthologies. In a year-end survey, *Publishers Weekly* reported that "anthologies are doing rather well these days," and my own count of mystery anthologies shows a total of thirty-eight published in the United States, Britain, and Canada—more than any other year in recent decades.

Anthologies usually are published in relatively small printings with little or no advertising, relying upon mystery bookstores and library sales to return a profit to the publisher. Some might aim for wider sales through publication as paperback originals or as so-called bargain books to be sold through the big chain bookstores. But for the most part the sales figures for an anthology never approach those of the mystery magazines.

The fact that anthologies can often turn a profit with sales of a few thousand copies might help explain why they are doing well and the mystery magazines are in trouble. During 1987 *Espionage* ceased publication entirely, after changing its size and bringing out three issues in a larger format. Published circulation figures showed both *Ellery Queen's Mystery Magazine* and *Alfred Hitchcock's Mystery Magazine* continuing to lose circulation, *EQMM* even more rapidly than *AHMM*.

The New Black Mask, an attempt to combine the regularity of magazine publication with the marketing techniques of a paperbound anthology, was forced to cease publication because of legal problems over use of the *Black Mask* name. It was reborn, phoenixlike, as *A Matter of Crime* and the first two issues showed great promise. However, the publisher's last-minute decision to increase the cover price from $5.95 to $6.95 may have had a negative impact on distribution and sales.

Mystery short stories continue to appear occasionally in

mainstream magazines and even in specialized publications like *The Yacht*. There is evidence too that the recent resurgence of the hardboiled mystery may be more than a passing fad. Semi-professional and fan magazines like *Hardboiled* and *Mystery Scene* are bringing tough, realistic stories to a receptive audience, and it may be more than a coincidence that the last four Edgar awards of the Mystery Writers of America have gone to short stories that could be considered hardboiled, either with or without private eyes.

There is no better evidence of the vigor of the mystery-suspense genre than the fourteen stories that follow. They represent both the classic and the tough. In this respect I'm especially pleased to welcome back two writers more closely associated with science fiction and fantasy. Isaac Asimov and Harlan Ellison both appeared in annual "best mystery" volumes during the 1970s, and now they return with two stories that represent the different directions the mystery has taken since its Golden Age.

As always, my thanks to those who helped in the preparation of this volume, especially Jane Langton, Eleanor Sullivan, John F. Suter, Mary Shura Craig, and my wife, Patricia.

Edward D. Hoch

THE YEAR'S BEST

MYSTERY AND SUSPENSE STORIES

1988

Q. ISAAC ASIMOV

THE STAMP

Isaac Asimov's contributions to the mystery short story are more in the nature of puzzle tales than fully developed detective stories, and for this reason it's been too easy for anthologists like myself to overlook them. It's only when one sees a full collection of Asimov's riddles, as in The Best Mysteries of Isaac Asimov *(Doubleday, 1986), that their sheer cleverness can be fully appreciated. The stories generally fall into one of two series, either the Black Widowers or Griswold, both of which number over fifty stories at this point. In the Griswold tale that follows, our sleuth comes up with a solution that recalls the very best of the Ellery Queen short-shorts.*

I said, rather jubilantly, "I've thought up a story."

To which Baranov at once said with fine skepticism, "I bet it stinks."

"Not at all," I said. "It's the kind *he* tells. Griswold." And I jerked my thumb in the direction of the old man, whose head was resting quietly against one of the tall wings of his armchair while one hand rested quietly, with its whiskey and soda, on the chair-arm on the other side. He was snoring very softly.

Jennings said suspiciously, "What's it about?"

"Well, it's like this. A rich man dies and leaves a distant relative something valuable—"

"What something valuable?" demanded Jennings.

"Who knows? That's unimportant. The point is that he hid it in a room filled with all sorts of bric-a-brac. Whatever it is is very small in addition to being very valuable, and the distant relative searches and searches for it and comes up with nothing. Absolutely nothing. He goes to this friend of his who, let us say, is someone like Griswold and tells him the story. At once the friend says, 'Why, it must be in such-and-such a place,' and, of course, it is."

1

Baranov said, "And where is the place?"

"For goodness sake," I said, "*I* don't know. I still have to fill in some of the details."

"Like what the object is and where it is," said Jennings. "You call that a story?"

Griswold stirred suddenly. "*I* call it a story"—he took a small sip of his drink and his icy blue eyes glared malevolently at me—"because it happened to me."

"What happened to you?" I said.

"That story you told. Precisely."

"You mean you're going to make up a story that will fit precisely my outline."

"I don't know about 'make up,' but it fits your outline."

"I dare you to tell me such a story," I said indignantly.

Since you express such enthusiasm [said Griswold] and are so anxious to hear it, I will gladly oblige you.

The central character in the tale I'm about to relate was Charles Plaggard, a prolific author of whom, doubtless, none of you have heard. For one thing, he wrote westerns and romances under pseudonyms, male for the westerns, female for the romances. And even if he had used his own name, none of you would have known him, since neither you nor anyone else of even the slightest pretensions to taste in literature would ever read him. However, that left a huge majority that lacked even those slightest pretensions and he became quite well off. Add to that some shrewd speculative investments that did well and you might say he even became quite rich.

As sometimes happens, however, worldly success did not satisfy Charles Plaggard. What he wanted was recognition. He wanted to be considered a great writer and a luminary of literature, and this he simply never got. He therefore planned to force himself, more or less, upon the world. In his will, he directed that the house he had lived in for three decades was to be converted into the "Charles Plaggard Literary Museum."

The five rooms that he occupied—it was a small but well appointed house—were to be kept in perpetuity in the condition in which they were left at his death, barring a certain minimum amount of maintenance in the way of cleaning and straightening up. A very generous salary was allowed for two people to maintain the house in this fashion and to keep it in service as a museum. Plaggard's work study was to be open to the public at fixed hours and Plaggard even dictated the exact words that were to be used to point out the various sights. Very laudatory words they were too.

All the books he had written were on the shelves in that study, and in every English-language edition, hard-covered and soft. They were in chronological order and all were first printings, for what that was worth.

There were also on display some of the manuscripts to his later books, though he had produced nothing at all in his final five years, having grown so absent-minded as to leave the suspicion he was approaching senility. There was also his old typewriter, his reference books, his stationery, a sheaf of correspondence—in short, all the paraphernalia one would think of.

All was done exactly as he directed. He had no wife, no family, no close relatives to contest the will, and, except for a few minor bequests to some servants and to a few local causes he was interested in, every bit of his estate went into this museum. It was not a successful museum; there were very few visitors. Still, the plan made him happy in his last years, and now, in the execution, it left each of the two overseers with a good salary and little to do. So it seemed an excellent thing all around.

However, Charles Plaggard had a second cousin once removed, who was his nearest living relative. Plaggard knew of him but had never met him. As for James Forrest, who was the second cousin once removed in question, he knew that Plaggard was *his* second cousin and knew also, rather dimly, that he was a writer, but it wasn't a matter that interested him.

Forrest was not mentioned in the will, nor would it occur to him to expect to be. Plaggard was a total stranger to him in any real sense but for the thin bond of relationship between them. Besides, Forrest had a career as a sales executive and was doing well. He had no compelling motive to look for bequests and inheritances. So Plaggard's death passed him by without a flicker. He only knew of it when he happened to notice a report on the obituary page of his newspaper.

But a year later, he received a letter from his dead cousin. No, this is not a ghost story, the supernatural doesn't enter into it. Plaggard had written it a few days before his death, but he had sent it off to the wrong address and the letter had wound its way through the inner recesses and murky underworld of the post office for a long time. Such letters sometimes disappear forever, and sometimes they are returned to sender within days. Occasionally, though, for no known reason, they lie low, then surface and reach their proper destinations after months, or years, or even in some rare cases decades.

Forrest read the letter—which was handwritten shakily but clearly—with astonishment. I have never committed it to memory, of course, but it went something like this:

"Dear Cousin Jim. It strikes me that since you are my only living relative I ought perhaps do something for you before leaving for my final port of call, in what will, my doctors inform me, in all likelihood be a week or less. I am determined to devote my estate to the establishment of an important museum which, I confidently hope, will finally give me the prestige I have long deserved.

"However, among my possessions there is an old misprinted stamp that I once picked up for next to nothing, and which I believe may be worth some really large sum to a genuine collector. It is crimson in color, is American, and is two cents in denomination. As to its worth, a hundred thousand dollars is not beyond the realm of possibility, and I would like for you to have it.

"I carefully hid it in my study some time ago. I am not at present in a condition to guard it properly, but I think it will be safe where I left it. Unfortunately, in the confusion of these last days I do not remember where I placed it, but I'm sure you can find it. Simply show this communication to my lawyer and he will allow you to look through the room in order to locate it."

As I said, Forrest was not on the lookout for bequests, but a hundred thousand dollars was nothing to be shoved aside, either. He consulted his own lawyer, who discovered old Plaggard's lawyer, and together they decided that the stamp might be searched for. Since the house was now a museum and the study was open to the public, the search would have to be conducted at those times when the museum was closed. It would also have to be searched for under the eyes of both lawyers and of the two people who maintained the museum and were responsible for its upkeep. Everything had to be handled with the greatest of care, of course, and put back exactly as it had been.

The study was searched steadily from 3:00 P.M. one Friday, when it was closed to the public, until 10:00 A.M. the following Tuesday, when it was reopened. During those hours, whenever Forrest took time out to eat or sleep or attend to natural functions, the room was sealed. When Forrest was actually searching, the two lawyers and the two overseers were present.

The search came to nothing. Although the room was filled with miscellany, it was not a really large one. The number of objects it held was finite and every single one of them was searched. Every book was taken up and its pages examined, its dust sheet removed if it had one, its binding inspected. Every sheet of paper was separated from every other, every object was inspected inside and out. Everything that could be lifted was, and its bottom and the space under it was studied—as was each drawer of the desk and the filing cabinets. Every movable bookcase was shifted so that Forrest could look behind it. The carpet was taken up, the sofa virtually taken apart. Even the windows were opened so that the sashes might be studied.

But after hours and hours of the most painstaking search, the result was nothing. It was worse than nothing, in fact, for each lawyer charged Forrest a thousand dollars for his time and both overseers had to be paid overtime.

Some weeks afterward, Forrest came to see me. He was a rather thin young man, not very tall, and he had the rather frustrated look about him one would expect under the circumstances. He had heard about me from a mutual friend and somehow he had the idea that I could see further into a puzzling situation than most. It has always puzzled me how this sort of thing gets bruited about.

In any case, he told me the story exactly as I have told it to you, and then he asked, "Can you help me out in this, sir?"

I thought about it for a while and then I said, "The old man has been dead a year. The stamp might have been located at any time during that interval."

"That's true," said Forrest, "but no one was looking for it. No one even knew it existed."

"It might have been found by accident and just thrown away as part of the mess that ought to be cleaned up. I presume no one would know by looking at it that it was valuable."

"That's true enough too," said Forrest, "but the two people in charge swear that no object like that was ever found, and they're the only two people who've ever done any cleaning. I believe them. If either of them had found the stamp and thrown it away, the news that he or she had thrown away a hundred thousand dollars would have shown clearly in his or her face. But they were both absolutely cool about the matter."

I nodded. "That makes sense," I said. "You must also remember, though, that the aged Plaggard may not have been entirely in his right mind when he wrote you that letter. He had hidden the stamp but didn't remember where. That rather shows the deplorable state of his mentality at the time. It's quite possible he had never hidden the stamp at all; in fact, he may never have had such a stamp at all. Writers tend to live in dream worlds at the best of times, and toward the end of life and the edge of senility they are surely not to be trusted."

That seemed to take Forrest aback, but he recovered and looked stubborn. "That may be so, but suppose it isn't? Is there anyplace I should have looked that I didn't look?"

That was asking a good deal, since I had never been in that study, didn't know what was there, and didn't know what and how Forrest had searched.

I said, "Tell me again all the things you did."

He did, and I thought very hard for a while. Finally I said, "A writer is concerned with his tools. He had perhaps untouched blank paper about?"

"Yes, white bond, onionskin, and second sheets. I took the trouble to look through all of them, page by page—and under them too."

"He had pens or pencils, I'm sure, and may have kept them in cups or cylinders?"

"Yes, he had a supply of pens upended in a cylinder. I took

them out, inspected the cylinder, and the pens too—and, listen, I'll tell you what I did. Some of the pens could be opened. Those I opened and took out the ink reservoir to see if the stamp had been spindled and placed inside."

"I doubt it," I said. "If it were a valuable stamp, he wouldn't want to fold it, spindle it, or in any way mishandle it. Small things can cause such a stamp to lose much value."

"I didn't find it inside the pens anyway."

"And you lifted the typewriter?"

"Yes, I did. And I turned it upside down and shook it and nothing fell out."

"I see. I imagine that in all the time since Plaggard died, no one has used the room as a writer might use it."

"Oh, no. The caretakers were firm on that. I asked if anyone but themselves had ever been in the room alone. They insisted that no one used the room. Only they themselves and sight-seers—what there were of them—and the two lawyers and I had entered. Nor had anyone ever done anything but look, except for some dusting and vacuuming and such things that they did to care for the place."

"A pity we can't examine a year's worth of vacuum dust-bags, but never mind. A thought occurs to me. Mr. Forrest—there's one thing you can do very easily. Just go there any time the workroom is open to the public. The caretakers know you and should be willing to let you do one little thing. If not, wait till they're not looking and do it anyway. That may get you your stamp."

He did as I told him, and had his stamp in five seconds. It was by no means as valuable as Plaggard had thought, but a sizable sum was involved, enough to pay off Forrest's expenses and to pay me a small fee for my help as well. —And there's the story."

Griswold took a long sip of his drink and I said sardonically, "And there's the story? You mean he tore that room apart, but just sitting in your own armchair and never having been in that room you could tell him the one spot in which he didn't look."

"Isn't that how it was in the story *you* told?" demanded Griswold of me.

"Yes," said Baranov, "but he didn't have the faintest idea of the solution."

"Nor do you, Griswold," said Jennings. "You've faked the whole thing out of the outline."

Griswold's mouth twisted in a lordly sneer. "Really? Then you want me to tell you where Forrest found the stamp?"

"If you can," I said. "And right now."

"Very well," said Griswold. "The most sacred object to a writer of the old school is very likely to have been his type-writer. Forrest lifted the typewriter, turned it upside down, and shook it—but he didn't *use* it. Neither did anyone else. So I told Forrest to go back and turn the platen of the typewriter—turn the roller around which the paper goes when it's in use. He did—and there, revealed on its underside, was the stamp."

Robert Barnard

3. THE WOMAN IN THE WARDROBE

Ever since his first novel, Death of an Old Goat, *(1974), the British mystery writer Robert Barnard has been building a body of work that ranks with the very best in the genre. Barnard last year produced perhaps his best short story yet, "The Woman in the Wardrobe," winner of the EQMM Readers Award voted on by readers of the magazine. Almost as good was "Breakfast Television" (EQMM, January), which brought Barnard his fifth Edgar nomination.*

It was after the funeral when the relatives and friends had gone and the house felt cold and empty that Geoffrey Harcourt felt his loss most keenly. *The beginning of my aloneness,* he thought. It was Monday too, the start of the school's half-term holiday. Of course, he could go along to the office—there was always work for a headmaster to do—but that would only be exchanging one emptiness for another. There were friends he could visit, but he knew that their avoidance of him was partly from the kindliest of motives, partly to spare themselves awkwardness. Geoffrey was a reticent man, not one to hawk around his sense of loss.

The vicar had told him how it would be and he had been right. In fact, the vicar phoned him that evening, knowing how low he would feel after the funeral. Geoffrey had been listening to Mahler. He had always said that Mahler was getting to be that bit overrated, but in his current state the *Ninth* said things to him that it had never said before. The things it said were not comfortable things, though. He got more comfort from his chat with the vicar.

"Try to keep busy," the vicar said in his normal voice, which

9

was a comfort after all the hushed tones. "There must be lots of books around the house that were Helen's rather than yours. The library would probably be grateful for them. Good second-hand clothes are always in demand, particularly in hard times like the present. We at the church could get rid of them for you. I don't mean that you should wipe the house clean of all reminders of her—heaven forbid—but you'll be glad in a month or two's time that you don't have those things still to do. —You're not brooding on this man, are you? The driver?"

"No," said Geoffrey truthfully. "There doesn't seem much point. I'd like to see him caught and banned from driving for life, but beyond that— We don't even know it was a man, by the way. We don't even know it was a Honda. That was just the witness's impression—a silver-blue Honda. No, I'm truly not brooding over him. It's just the emptiness."

"I know, old chap. As I say, just try to keep busy. I'll come round in a few days and see if you've got anything for us."

So for the rest of the evening Geoffrey combed through the various bookcases that dotted the house. He found twenty or thirty books—novels, travel books, books connected with the sociology course Helen had been doing at the City Polytechnic. He made them up into a rough parcel and told himself he would ring the library next day. Certainly the activity had kept his mind occupied.

In the morning, after breakfast—the time of day when he and Helen had been most entirely together—he decided to tackle the clothes. He could not really see that he need keep anything at all. He would shrink from asking any of his or Helen's relatives if they would like anything and he was certain they would in any case have refused. Helen's interest in clothes was strictly utilitarian—she bought what would wear well, what was suitable for a headmaster's wife, there was no sentimental feeling involved. His mind was crowded with memories of Helen, but what she had worn on those occasions he would have been quite at a loss to say.

He put two old suitcases on the bed and opened the half of the wardrobe that contained the drawers. He piled under-clothes and nightgowns, tights and hats into one case—and though he did it quickly and expertly, he was surprised to find when he had finished that he was nearly crying. Should he make himself a cup of coffee? No. He would finish first. Ten minutes would do it easily.

He threw open the other door. His first emotion was merely a dim kind of puzzlement: something was not quite right. It was only after a few seconds that the full impact hit him. Here were all the clothes that he, absent-mindedly, knew so well—dresses and suits she had worn to the school meetings, the three-quarter-length gown she wore to their very occasional dinner-dance. But here too— He went forward and fingered them wonderingly.

In the darkest, innermost part of the wardrobe were clothes he had never seen. Clothes he could never imagine Helen wearing. They were bright, sensuous clothes, in rich materials—silks, cashmeres. He kept feeling them, as if that would make them real. He could not take his bewildered eyes off them. These were the clothes of a woman of the world: smart, fashionable clothes. He had seen women dressed like this in Bond Street. He could imagine the woman who owned them in the stalls at Covent Garden, dancing at the Dorchester. That evening dress—it shimmered; it was positively glamorous.

He shut the wardrobe door sharply and leaned his head against it for a moment. Then he went downstairs to make that cup of coffee. He sat down at the kitchen table to drink it and tried to collect his thoughts.

He rejected almost as soon as it entered his head the idea that she was storing the clothes for a friend. What friend had she that would wear clothes like *that?* Why would she be asked to store only the expensive, fashionable clothes? No, they were Helen's. She had known that, short of her being very ill, he would never think of looking in her wardrobe.

What did she want them for? Did she wear them during the day while he was at school? Did she float around the house in a dream of aristocratic elegance, imagining herself at cocktails in Mayfair, dancing the night away at some aristocratic sprig's twenty-first? It seemed so unlike Helen. His wife had been a competent, down-to-earth, no-nonsense woman. So he had always believed.

He steeled himself to go back to the bedroom. He took the clothes from the wardrobe, ran his hand over their softness, felt their textures, admired their cut. He was no expert, had always had to remind himself to comment on his wife's appearance if they were going out, but these clothes seemed to him immensely stylish: they were the sort of clothes worn by women who were rich, confident, and attractive. Helen had inherited a house in suburban London when her mother died and had sold it at the current inflated prices.

But the problem was not where she had got the money from. It was why she had felt the desire.

That afternoon, he rang the City Polytechnic. He got on to the admissions secretary at once.

"Hello. My name is Geoffrey Harcourt. I'm ringing about my wife, Helen Harcourt."

"Oh, yes, I remember her well," said a friendly female voice. "We had many good chats when she was deciding on her course."

"I think she told me about them. I'm afraid she's dead."

"Oh, dear! I *am* sorry! Had she been ill for some time?"

"It was a road accident. A hit-and-run driver."

"How *awful.* It must have been a terrible shock for you."

"It was. I just thought I'd ring to inform you, so you can take her off your books."

There was a pause of fully three seconds before the woman said: "Yes, of course. We'll do that. And once again, I *am* sorry."

Geoffrey knew what that pause meant, knew what the woman had been about to say and had stopped herself from saying: Helen had not been on their books for some time.

His night was awful. He lay on the double bed they had shared, feet away from the wardrobe. Nightmarishly, it seemed to him that in the wardrobe he had discovered another woman, a woman who was his wife and not his wife. Helen had had another life unknown to him, in which she was glamorous, fashionable, even seductive. It was as if some sudden crisis or involuntary action had revealed to him a side to his own nature of which he had always been unconscious. Helen was not *like* that, he kept saying to himself, had no desire for that kind of life. But she *was,* she *had,* said the wardrobe.

By next morning he knew he could not leave things there. He had to *know.* He had a gray, old-fashioned Puritan conscience. What his discovery was whispering to him was that somehow he had failed Helen. Still more, that meant he had to *know.*

Over breakfast, feeling furtive and grubby, he went through Helen's checkbook and the monthly statements of her credit-card company. So far as he could see, there were no hotel bills. When Helen had started staying overnight on Thursdays ("There are so many evening activities that I'm missing out on and British Rail has practically cut out all the trains after nine"), she told him she had found a little bed-and-breakfast place in Bloomsbury that was clean and cheap. There were no check stubs to bear this out. Nor were there checks made out to more glamorous hotels. There were, though, largish sums on the statement paid to Harrods, Selfridges, and a shop called Amanda's, which was in Knightsbridge. The clothes, obviously.

His mind honed in on the sociology course. They had discussed it quite a bit at first, hardly at all recently. The subjects had become too esoteric and, besides, Geoffrey had the natural contempt of the academic mind for such a subject. It had been a one-day-a-week course, aimed at part-time students and people with special needs. When she had started, she had gone on Wednesdays. Some way into first year, she had said that the day had been changed to Thursdays. But wouldn't that have been immensely disruptive of the students' arrangements, and wouldn't the timetable readjustments have been difficult or impossible? She had changed to Thursdays because—

But no. Best to put any such thoughts aside. Stick to facts. Keep a firm grip on reality. He had to look at the newspaper to establish that the day was, in fact, Wednesday.

He took the car up to London. He couldn't face the sympathy and inquiries of the people at the station. At Carbury, the small Essex town where he lived, everyone knew everyone.

He drove to the City Polytechnic, then round and round it for twenty minutes until he saw a car pulling out. He nosed into the parking space and walked into the Poly. In the foyer, he prowled around until he found the notice-board with the timetables. With his practiced headmaster's eye he skimmed over the mass of detailed information (so many courses, so little knowledge) till he came to Sociology (Special Needs). If Helen had continued, she would now be taking—had said she *was* taking—the third-year course.

He was right. The course was on Wednesdays. The group was currently engaged in a seminar on The Battered Child Syndrome in Room 347B. They would be out at twelve o'clock. He took the lift up to the third floor and walked through the tedious, anonymous corridors. More like a business firm or a rather run-down hotel than a place of education, he thought. How had Helen fitted in here? Had she ever felt at home? He stationed himself near 347B, feeling like a novice plainclothes policeman.

When the seminar broke up, the students trailed out, looking bored. It was difficult to imagine how a terrible, touching subject like battered children could be made boring, but the lecturer seemed to have managed it somehow. About a third of the students were the normal college-age young, others were in their twenties or thirties, the rest Helen's age or older. He picked out a sympathetic woman of about forty and went hesitantly up to her.

"Excuse me, I wonder if you can help me. I'm looking for someone who knew Helen Harcourt when she was a student here."

The woman turned and smiled. "Oh, yes—I knew Helen."

"Well?"

"As well as anyone here, I suppose. Those of us who'd reached the forties mark tended to get together between classes. Why?"

"I'm her husband. Helen died in a road accident last week."

"Oh, *dear*. How tragic. She was so gay and vital."

"Look, would you let me buy you lunch? Is there anywhere around here?"

"I'll let you buy me lunch, but in the canteen," she said. "It's not too bad. I don't know what you want of me, but it can't be worth the price of a restaurant meal."

Over two plates of shepherd's pie and peas, Geoffrey put his cards on the table.

"Since my wife died, I've discovered things about her I never knew before. I didn't know she'd given up her course here, for example, and there are—other things. She had a life for one day a week of which I knew nothing. Please believe it's not anger or pique that makes me feel I have to know. You won't be betraying Helen in anything you tell me. I just want to find out how I failed her."

The woman nodded. "I can understand that. But truly I know nothing that could 'betray' her in any way. We weren't that kind of friends, and she was only here for a term and a half, you know."

"That's what I guessed. Why did she give it up? She seemed so enthusiastic at first."

"Oh, she was. We all were. But the teaching is not too good, and some of the subject areas seem just plain potty. I remember Helen once said to me that she wondered whether what we were studying *was* a subject at all. In fact, quite a lot of us wonder why we go on. Just to get a bit of paper at the end, I suppose."

"And that was the reason she stopped?"

"I don't know the reason she stopped. But she was expressing boredom, and then one week she wasn't there. She never came again."

"I see. Tell me, did she have any special friends?"

"Well, we're all quite good friends. The young ones tend to keep to themselves, but they're really quite *kind* to us.—I see what you're getting at, of course." She thought. "There was a man—oh, dear, what was his name? There was a Polytechnic party and dance, early in second term that year—"

"Yes, I seem to remember. Helen took the car and drove back very late. I was asleep when she got back in."

"I'm sure it meant nothing special, but she danced a lot with this man. He gave up the course about the time she did, I think, which is why I can't remember his name. He was five or six years younger than Helen, but they seemed to find each other a lot of fun. His business had collapsed, but he was hoping for a job on ICI, on the personnel side. This course was a sort of stopgap. As far as I remember, he got the job and stopped coming."

"There's nothing else you can remember about him—about them—that might suggest—"

"That they were having an affair? That is what we're talking about, isn't it? Oh, dear, I *do* feel this is a betrayal.

"It was so much more, at that stage, a matter of a shared sense of humor. I remember once, when we were all sitting talking in here, this man gave us a marvelous account, with miming and accents and all, of this hotel in Bloomsbury—the Durward, that was it—where they still do real old-fashioned teas, with dainty sandwiches and tea-cake and muffins. And they have dancing after dinner with a palm-court orchestra and lots of faded elegance. I remember your wife laughing till she ached and saying, 'Just like Bertram's Hotel. I'd love to see it.' And this man promised to take her one day. What *was* his name?"

"Would anybody else remember?"

"They might do." She looked around and darted to a table with three or four older students. "His name was Roger Michaels," she said when she returned. "He'd owned a small toy factory but the recession had closed it. And it was ICI he went to." She leaned forward very earnestly. "You do realize I've no *evidence.*"

"Oh, of course. It could be someone else entirely. Someone she met on the train, for instance. It could be no one. By the way, what did he look like?"

"Dapper. Well set up, but not tall. Lively, always darting here and there. Lots and lots of jokes."

I've never been good on jokes, thought Geoffrey sadly. It seemed as though some great weight was pressing on his back, squeezing the breath out of him. How I failed her, he thought. He had known his wife had been kind, generous, considerate. Now he also knew she had craved color, gaiety, and laughter. How totally he had failed her.

It was still early afternoon when he got back to his car. He thought he had enough information to track this Roger Michaels, but first there was something else he could try to see if he was on the right track. He had lied when he said to Helen's friend that there could be no one, no affair. The clothes were the clothes of a woman in love. But was Michaels the man?

He drove to Bloomsbury, and once again drove round and round before he found a parking space. Then he marked time in Dillons and Foyles until it was four o'clock and tea would be served at the Durward.

It was overpoweringly genteel, like Harrogate in the thirties. A pianist played Gershwin and Ivor Novello quite softly, and the sandwiches and cakes nestled on lacy doilies in silver baskets. Only the staff was wrong: a heterogeneous collection of nationalities. But Geoffrey was lucky—he had a genial, potbellied Cypriot with an East London accent. When he was halfway through his tea, he fished from his wallet the photograph of Helen, taken on holiday the year before in Verona, and he beckoned the waiter over.

The waiter's first reaction was to shake his head. "No. No, I can't say I have. Wait—wait a minute, though. I think that must be Mrs. Rogers, so called. Yes—I'd bet my— Mind you, she looks very different there. Quite dowdy, really, as if she'd tried to deglamorize herself. Our Mrs. Rogers— What's this all about, mate? Private detective, are you? I suppose it'll be the real Mrs. Rogers, or whatever her name is."

"When are you off?"

"I finish at six, thank Gawd."

"Care for a drink?"

"I wouldn't say no."

"Meet you outside at six. . . ."

Settled into the Jug and Bottle, just off the Tottenham Court Road, and after a tenner had passed between them, the waiter told Geoffrey all he knew.

"Somehow I always had the suspicion they weren't married. I saw him sign the register when they first stayed the night and he didn't do it confidentlike. What ho! I thought, your name isn't Michael Rogers. Since then, I've noticed he always pays cash, never check or credit card."

"But they register as husband and wife?"

" 'Course they do. What do you think? Mind you, it is a bit out of the usual run of liaisons. Because when you look close, you realize she's older than him. Glamorous, very smart, altogether the superior article, but older. I put her down as a lady from the provinces—and I do *mean* a lady, and a well-heeled one—having a fling in London. Though it's more than that too. You can see she's in love."

The waiter, drinking deep, did not see Geoffrey flinch.

"Do they come to the Durward every week?"

"Oh, yes, they have been doing. 'Cept in the holidays. I put it down to one or the other of them having kiddies home from boarding school."

"So they come every Thursday?"

"That's right. Not last week, but it's probably half term or something. Yes, they come down and have tea in the Garden Room, same as you just done."

"What do they do in the evenings?"

"Sometimes they have dinner at the Durward, and a dance afterwards. But Thursday nights is not very lively. Mostly they go out. Taxi called from the desk, then off to the Savoy or wherever. She in long dress, hair done, beautifully made-up. My God, she can look a stunner! I don't wonder he was taken."

"You said that she's in love. Is he?"

"Oh, I think so. Not a doubt of it. At least until recently—"

"There has been a change?"

"Well, there has and there hasn't. On the surface, everything's been the same. But they've got more serious—had long conversations in low voices over the tea-table. Once I could see she was distressed, though being a lady she was always the same to me if I came up to see if there was anything they wanted. He wasn't upset in quite that way, and I put the change down to him trying to wind up the affair—in the nicest possible way. Say what you like, that's what usually happens when the woman's the older one. Mind you, thinking back on it, he could have been telling her that his wife was suspicious and they'd have to go careful for a bit."

No, Geoffrey thought—he'd used her and was giving her the brush-off. He was conceiving an intense dislike for this Roger Michaels, who worked for ICI and had this great store of jokes. What he felt—he told himself with the bleak honesty of someone whose emotional voltage was low—was not jealousy. Or not primarily jealousy. It was indignation on Helen's behalf. He saw her now as someone who had for years modified her personality to suit the gray, even life which her marriage had offered her, but who had had that other, more daring self waiting to spring out. And when it had done, she had been used by a thoughtless or heartless man and then thrown aside.

"I feel guilty about this," said the waiter, standing up and patting his back pocket, "but a tenner's a tenner. I don't know what the lady who's paying you is like, but *my* pair are nice people. And *she* is a beautiful woman."

I never knew I was married to a beautiful woman, thought Geoffrey sadly.

Next morning, the great weight of failure, of lack of understanding, seemed as crushing as ever. Before breakfast, he drove to his school.

It was like a ghost school—though later, he knew, one of the secretaries would be coming in. He took the L-to-R volume of the London Telephone Directory from the office and drove home. He spoke to nobody. Still less, now, did he wish to have a heart-to-heart with anyone about his loss.

Michaels, fortunately, was not a common name. With the data he had on him, Geoffrey could make a guess at the sort of area he might live in, and from the handful who had the initial R he struck gold with his second call. It was to the R. Michaels who lived in Grafton Avenue, Surbiton.

"Could I speak to Mr. Michaels, please?"

"I'm afraid my husband is away at his job from Mondays to Fridays. Can I help?"

It was a hard, tight little voice, quite neutral in accent.

"Perhaps you can. I'm with *The Economist,* and we're doing a survey of British toy manufacturers—"

"Oh, my husband got out of that long ago. Nearly two years. He saw the way the wind was blowing. He's got a very good job with ICI now."

"Thank you. That tells me what I wanted to know. I shan't need to trouble you again."

On an impulse, when he had put the phone down, he looked up the number for ICI and got on to the personnel department.

"I'm sorry, but Mr. Michaels isn't here at the moment," a cool competent voice told him. "His main work is with our businesses in the north. He drives up there on Monday mornings and he only comes in here on Fridays, though I believe he drives down on Thursday afternoon."

When he had put the phone down, Geoffrey began wondering about Roger Michaels's arrangements with Helen. Did they meet somewhere, then go on to the Durward together? That seemed likely. Had he been expecting to meet her last Thursday, and would he be waiting again today? Or had he, as the waiter conjectured, broken it off—disguising it, perhaps, as a temporary break while his wife was suspicious, but in brutal reality ditching her?

By now he had made up his mind. At some time in the future, he was going to have to have a talk with Roger Michaels.

But first he wanted to suss out the lie of the land, sniff out the character of his everyday life. He found Grafton Avenue easily in his *London A–Z*. There was nothing to prevent him driving there at once. Half term had still some days to run and doubtless any problems that came up were referred to the deputy head.

When he got to Surbiton, he found that at least here parking was no problem. There didn't seem to be much else to be said for the place. He put the car in the next street and walked casually along Grafton Avenue. The Michaels' house was not very different from what he had expected: a standard detached house, probably built in the fifties, with a tiny, neat front garden and no character whatsoever. The same was true of all the houses in the street: suburbia personified. The only relief from the architectural monotony was a small square of public garden on the opposite corner of the avenue. Geoffrey walked in it for a bit, his eye on Roger's house, but there was no sign of life.

Was Roger a pub man, he wondered. Yes, it did sound as if Roger was probably a pub man. Men with streams of jokes usually were. Two streets away, Geoffrey could see the outlines of a thirties roadhouse, Brewery Anonymous in style. Could that be Roger Michaels's local? It seemed worth a try.

It was still a good half hour before the lunchtime rush and the landlord was ready for a leisurely gossip.

Thinking of moving round here, was he? Well, he always did say you couldn't find a nicer area. Lovely houses—well, he would have seen that. Nice people too, if it came to that—a very good *class*, if Geoffrey knew what he meant. What line of business was Geoffrey in himself? Schoolmastering? *Head*master! Well, he could practically guarantee he would fit in perfectly. Did he have any connections in this area?

"Oh, no," said Geoffrey airily, "not really. Though I've just remembered I do know a chap who lives around here somewhere. Man called Roger Michaels."

"Roger! One of the best. He's one of our regulars. Well, not regular, because these days he's up north from Monday to Friday. But he'll be in on Friday or Saturday, and he and his wife come in on Sunday lunchtime without fail. Come in about half past twelve, have a couple, then leave about half past one, when the roast is done."

"Great chap, Roger," said Geoffrey with painfully assumed heartiness.

"Lovely man. Really funny. I'd say he was a real wit. He gets a little circle round him when he comes in here and he has them splitting their sides."

"Bit of a lad too, I believe," said Geoffrey.

"Oh, we wouldn't know about that round here," said the landlord with professional caution. "While he's home, his wife keeps him on a very tight leash. Between you and me"—he leaned forward over the bar and hushed his voice—"she has the reputation of being a bit of a b-i-t-c-h. Mind you, if he has his fling now and then I'm not alto*gether* surprised."

"No?"

The landlord lowered his voice again.

"Couple round here had their Silver Wedding. Went to the Savoy for a bit of a splash. They saw Roger there with a woman—a real corker, so they said. 'Course, it could have been his sister." The landlord smirked. "Nothing was said. Just one or two dirty snickers. The fact is, his lady wife's not greatly liked. And you can say what you want about Roger, he's a man people take to."

Then the bar began to fill up.

Geoffrey went back to the roadhouse on Sunday at lunchtime.

The bar was full this time and he was served by a barmaid. He stationed himself by the window. From here he couldn't see the Michaels' house, but he could see the end of Grafton Avenue. Most of the couples who came for a drink drove, but surely the Michaelses would not. At about half past midday, he saw a couple walking from Grafton Avenue. They were apparently affectionate, but there was something forced about it, even from a distance. He walked like a man with something on his mind. She took his hand in hers, but that only increased the sense of strain. As they approached the pub, Geoffrey downed his drink and escaped out the back.

In the car, he found he was drenched with sweat. That, certainly, had not been the time or the place for an encounter. He had to get Michaels on his own, in some place where neither of them was known. But how could that be arranged?

On Sunday night, Geoffrey rang his deputy head. He found he just couldn't face school in the morning, he said. He'd intended coming in, but somehow the thought of school assembly, with all the children looking at him, was more than he could bear. He might slip in inconspicuously later in the day, or he'd be there without fail on Tuesday. His deputy was very sympathetic and said she quite understood.

It was very dark when Geoffrey left the house on Monday morning—still night, in fact. Roger Michaels's time of departure for the north could be anything from six onwards. In fact, Geoffrey was in position in the little patch of public garden by five past. He had left his car just round the corner from Grafton Avenue.

At about twenty past, a light came on in the landing of Number 26, and soon there seemed to be lights on in the back of the house downstairs. What was he doing? Making himself coffee, or making himself breakfast? Geoffrey hoped it was the former. When he had thought about their encounter, he had envisaged it taking place in some motorway cafeteria where Roger had stopped for breakfast. Daylight broke over Surbiton. He must have made himself something to eat. But even so, he would stop for a cup of coffee, surely, at some stage in his journey?

It was just after seven when the front door opened. Geoffrey saw Michaels's back as he closed the door, then a side view as he walked to the garage. Middle height, little moustache, firm walk. Geoffrey fingered his car keys as he heard the garage doors opened. Then another wait. What was the man *doing?* Finally a car started and began backing out.

The rush of blood to Geoffrey's head was so blinding he had to lean against a tree. It was a silver-blue Honda. There it stood, in the middle of the road, as Roger got out to close the garage doors. A silver-blue Honda. He had killed her. Deliberately run her down. The coincidence was too glaring to believe otherwise. Suddenly decisive, Geoffrey ran to his car, started it, and when the Honda had driven past silently put it into gear and followed at a safe distance.

All the way, through suburb after dreary suburb and towards the M1, Geoffrey was thinking. He had tried to throw her over and she had not taken it lying down. She had got troublesome. She had threatened to go to his wife. He couldn't imagine Helen being troublesome, but then the whole of Helen's other life was something he could only conceive of by imagining a quite different sort of woman. She was a woman of forty, hopelessly in love with a younger man. A desperate woman will adopt desperate means. He, on the other hand, had just been having a fling on the side. His marriage was important to him. Why? Did the wife have money?

Helen had been driving down between town and home, on a stretch of highway where a spurt of speed was possible. She had been giving her cookery class as usual—something she always did on a Tuesday night. Anyone could have known this, but it was something Michaels would doubtless have known very well. He must have driven down from the north, parked there, waited for her to pass, then driven into her at speed and driven on. Geoffrey felt that great, choking well of anger in him, still as strong as when he had seen the car.

At last they got to the motorway. Roger was not a fast-lane man, Geoffrey was relieved to find. He kept on the inside, driving carefully. Was he naturally a fast-lane man but one with something on his mind? On and on they went, towards the Midlands, towards the north. He was not going to stop! Geoffrey felt a growing surge of frustration, pushing his anger to boiling point. He was not going to stop! Where was he going to be able to confront him—tell him face-to-face he knew what he had done?

They were nearing a flyover. On an impulse Geoffrey accelerated. He drew level with the Honda and stayed level. Roger was driving steadily, carefully. A flicker crossed his face. He had realized that the car beside him in the next lane had been there too long. He turned his head and saw Geoffrey's face looking directly at him. Geoffrey saw his jaw drop. Michaels had recognized him. So Helen had shown him pictures. His jaw was working. He seemed about to say something. Then all of a sudden, his car was out of control, swerving to the left, off the road, through the flyover's safety barrier and down to the ground or road beneath. Geoffrey's last view had been of a face crazed with terror.

He drove on till he came to a lay-by. He sat for some minutes with his head in his hands. He had done nothing. His car had not touched the Honda. And yet—what had been his motive in driving up beside him, staying beside him in the second lane? To get a good look? Or with the subconscious desire that something like this would happen?

At any rate, some kind of justice had been done. Ten minutes later, almost cool again, Geoffrey drove to the next junction, then turned and headed south. There were police and AA men on the flyover, and down below he could hear the shriek of an ambulance.

Geoffrey drove to Surbiton on the next Saturday to buy a local paper. There was a brief notice of the accident, with the news that it had involved no other deaths, though a passenger was injured in a car on the road below which had been slightly grazed by the falling Honda. Geoffrey was relieved it was not worse. He went back to Surbiton the next Saturday, and the one after that, but it was not till the third Saturday that he found a report of the inquest.

The coroner, before accepting a verdict of accidental death, set out the facts admirably. The dead man was still young, was happily married, and had quite recently embarked on a promising career with a first-rate company. Unfortunately, his job necessitated a great deal of traveling. There was no evidence that Mr. Michaels had been drinking, either on the morning or the night before. Nor was there any evidence that his judgment could have been impaired for any other reason—for example, drugs. The relevant facts were that Mr. Michaels had not had a great deal of sleep the night before and had begun his long journey early in the morning. It was clear that the accident had been caused by a momentary lapse in concentration.

The coroner also noted the fact that in her evidence Roger Michaels's widow had suggested that a contributory factor in the accident was the fact that her husband was driving a car to which he was not accustomed. His company Volvo was in the garage for an extensive refit and he had been forced to take her car.

GEORGE BAXT

STROKE OF GENIUS

*Perhaps no mystery writer knows the New York literary
and theatrical scenes as well as George Baxt, and no one
can write about them with such cutting wit. Here's Baxt
at his best in a story that was nominated for an MWA
Edgar award.*

Gregory Barlow had always secretly admired Vernon Bigelow.
Vernon was rich, he was an investment counselor. Gregory was
always struggling to scratch out a living, he was an author.
Vernon lived in a four-bedroom triplex on Fifth Avenue, facing
Central Park, the zoo, and assorted muggers. Gregory lived in a
cold-water walk-up railroad flat, which he shared with several
mice and an assortment of roaches, overlooking a filthy, con-
gested stretch of Ninth Avenue, a motley group of Spanish-
speaking neighbors (all of whom owned blaring portable radios), and a select group of crack dealers. Gregory wasn't
jealous of Vernon. He had accepted his lot from that moment as
an infant when his eyes finally came into focus and realized the
gurgling man and woman cooing at him were his parents.

Actually, most of Vernon's wealth was inherited—from his
parents, his grandparents, a doting aunt, a crooked uncle he
was quietly blackmailing, and a first wife (of four) who was
darling enough to be hit by a Trailways bus at the corner of
Fifth Avenue and Forty-second Street and die instantly. ("Whatever do you suppose she was doing *walking?*" asked Corinne
Barlow, Gregory's dreadful niece, who was that kind of despi-
cable snob only poverty could breed. It was Corinne who had
introduced her uncle to Vernon Bigelow.)

"Unk, I've got a new girlfriend," Corinne had said that Colum-
bus Day noon over a cup of instant decaffeinated in her uncle's
weary little kitchen. "*Very* rich. Well, that is, her father's very
rich. Her father's Vernon Bigelow."

Gregory was busy finishing the *New York Times* crossword puzzle, which had another of its glaring errors: "Anna Lucasta" by O'Neill. "The idiots!" raged Gregory.

"Which idiots?" asked Corinne, steadying her cup of coffee, which had been set quivering by her uncle's hand crashing down on the table.

"Crossword-puzzle idiots! 'Anna Lucasta' was written by Philip Yordan, not by Eugene O'Neill. And they've got Della Reese in it again!"

"Don't you want to hear about my girlfriend?" Gregory said nothing and Corinne ploughed onward, as he knew she would regardless. "I met Elyse Bigelow at that trendy new disco down on Avenue A, The Greedy Sow."

"So you dislike her already?"

"No, that's the name of the disco. Anyway, Elyse was trying to score with my date, and I was hoping she would because if he greeted anyone with 'Hi guys' once more I'd slit his throat. Anyway, to make a long story short—"

"Too late."

"—I introduced myself to Elyse and told her straight off if she wanted Harvey she was welcome to him, and she just screamed with laughter and threw her arms around me and kissed both my cheeks as though she'd just pinned me with the Croix de Guerre and asked if I'd like a cup of coffee and some girl talk. So I said yes and the next thing I know I'm in a stretch limousine longer than—"

"Your story."

"—the Holland Tunnel and then I'm in her apartment on Park Avenue, the foyer of which could house a small chic restaurant—"

"Oh, get on with it, for crying out loud!"

"Well, so by now I was sure she was rich, and when she told me her father was *the* Vernon Bigelow—"

"As opposed to *the* Stone of Scone."

"Well, surely you recognize his name?"

"Yes, I recognize it." One of Gregory's secret vices was gossip columns, especially the so-called society columns. It was always the same names and the same restaurants. Bill Blass this, Pauline

Trigere that, Pat Buckley here, Swifty Lazar there, Bianca Jagger, etc., etc., and usually tucked in somewhere was Vernon Bigelow.

"Well, aren't you impressed?"

"I can't tell you about the last time I was impressed because even the thought of it makes me blush. The only hint I'll give you is that it involved a well known authoress of trash novels and the UCLA football team, eight of whom suffered heart attacks and never played again—at least not football."

"Anyway, Elyse and I have been seeing a lot of each other and she's introduced me to some really terrific guys. I've been dating one of them pretty steadily."

"And he's very wealthy."

"Well, I can't say for sure, but Elyse says he has his cavities filled with platinum. Anyway, Unk"—Gregory loathed her calling him Unk as much as he loathed her purplish orange hair that stuck up in ugly spikes and the way she painted her face like it belonged on an Incan totem pole—"I've met Vernon and I've told him all about you. How your books and short stories make a little money—"

"A very little money, be sure to specify."

"—and that you own some awfully good art that I'm sure is worth a good deal of money." When she smiled, she looked like a piranha in heat, and she was smiling. Gregory wondered how surprised she'd be if he socked her.

"Corinne, my few works of art are a lifetime's accumulation"—Gregory was in his early sixties—"acquired by missing meals, skipping dates, not buying new clothes when necessary, and I'll skip the rest of the hearts and flowers. They're my only assets. There were more but I had to sell some during some of my leaner periods"—he looked around at his sorry surroundings—"such as now."

Corinne paled and her voice grew husky. "You're not going to sell one of them? Not the Vickery or the Shahn or the Cadmus—or that darling Roger Baker feather?"

"What business is it of yours?"

Corinne recognized the danger when her uncle's eyes narrowed into slits. "Well, they—they do brighten up this place."

"You don't."

"Oh, Unk." She didn't realize how revolting he found her

when she grew flirtatious with him. "Vernon wants to meet you. He has a *huge* art collection and he has a publisher who wants to do a book on them. You know, a coffee-table book."

"Good heavens, do the rich still have coffee tables?" Gregory flung the newspaper aside, collected the cups and saucers, and carried them to the sink. Corinne had to shout over the torrent of running water as he fell to the washing up.

"He says he'll pay you well if you help him with the writing."

Gregory turned off the tap and looked at his niece over his shoulder. She looked like a floral offering at a Mafia funeral. "You mean he wants me to ghost the book for him?"

"You could use the money, couldn't you?"

"I've no other means of income at the moment," he told her, "short of attempting to sell you to the Arabs."

So Corinne set up a meeting with Gregory and Vernon, to be held at Vernon's private club, so chic and so private that the building was unnumbered. Gregory found it with the help of a compass and a seeing-eye dog, or so he liked to tell people. Amazingly, he and Vernon hit if off at once. Vernon was a tall, slim, good-looking man, who although he was fifty-nine didn't look a day over sixty-five. As the afternoon wore on and out, he regaled Gregory with tales of his daily regimen—fifty pushups in the morning, hot water with tea and a slice of melba toast for breakfast, then five miles, jogging in Central Park with a friend of his. In the afternoon after work, he went to his gym where he worked with the barbells and the weights before an hour with his karate instructor. Gregory admired all this. His own idea of exercise was inserting a cassette in his VCR and then adjusting the tracker before settling back on the couch with a very dry vodka martini on the rocks. Vernon, of course, didn't drink, except for an occasional white-wine spritzer when he dined at the White House. ("Those two are such squares," he confided to Gregory, who was learning nothing new. "When I asked her what she thought of Tutu of South Africa, she said, 'Too too divine.'")

In the fourth hour of their meeting, Vernon finally brought up the subject of the book. In ten minutes, they struck a deal, almost all of it surprisingly in Gregory's favor. In fact, the sum of money Vernon promised made his head swim, his eyes cross, and his mouth go dry. He couldn't believe it when Vernon whipped out his checkbook and wrote him a handsome advance. At last, thought Gregory, I can buy a microwave oven! A baked potato in seven minutes! Heaven!

Vernon became genuinely fond of Gregory and they started to see a lot of each other. He even visited Gregory in his Ninth Avenue apartment and commented, really meaning it, "Now this is real cozy." He admired Gregory's small but tasteful collection of art as opposed to his own vast one bought either for investment or the glamor of the artist's name. "Face it, Greg," he said one Sunday at brunch in Gregory's apartment, "I've got no real taste. I have the money with which to buy taste, but I don't even know which kind of taste to buy. Why don't you help me buy some stuff?"

"That still wouldn't be your taste. It would be mine."

"So what? You're the only one I can trust. I certainly can't trust that greedy daughter of mine."

"I didn't get that impression," said Gregory, lying.

"Like hell you didn't. You can tell every time she looks at me her mouth is watering. Just like every time your niece looks at your art collection, her eyes turn into dollar signs. Thank God I've got my health and can look after myself. No one's going to do me out of what's mine."

Vernon Bigelow suffered a crippling stroke that night while getting into bed. It paralyzed his left side and he lost his power of speech. His mouth was twisted cruelly out of shape and he couldn't control the drool that dripped out of the sides. It was said that it was while he was being transported to the hospital that Elyse had herself declared his conservator and gained control of his wealth.

When Gregory was permitted to visit Vernon, he couldn't believe the human wreckage in the wheelchair was the man he had secretly admired. Vernon had some strength left in his right hand and managed to scrawl a note to Gregory: "Beware relatives." Gregory was grateful when after only five minutes with Vernon, the nurse asked him to leave. He patted Vernon's

right hand, promised to come back soon, and almost burst into
tears when Vernon's eyes erupted.

Beware relatives.

Gregory slowly walked the two miles from Vernon's chic
hospital on the East Side to his apartment on the other side of
Manhattan deep in thought. He thought of himself in Vernon's
situation and of the rapidity with which his niece would un-
doubtedly go about taking control of his art collection and
what little else he had of value. Many of his books were first
editions, and there were his own novels and stories. On occasion he'd received options from television and film companies,
usually a nick-of-time bonanza just when he was on the verge
of selling a painting. He recognized now that Vernon hated his
daughter, and that the seeds of that hatred had probably been
sown long before the stroke.

I hate Corinne, Gregory thought.

He took a deep breath. He truly did hate Corinne. Her
stupidity, her snobbishness, her mode of dress, her face and
hair, her lack of ethics, and the paucity of her ambitions other
than to covet what little he owned. Thinking about her, he
began to feel a little weak. He sat down on a park bench on
Central Park South. It was there, a few minutes later, that a
policeman found him.

He would later remember that when he tried to reach into
his left jacket pocket for a handkerchief, he couldn't find his
pocket. He remembered touching his left hand with his right
hand and realizing the left was totally numb. He had wanted his
handkerchief because he was drooling. He remembered trying
to stand, but his left leg wouldn't support him and he fell back
on the bench, struggling for breath. He tried not to panic, but
when he wanted to shout for help all that came out of his
mouth were meaningless, guttural noises.

When the policeman saw him, he recognized the symptoms
of a stroke and called for help on his walkie-talkie.

Two months later, Gregory was back in his apartment in a
wheelchair, at the mercy of his niece Corinne and a kindly
neighbor, a young Puerto Rican man who by happy chance was

an orderly at St. Clare's Hospital and knew how to deal with stroke victims.

His name was Rosario and he shopped for Gregory (who, much to Corinne's anger, trusted Rosario with his bank card), cooked for him (though Gregory had little appetite), and, most importantly, tried to teach him all the methods of rehabilitation taught to stroke victims. Though Gregory appeared to make little progress, Rosario never lost patience with him. Sometimes Rosario's girlfriend, a professional manicurist, would come in and run a cassette on the VCR and watch with Gregory. He liked her company. She always smelled good, and she hummed a lot and talked back to the screen. ("Dat dere Meryl Street. Looka her. No blood. No notting. Why she a star?") She particularly favored violence. ("Keel heem! Slit heez throat! Ahhh! Looka da blood!")

Then Corinne would arrive and spoil it all. Once she brought Elyse with her and the two of them talked as though he had also lost his sense of hearing.

Elyse: "A smart lawyer could help you get your hands on these pictures."

Corinne: "I have to be careful. His lawyer's a shrewdie. But Unk's money is running low. I've been checking out charity homes. He once had a flop play on Broadway and still belongs to the Dramatists Guild. They're affiliated with an actors' home out in New Jersey. Once I can get him into a place like that, I'll have control of everything he's got. I've found out what the Vickery, the Shahn, and the Cadmus are worth." She whispered her findings to Elyse. Gregory couldn't hear, but he didn't have to. He knew their value.

Moments later, Corinne was staring down at him while Elyse stood impatiently in the doorway. "I have to go now, Unk. I'm sure one of your spic friends will be looking in on you and help you get into bed. Elyse and I are invited to a cocktail party for Jackie Collins's new best-seller, *Goodbye Is Not Forever.* It's been bought for a miniseries to star Loni Anderson and Herve Villechaize."

I'm going to kill you, Corinne.

"Oh, I can't stand it when your eyes tear up, Unk—"

"Come on, Corinne, let's get moving," Elyse said from the door.

When they had gone, locking him in, Gregory went to work on the therapy Rosario had taught him with fresh determination.

Four weeks later, Corinne came to visit Gregory and found the door unlocked. As she pushed the door open, she realized the lock had been jimmied. Her heart pounded: Someone's broken in! Then her heart leapt: Maybe Unk's been murdered! She found Gregory lying on the bed, the wheelchair overturned, the drawers opened and ransacked. Not bothering with Gregory, she rushed to check the artwork.

Finding nothing stolen, she cried, "Oh, God! Poor Unk! Are you all right?"

As she helped him off the bed into the wheelchair, he motioned for a pad and pencil and scribbled, "Police—wristwatch—cufflinks—cash."

Rosario arrived soon thereafter and said something in Spanish, hurriedly checking Gregory for bruises and for his pulse beat, while Corinne phoned for the police. A squad car pulled up in front of the tenement in record time, sending most of the neighborhood scurrying for cover.

Corinne explained to the two officers her uncle's incapacitation and showed them what he had scribbled. One of the policemen turned to Gregory and explained, "In cases like this, the perp is usually hard to trace, but we can try. I know this is difficult for you, Mr. Barlow, but why don't I ask questions that you can answer by nodding your head or shaking it yes or no, okay?"

Gregory nodded yes.

In fifteen minutes, the police knew the thief was white, in his early twenties, about six feet tall, and thin, that he had menaced Gregory with a knife, had slapped his face twice, and had come in through the front door, which Gregory had heard him jimmying but had been unable to do anything about. Also that he had taken sadistic delight in telling Gregory he'd be back.

"He comes back again I'll break his neck," said Rosario, while

Gregory wondered by what stroke of luck Rosario would be in attendance if and when the thief struck again.

After the police and Rosario left, Corinne was talking aloud to herself. "This settles it! You've got to go into a home—it's too dangerous here! Stop making those awful noises, Unk. It's out of your hands and that's that. God, I can't even lock the door behind me this time. Oh, the hell with it! I've got to meet Woody and Mia at Elaine's and they hate it when I'm late!" She stormed out the door, slamming it behind her.

Oh, my niece—how I hate you. How I truly hate you.

The following Tuesday, Corinne came to see Gregory. "It's not easy getting you into this place, you know, Unk. There are so many ill, infirm, and needy actors—"

All starring in television series, thought Gregory.

"—waiting to get into the home. But by some pull, you're now number twelve on the waiting list. God willing, it'll only be a matter of a few months before I can lock you—get you into the place. And you'll be safe and looked after for the rest of your life. I've talked to your lawyer about being appointed your conservator and he seems to think *he* should be, but *my* lawyer says I'm in the favored position, being a blood relative. Why don't I wheel you into the kitchen and I'll make some tea." Gregory very much wanted to be wheeled into the kitchen, but not for tea. "While the kettle's boiling, I'll just go into the living room and start an inventory of everything."

When Corinne heard the kettle whistling, she put her pad and pencil aside and got up from the sofa. She turned to walk to the kitchen and that was when Gregory plunged the steak knife into her heart. He adored the look of surprise on her face because he knew she adored surprises. Deciding to leave the knife in her heart because it would look more dramatic, he lowered her body to the floor and set about disarranging the room. He went to the kitchen to take the kettle off the fire, then to the bedroom to ransack the drawers. He carefully hid some worthless jewelry and cash Rosario had brought him the day before in the same place he had hidden the things when he had staged the earlier robbery.

What an actor I could have been! he exulted. From that first moment over a month ago when Rosario's therapy had begun to pay off, Gregory began to formulate Corinne's murder. It was his fingers that first came back to life. A few days later he could move the hand effortlessly. At the same time, his mouth started returning to normal. And, oh, that wonderful morning when his left leg returned to him and he was able to get out of bed unassisted!

But the masquerade was far from over. He settled onto the bed and twisted his body and mouth back into the shape of himself as a stroke victim. Soon Rosario would come. He would find the door ajar, fear the worst, and find it. There would be the police—probably photographers and newsmen as well because Corinne was a celebrated freeloader now, and also perhaps some mention of his being a novelist. With some of his titles thrown in, maybe there'd be fresh interest from some paperback house. He'd never been paperbacked, ever.

He remembered to strip off the gloves he'd worn for the murder and tucked them under the mattress, thinking about how much time to give himself before overcoming the symptoms of his stroke. Perhaps he'd begin in a few days with the partial return of his speech, then the use of his left hand, then the leg, and finally the mouth, and then—

And then Vernon. He'd see what he could do for Vernon.

His reverie was interrupted by Rosario's cry of horror from the doorway that opened onto the sitting room. He'd seen the dead Corinne. This is it, thought Gregory gleefully—it's show time!

BRENDAN DuBOIS

ⅴ FINAL MARKS, FINAL SECRETS

We welcome Brendan DuBois's first appearance in this annual collection, with a powerful story of a remembered childhood. DuBois, a frequent contributor to the mystery magazines in recent years, is at his best with these "memory" stories, and attention should be called to another of them, "Still Waters," from the September issue of EQMM.

It started again, a month after I married my wife Annie. We were in our new apartment in a small North Shore town outside of Boston, and we were playing a game newlyweds probably think up all the time. It was Annie's idea and though I smiled and played along with her, it felt like a cold ice cube was being run up and down my back.

The game was called "Secrets," and we went back and forth, telling each other past secrets we had kept from our families and our friends, but not from ourselves. No, not that, at least. We were in the living room and the sliding glass door to the deck was open, and I saw fireflies dance and blink over the Bellamy River as we played. I looked away, suddenly not liking the door being so open. Strawberry daiquiris in hand and candles on an oak dining table, we talked the night away. Annie had just told me of a time when she was seventeen and had spent the night in Boston, partying, when she was supposed to be with a high school friend. And before that, I had told her about my first and only shoplifting offense, when I was twelve and stole a *Playboy* just for a chance to see what was hidden behind those glossy covers.

I took a leisurely sip from my frozen strawberry drink, which was in a delicate and long glass, one of the countless wedding gifts from nameless aunts or uncles that cluttered our apartment. I wondered how long it would take before "Uncle Ray's table" became our table, and I wondered how long before the game was over. But in the candlelight Annie's blue eyes were laughing at me.

"C'mon, Lew, it's your turn for a secret," she said. "You know secrets aren't healthy for a modern marriage."

The flickering light made her blonde hair sparkle and looking at her I had a warm feeling that everything, at long last, was right. I had met the right woman, I had made the right choices, and things were going to be perfect. Annie was a layout artist for an advertising company in Boston, while I was a wire editor for one of the city's two largest newspapers. I had gone many miles to get here, and I hoped I was happy.

"Sorry," I said. "My life isn't that sordid. I'm squeaky clean; even your parents think so."

She stuck out her tongue. "Maybe, Lew, but your parents told me a few secrets. Especially your mother."

The ice cube was back. "My mother?"

"Right." Annie picked up her matching glass and took a long swallow, and put her drink down. A breeze from the river made the candles flicker. She gave me an arch look with her eyebrows. "Your mother. About the time you were at that Catholic high school and forged your report card."

I tried to smile but I failed. I picked up my glass and there was a sharp *crack* and my hand felt suddenly cold and then warm. Annie screamed and I looked down, and part of the shattered glass was still in my hand. The dull pink of the frozen strawberry was dripping down my wrist, joined by the shockingly bright red of something else. Good God, I thought. He's come back.

Lewis Callaghan was fourteen years old and was certain of one thing—by tomorrow, Saturday, he would be dead.

He slouched low in his classroom seat, trying to be as inconspicuous as possible, though it felt like a spotlight was trained on him. Like every other male in St. Mary's High School in North Manchester, he wore black shoes, black pants, a white shirt, and a blue necktie with S.M.H.S. in gold thread in the center. The windows were open for the first time that year, promising spring with a warm breeze and the smell of wet earth, but he could only concentrate on one thing—what he held in his sweaty hands.

It was a folded piece of white cardboard, with the school seal on the outside and his handwritten name and "Grade 9" underneath it. Inside were columns listing school subjects and inside the report card was his death warrant.

He sank lower in his seat.

A few hours ago he had watched Sister Juanita, sitting behind her large wooden desk in her flowing black and white habit, as she reached into a side drawer and came up with the blank report cards for that semester. She had slowly transferred the marks for each student from a leather-bound ledger on her desk to the blank cards, and once she had looked up at him and glared at Lewis with those cold blue eyes of hers. At that look his heart felt like stone. He was dead.

Lewis opened the report card just a bit, ashamed of what was in there, not wanting anyone else to see the scarlet mark. History, B +. Geography, B. English, A. Religion, A. French, B. And Algebra, F.

F.

His hands felt dirty. God, he had never gotten a D in his life, never mind an F. His parents were away visiting his aunt and uncle in Rhode Island and were due back tomorrow, and that was the day he was going to die. He was sure of it. Up on the pale green wall, over the clock that said he had ten minutes left of the school day, was a crucifix. He said a Hail Mary, remembering the miracles he had read about in religion class. Please God, just this once.

He opened the card again. It still said F.

Around him the other students—the boys dressed like him, the girls in their plaid skirts and blazers—doodled in notebooks or read. He heard someone whisper at the back of the class and Sister Juanita looked up as the whispering stopped. He felt like shaking his head as he looked at his classmates. He wasn't really close to any of them. They seemed so . . . silly, though that really wasn't a good word. It was just that Lewis had it all planned, knew exactly where he was going, and these kids were satisfied with what they had, happy at the thought of living in North Manchester the rest of their lives.

But not Lewis, he thought. As long as he could remember he had always gotten A's in English and he was counting on that to take him places after high school and college. He wanted to be a newspaper reporter, talk to governors and astronauts, presidents and criminals, and see his name on the front page of a big newspaper. This summer one of his cousins in Rhode Island had gotten him a job as a copy boy at the Providence *Journal.* Mom hadn't been so crazy about the idea of his spending a summer away from home, but Dad thought it was great. A summer working at a real newspaper, watching the giant presses roll out newspapers still damp with ink, and knowing the people who put those words on paper. It seemed like a dream.

The final bell rang and he mechanically put the report card in the center of his history book and went out to the hallway, picking up his corduroy coat along the way. Yep, a dream all right. F, F, F. Once his parents saw that, so long summer job. And who knew if Cousin Paul would be able to arrange that copy boy job again.

His hands felt grimy from handling the report card so he went to the basement, where the lavatories were. The boys' bathroom was empty and he washed his hands in one of the large, dirty porcelain sinks. Over the sinks were large windows cranked open with a hand wheel, and the center one was open. In spite of it all he smiled at the sight. Poor Mr. Flaherty still hadn't gotten that window fixed, despite how many complaints from Sister Alicia, the principal.

The basement of the school held storage rooms, the nurse's office, a jumble of old desks and chairs, and the boiler room, where Mr. Flaherty held court. Lewis stopped outside the boiler room, jacket slung over one arm. The door was open and along a short brick-lined hallway was a row of trash cans. One of the prized chores in school was dumping the classroom wastebaskets because it meant a trip to the boiler room and a chance to talk to Mr. Flaherty. And if he was in a good mood, he'd let you dump the trash right into the incinerator, which was at the end of the brick hallway. That door was also open and Lewis watched the roaring of the flames and the red and orange glow of the coals. That must be what hell looks like, he thought. Spending forever there, with the coals against your skin, burning and burning.

Mr. Flaherty stepped out from his workroom, which led off from the hallway. He wore dark green chino work pants and shirt, and his hands were browned and permanently stained with grease. He was almost completely bald and his black-rimmed glasses were held together with masking tape.

Before he spoke Lewis could smell him, smell the thick odor of mouthwash. "You need something?" he demanded.

Mr. Flaherty was not in a good mood. Lewis thought quickly for a moment and said, "The window in the boys' bathroom still won't close."

The janitor snorted in distaste. "That nun principal send you down on that? Let me tell you, kiddo, bad enough I spent twelve years learning from the likes of her, now I have to work for her, too. Now you run along, 'fore I take a hand to you."

He ran along.

At home his older brother Earl had left a note, saying he would be out with friends that night. Drinking, no doubt. Lewis didn't care. Their parents wouldn't be back until tomorrow.

He rambled through the empty house and in the kitchen he ate some chocolate chip cookies and drank a glass of milk. He sat on a high wooden stool and through the kitchen window he watched the sun set out beyond the dull brown hills that ringed North Manchester. Occasionally he glanced over at the small wall clock and checked the time. 5:00 P.M. 6:10 P.M. 6:30 P.M. The minutes were sliding away. He looked over at the counter where Mom made her Italian dinners and pizza or fish every Friday night. The dull white report card sat in the middle of the counter, mocking him.

Maybe, he thought, maybe we could tell Mom and Dad we lost the report card. Or the nuns couldn't find it and would give him a new one on Monday. It might work.

He slapped his hands with disgust on the counter and walked out the back door to the rear lawn. Sure. It'd work. But only for a couple of days. And what would those be like? Skulking around the house, wondering if his parents believed him, wondering if maybe they'd call up the convent to complain or double-check. And then it would be worse, much worse, if they found out that deceit. Lewis sat down on the stone steps and drew up his knees to his chin. He felt like he was six. He was panicking, his chin was trembling, and his eyes were teary. And over what? An ink mark on a piece of cardboard. That was all. He took a deep, shuddering breath, and thought, yeah, that's all. He imagined Mom and Dad coming home tormorrow. Looking at the report card. The tense looks. The yelling. Maybe even a slap or two across the face. Then the phone calls. One to the school, demanding to know how he screwed up. And one to Cousin Paul, canceling the summer job. All because of one lousy mark.

The night air was still warm, strange for March. Stars were starting to appear against the dark sky and the color reminded him of Sister Juanita's habit. He recalled how she reached into her bottom desk drawer, pulling out the blank report cards and filling in those marks, and he remembered wondering, which one of those will be mine? Which one of those will bear that damnable F? He shook his head and tightened his grip on his knees, and the smell of the school soap on his hands made him think of something, of something in the boys' bathroom, and in a very few minutes he had locked the house and was walking back into town.

This sure is crazy, he thought, huddled against the cold brick of St. Mary's High School. And all because of algebra. Something about it never clicked with him. He could understand numbers all right, multiplication and division and fractions. But letters instead of numbers? X's and Y's? It was like part of his brain was dead, that it couldn't even begin to grasp the meaning or basic function of algebra. So he had gone from a B to a C and now, that blasted F.

The wind picked up, stirring dust and dead leaves from last year around his feet. He was at the rear of the school, in the fenced-in asphalt lot where gym and recess were held. In front of him were three windows, and the middle one moved easily enough in his hands. All he had to do was swing himself in, put his feet on the bathroom sink, and he'd be in. Clipped to his belt was an old Boy Scout flashlight. And then . . .

He turned around again. God, can I do this? Will I go to hell? Not only are we trespassing, we're stealing and lying. Because inside the school was Sister Juanita's desk, and it would be easy enough, yes, so easy, to steal a blank one and forge a new card. One with a C in algebra instead of an F. Forge it and give it to his parents tomorrow, apologize for not doing better. Get some good-natured kidding from Dad, and on Sunday, forge Dad's signature on the real card, pass it in, and start working like the devil himself to do better next semester.

Against the brick wall his hands were trembling. It was very dark and there had been hardly any traffic on the short walk to the school. Up and over. That's all it would take. Or face parents tomorrow with the real thing, and spend a summer here instead of Rhode Island. He tried deep breathing to calm the trembling but instead it made his head dizzy. Such a small town. It only took a few minutes to walk from one end to another, and it wasn't for him. He imagined living in a big city, bigger than Manchester or Boston, where it was hard to sleep at night because of the traffic and the music. He wanted that so bad it was almost something he could grab. He closed his eyes and tried to imagine hell again, the burning coals and fire, but all he saw was the red of the mark. F.

He flipped down the window and clambered inside, reaching out with his feet to the sink. His feet flailed in the empty air and he started sliding on his stomach on the window, banging his chin in the process, and he bit his tongue. He almost cried out, imagining falling to the cement floor and breaking a leg, but one foot touched the sink and in a few seconds he was there.

The bathroom was dark and there was a sharp odor of chemicals. Mr. Flaherty must've cleaned it before leaving. He touched the flashlight on his belt and rubbed at his chin. A scratch was there, one that stung, and he looked up at the window. Could he make it back up there when he was done? He touched the cold porcelain of the sink. He'd have to. There was nothing else left. In the lavatory another sink was dripping, the loud noise sounding like a series of gunshots.

He stood at the doorway, wondering why his legs were

shaking so. This is stupid, he thought. We've been down here dozens of times, hell, *hundreds* of times before. Why the shaking legs? Why the dry mouth that wouldn't go away? Why did his hands itch, as if they wanted a gun or a club to hold? To his right were the stairs and to the left were the piles of furniture, storage rooms, and the boiler room. God, I'm so scared, and it was because of the time and place. During the day when there was light and hundreds of other kids here, the school seemed to be alive. Now it was so dark it almost hurt his eyes to squint, and the only sounds were from dripping water and the occasional creak or groan from the pipes.

Can a school be haunted?

Lewis started up the stairs, a hand gliding along the cold metal of the bannister. He noticed the dusty smell of the school—the dirt, the chalk dust, the sweat from all the kids roaming around during the day. The stairs were gritty from dirt and he was halfway up the first flight when the noise made him freeze and grab onto the bannister with both hands.

Below him a door had slammed.

He forced himself to look. Below and at the other end of the basement a red glowing light was coming out of an open door, and the bannister was sweaty in his hands as he tried to imagine what was there. A fire? The devil? Some footsteps echoed out and the door closed, and he heard muttered cursing as Mr. Flaherty stepped out and slowly walked up the other stairs. Oh Lord, Lewis thought. Mr. Flatherty's still here and he's drunk. And he had heard whispered stories out in the playground about Mr. Flaherty's temper when he was drunk. He tried not to move but his arms were shaking as he watched Mr. Flaherty ascend the other stairs, his way lit by streetlights from outside. Lewis let out a breath of air when he heard another slam. The door outside. Mr. Flaherty must be outside. That's all.

The lavatory was still there, with the open window that led out. And out there was a real report card, with a real failing grade. He started back up the stairs.

At the first floor corridor he saw he didn't need his flashlight. The outside streetlights lit up enough of the interior but when he started up the hallway, hugging close to the wall, something struck his face and he stopped, listening to a clattering noise that seemed to go on forever. He reached up and touched a swinging coat hanger that his head had struck. Idiot, he thought. Le'ts make some more noise. He waited a few more minutes and then kept on going down the hallway, but this time he stayed in the middle. His heart was pounding so hard he couldn't make out the individual beats. The sound was one giant roar that filled his ears.

The door to Sister Juanita's classroom was partially opened and he slowly opened it farther, the creaking of the hinges echoing in the room. The room and the rows of desks seemed smaller in the nighttime, less real, like it was all a bad dream. Sister Juanita's desk was in the far corner, the American flag next to it, and the blackboards seemed like polished stone in the faint light. His chest felt as if it was going to burst and he licked his dry lips as he walked across the classroom floor. At every step a floorboard creaked.

At the desk he wondered what Sister Juanita might do if she found him here. If she came in right now, habit swishing and flowing, the rosary beads clicking, switching on the overhead lights. What would she do? Grab him by the hair, no doubt, and hit him a few times. Call home and maybe speak to his older brother Earl, or even demand the phone number of his aunt and uncle in Rhode Island. He wiped his hands on his jacket and leaned forward, not quite believing he was actually going to go through Sister Juanita's desk. It was stealing.

But his hand moved forward anyway, touching the polished wood of the lower desk handle. He tugged at it and the drawer wouldn't budge. He tugged again, harder, and then knelt down and used both hands.

Damn! He sank forward on his knees. The drawer was locked. He jerked at it a few times, his hands finally slipping off the handle in the effort. It was locked, and he had done all of this for nothing. Tomorrow he was still going to be dead. This time he sat down against the desk and drew up his knees and cried into his hands, muffling the tears with his coat sleeve, the musty smell no comfort at all.

In a while he was done, his face dried, his eyes watery and aching from the sharp sting of his tears. He was about to get up and slink downstairs when he tried to remember one thing, what Sister Juanita did every morning. She would sweep into class and nod at the kids, her books and ledger in her gnarled hands, and then she'd sit down, open the center desk drawer, and then . . .

Still on his knees, he moved over to the center drawer, pushing her swivel chair out of the way. He tugged at the center drawer and it slid easily out, and from inside the desk there was a click, as a mechanism of some sort was released. He tried again with the lower drawer and it came out with no problem at all.

The flashlight was in his hands and the strong light made him blink. Inside the drawer were pencils, pens, an ink pad, two blackboard erasers, a pile of envelopes, and there, almost at the bottom and bound with an elastic band, the blank report cards. His prize. He gently pulled one free and replaced everything in the drawer, and then closed both drawers shut, also moving the swivel chair back. He put the blank report card down his shirt, and even though it was cold and scratchy on his skin, it felt wonderful. He was going to make it.

And he was halfway out of the classroom when the voice came. "Hey, you! Stop that!"

He closed his eyes. Caught. He couldn't move, waiting for the hand on his shoulder, the slap on the face, the fingers tugging at his ear. The failure and now all of this. He should have stayed home, for what could he ever do now? He started praying but instead of the formal Hail Mary or Our Father, he just said, Oh Lord, over and over.

The voice came again, louder. "Stop that, now!" He opened his eyes. He was still alone in the room. The voice was coming from outside. Without knowing why he was doing so, he walked over to the row of windows, just above the bright gray of the radiator. One window was still open and he looked down through the screen, at the fenced-in yard where he had been a hundred hours ago. The corner streetlight cast an odd glow over the asphalt and Mr. Flaherty was there, a bottle in one hand, his other hand raised. He wasn't alone. Two young men were in front of him, laughing and poking at him with their hands. They had long hair and both wore dungaree jackets.

Lewis held his breath. No one could see them from the street. Only Lewis was watching. Mr. Flaherty tried to stumble away and the men were with him.

One said, "C'mon, Curt, grab the bum's wallet and let's screw."

Mr. Flaherty turned. "No, you won't," and he brought the bottle down on Curt's shoulder. The young man yelped and cursed and Lewis bit his lip, trying not to scream, trying not to cry out. Suddenly Mr. Flaherty was sitting on the asphalt, his legs splayed out, both hands clasped to his chest.

"Here," the young man said, reaching out with a hand, the streetlight glittering sharply on what was there, and he punched Mr. Flaherty twice in the chest again. He coughed and in an instant the two men were running away, heading for the street. They both turned in unison, as if they were brothers, and looked back at Mr. Flaherty, self-satisfied grins on their young faces.

Lewis held onto the wooden windowsill with both hands, not moving. Below him Mr. Flaherty sat on the asphalt, stock still, hands at his chest. Then Mr. Flaherty started weaving slightly, from side to side, and he slowly rolled over to the hard surface of the asphalt, as if he was suddenly exhausted. A leg twitched, and then he was still.

Out on the deck later that night I sat and looked out at the stars, and I tried not to look at the back yard, which fell toward the slow-moving Bellamy River. I tried to keep my gaze up at the stars, trying to remember the constellations, but like so many things I failed at it. My right hand throbbed with a dull ache where an emergency room doctor had cleaned and stitched my wound. There was a taste of dead ashes in my mouth, despite the half-drunk bottle of beer in my hand. What Annie had said brought it all back.

I never mentioned it to anyone, not even the police. How could I explain what I was doing in school at that time of the night? The forgery had gone on, I had gotten that summer job and others, and I had gotten here, to where I wanted to go so bad. But it never had been like I had planned. At some points in my life, like my high school and college graduations, at my first newspaper job and the time I won a journalism award two years

ago, I could never quite enjoy what I had achieved. It was
always spoiled by the thought of how I had gotten there, over
the corpse of Mr. Flaherty. At those times when I was supposed
to be happy, and when I had a little too much to drink, I always
imagined I saw someone just stepping out of a door, or ducking
behind a group of people. And this someone would always be
wearing faded green chinos.

Annie came out, sitting next to me, a soft hand on my
shoulder. "You okay?"

"Not bad," I said, trying to keep my tone light. "We ought to
call your Aunt Mary and complain about those glasses."

"Maybe so," she said, and her voice was low.

We sat there for some minutes, until I couldn't stand it any
more, and I said, "What did Mom say about my report card?
She's never mentioned it to me, not ever."

Annie shrugged her shoulders. "She told me at my bridal
shower that you were her best-behaved son, except for that
report card your freshman year. Some nun had talked to her at
a school function, congratulating her on making you work
harder. I guess you went from an F to a B in one semester."

Which was true. "That's right."

"And that was the first time she had ever heard about it, but
by that time you were in Rhode Island and she never bothered
to bring it up. Your mom gave me the idea she thought it was
kinda funny."

My throat was dry, despite the beer. Kinda funny. "Oh."

She touched my shoulder again, a soft flicker. "What happened, back then? It really bothered you, didn't it?"

I looked over at Annie and thought, well, maybe it's time to
tell someone what happened back then. Maybe it was time to
stop the lies. In her eyes I saw a look of love and concern, and
I knew it was for a man she thought she knew everything about.
And what would my wife then think, if she knew how I stood
there and watched a man bleed to death, for a report card
mark? I had wanted a wife like Annie all my days, but some
secrets would always have to stay secrets.

"What's wrong?" she softly asked again.

The night air seemed cooler and my hand still ached.

"Nothing," I said, lying for the first time as a married man. I took a drink from my beer and looked down at the bushes and the yard out beyond the deck, and in the darkness I thought I saw someone move.

HARLAN ELLISON

SOFT MONKEY

To call Harlan Ellison the finest writer of short fantasy in our time would be to limit him needlessly. He is a teller of strange tales, like Edgar Allan Poe and Ambrose Bierce before him. Most often the stories are fantasy, but he is also capable of turning to crime and suspense with stunning results. A previous effort in the genre, "The Whimper of Whipped Dogs," won the 1973 MWA Edgar award. This story, which appeared almost simultaneously in The Black Lizard Anthology of Crime Fiction *and* Mystery Scene Reader, *both edited by Ed Gorman, repeated that earlier success, capturing Ellison's second MWA Edgar for best short story of the year. About the story, Ellison has written, "Psychologists specializing in ethology know of the soft monkey experiment. A mother orangutan, whose baby has died, given a plush toy doll, will nurture it as if it were alive, as if it were her own. Nurture and protect and savage any creature that menaces the surrogate. Given a wire image, or a ceramic doll, the mother will ignore it. She must have the soft monkey. It sustains her."*

At twenty-five minutes past midnight on 51st Street, the wind-chill factor was so sharp it could carve you a new asshole.

Annie lay huddled in the tiny space formed by the wedge of a locked revolving door that was open to the street when the document copying service had closed for the night. She had pulled the shopping cart from the Food Emporium at First Avenue near 57th into the mouth of the revolving door, had carefully tipped it onto its side, making certain her goods were jammed tightly in the cart, making certain nothing spilled into her sleeping space. She had pulled out half a dozen cardboard flats—broken-down sections of big Kotex cartons from the Food

Emporium, the half dozen she had not sold to the junkman that afternoon—and she had fronted the shopping cart with two of them, making it appear the doorway was blocked by the management. She had wedged the others around the edges of the space, cutting the wind, and placed the two rotting sofa pillows behind and under her.

She had settled down, bundled in her three topcoats, the thick woolen merchant marine stocking cap rolled down to cover her ears, almost to the bridge of her broken nose. It wasn't bad in the doorway, quite cozy, really. The wind shrieked past and occasionally touched her, but mostly was deflected. She lay huddled in the tiny space, pulled out the filthy remnants of a stuffed baby doll, cradled it under her chin, and closed her eyes.

She slipped into a wary sleep, half in reverie and yet alert to the sounds of the street. She tried to dream of the child again. Alan. In the waking dream she held him as she held the baby doll, close under her chin, her eyes closed, feeling the warmth of his body. That was important: his body was warm, his little brown hand against her cheek, his warm, warm breath drifting up with the dear smell of baby.

Was that just today or some other day? Annie swayed in reverie, kissing the broken face of the baby doll. It was nice in the doorway; it was warm.

The normal street sounds lulled her for another moment, and then were shattered as two cars careened around the corner off Park Avenue, racing toward Madison. Even asleep, Annie sensed when the street wasn't right. It was a sixth sense she had learned to trust after the first time she had been mugged for her shoes and the small change in her snap-purse. Now she came fully awake as the sounds of trouble rushed toward her doorway. She hid the baby doll inside her coat.

The stretch limo sideswiped the Caddy as they came abreast of the closed repro center. The Brougham ran up over the curb and hit the light stanchion full in the grille. The door on the passenger side fell open and a man scrabbled across the front seat, dropped to all fours on the sidewalk, and tried to crawl away. The stretch limo, angled in toward the curb, slammed to a stop in front of the Brougham, and three doors opened before the tires stopped rolling.

They grabbed him as he tried to stand, and forced him back to his knees. One of the limo's occupants wore a fine navy blue cashmere overcoat; he pulled it open and reached to his hip. His hand came out holding a revolver. With a smooth stroke he laid it across the kneeling man's forehead, opening him to the bone.

Annie saw it all. With poisonous clarity, back in the V of the revolving door, cuddled in darkness, she saw it all. Saw a second man kick out and break the kneeling victim's nose. The sound of it cut against the night's sudden silence. Saw the third man look toward the stretch limo as a black glass window slid down and a hand emerged from the back seat. The electric hum of opening. Saw the third man go to the stretch and take from the extended hand a metal can. A siren screamed down Park Avenue, and kept going. Saw him return to the group and heard him say, "Hold the motherfucker. Pull his head back!" Saw the other two wrench the victim's head back, gleaming white and pumping red from the broken nose, clear in the sulfurous light from the stanchion overheard. The man's shoes scraped and scraped the sidewalk. Saw the third man reach into an outer coat pocket and pull out a pint of scotch. Saw him unscrew the cap and begin to pour booze into the face of the victim. "Hold his mouth open!" Saw the man in the cashmere topcoat spike his thumb and index fingers into the hinges of the victim's jaws, forcing his mouth open. The sound of gagging, the glow of spittle. Saw the scotch spilling down the man's front. Saw the third man toss the pint bottle into the gutter where it shattered, and saw him thumb press the center of the plastic cap of the metal can, and saw him make the cringing, crying, wailing victim drink the Drano. Annie saw and heard it all.

The cashmere topcoat forced the victim's mouth closed, massaged his throat, made him swallow the Drano. The dying took a lot longer than expected. And it was a lot noisier.

The victim's mouth was glowing a strange blue in the calcium light from overhead. He tried spitting, and a gobbet hit the navy blue cashmere sleeve. Had the natty dresser from the stretch limo been a dunky slob uncaring of what *GQ* commanded, what happened next would not have gone down.

Cashmere cursed, swiped at the slimed sleeve, let go of the victim; the man with the glowing blue mouth and the gut being boiled away wrenched free of the other two, and threw himself forward. Straight toward the locked revolving door blocked by Annie's shopping cart and cardboard flats.

He came at her in fumbling, hurtling steps, arms wide and eyes rolling, throwing spittle like a racehorse; Annie realized he'd fall across the cart and smash her flat in another two steps.

She stood up, backing to the side of the V. She stood up: into the tunnel of light from the Caddy's headlights.

"The nigger saw it all!" yelled the cashmere.

"Fuckin' bag lady!" yelled the one with the can of Drano.

"He's still moving!" yelled the third man, reaching inside his topcoat and coming out of his armpit with a blued steel thing that seemed to extrude to a length more aptly suited to Paul Bunyan's armpit.

Foaming at the mouth, hands clawing at his throat, the driver of the Brougham came at Annie as if he were spring-loaded.

He hit the shopping cart with his thighs just as the man with the long armpit squeezed off his first shot. The sound of the .45 magnum tore a chunk out of 51st Street, blew through the running man like a crowd roar, took off his face and spattered bone and blood across the panes of the revolving door. It sparkled in the tunnel of light from the Caddy's headlights.

And somehow he kept coming. He hit the cart, rose as if trying to get a first down against a solid defense line, and came apart as the shooter hit him with a second round.

There wasn't enough solid matter to stop the bullet and it exploded through the revolving door, shattering it open as the body crashed through and hit Annie.

She was thrown backward, through the broken glass, and onto the floor of the document copying center. And through it all, Annie heard a fourth voice, clearly a fourth voice, screaming from the stretch limo, "Get the old lady! Get her, she saw everything!"

Men in topcoats rushed through the tunnel of light.

Annie rolled over, and her hand touched something soft. It

was the ruined baby doll. It had been knocked loose from her bundled clothing. *Are you cold, Alan?*

She scooped up the doll and crawled away, into the shadows of the reproduction center. Behind her, crashing through the frame of the revolving door, she heard men coming. And the sound of a burglar alarm. Soon police would be here.

All she could think about was that they would throw away her goods. They would waste her good cardboard, they would take back her shopping cart, they would toss her pillows and the hankies and the green cardigan into some trashcan; and she would be empty on the street again. As she had been when they made her move out of the room at 101st and First Avenue. After they took Alan from her . . .

A blast of sound, as the shot shattered a glass-framed citation on the wall near her. They had fanned out inside the office space, letting the headlight illumination shine through. Clutching the baby doll, she hustled down a hallway toward the rear of the copy center. Doors on both sides, all of them closed and locked. Annie could hear them coming.

A pair of metal doors stood open on the right. It was dark in there. She slipped inside, and in an instant her eyes had grown acclimated. There were computers here, big crackle-gray-finish machines that lined three walls. Nowhere to hide.

She rushed around the room, looking for a closet, a cubbyhole, anything. Then she stumbled over something and sprawled across the cold floor. Her face hung over into emptiness, and the very faintest of cool breezes struck her cheeks. The floor was composed of large removable squares. One of them had been lifted and replaced, but not flush. It had not been locked down; an edge had been left ajar; she had kicked it open.

She reached down. There was a crawl space under the floor.

Pulling the metal-rimmed vinyl plate, she slid into the empty square. Lying face up, she pulled the square over the aperture, and nudged it gently till it dropped onto its tracks. It sat flush. She could see nothing where, a moment before, there had been the faintest scintilla of filtered light from the hallway. Annie lay very quietly, emptying her mind as she did when she slept in the doorways; making herself invisible. A mound of rags. A pile of refuse. Gone. Only the warmth of the baby doll in that empty place with her.

She heard the men crashing down the corridor, trying doors. *I wrapped you in blankets, Alan. You must be warm.* They came into the computer room. The room was empty, they could see that.

"She *has* to be here, dammit!"

"There's gotta be a way out we didn't see."

"Maybe she locked herself in one of those rooms. Should we try? Break 'em open?"

"Don't be a bigger asshole than usual. Can't you hear that alarm? We gotta get out of here!"

"He'll break our balls."

"Like hell. Would he do anything else than we've done? He's sittin' on the street in front of what's left of Beaddie. You think he's happy about it?"

There was a new sound to match the alarm. The honking of a horn from the street. It went on and on, hysterically.

"We'll find her."

Then the sound of footsteps. Then running.

Annie lay empty and silent, holding the doll.

It was warm, as warm as she had been all November. She slept there through the night.

The next day, in the last Automat in New York with the wonderful little windows through which one could get food by insertion of a token, Annie learned of the two deaths.

Not the death of the man in the revolving door; the deaths of two black women. Beaddie, who had vomited up most of his internal organs, boiled like Chesapeake Bay lobsters, was all over the front of the *Post* that Annie now wore as insulation against the biting November wind. The two women had been found in midtown alleys, their faces blown off by heavy caliber ordnance. Annie had known one of them; her name had been Sooky and Annie got the word from a good Thunderbird worshipper who stopped by her table and gave her the skinny as she carefully ate her fish cakes and tea.

She knew who they had been seeking. And she knew why they had killed Sooky and the other street person; to white men who ride in stretch limos, all old nigger bag ladies look the same. She took a slow bite of fish cake and stared out at 42nd Street, watching the world swirl past; what was she going to do about this?

They would kill and kill till there was no safe place left to sleep in midtown. She knew it. This was mob business, the *Post* inside her coats said so. And it wouldn't make any difference trying to warn the women. Where would they go? Where would they *want* to go? Not even she, knowing what it was all about . . . not even she would leave the area: this was where she roamed, this was her territorial imperative. And they would find her soon enough.

She nodded to the croaker who had given her the word, and after he'd hobbled away to get a cup of coffee from the spigot on the wall, she hurriedly finished her fish cake and slipped out of the Automat as easily as she had the document copying center this morning.

Being careful to keep out of sight, she returned to 51st Street. The area had been roped off, with sawhorses and green tape that said *Police Investigation—Keep Off.* But there were crowds. The streets were jammed, not only with office workers coming and going, but with loiterers who were fascinated by the scene. It took very little to gather a crowd in New York. The falling of a cornice could produce a *minyan.*

Annie could not believe her luck. She realized the police were unaware of a witness: when the men had charged the doorway, they had thrown aside her cart and goods, had spilled them back onto the sidewalk to gain entrance; and the cops had thought it was all refuse, as one with the huge brown plastic bags of trash at the curb. Her cart and the good sofa pillows, the cardboard flats and her sweaters . . . all of it was in the area. Some in trash cans, some amid the piles of bagged rubbish, some just lying in the gutter.

That meant she didn't need to worry about being sought from two directions. One way was bad enough.

And all the aluminum cans she had salvaged to sell, they were still in the big Bloomingdale's bag right against the wall of the building. There would be money for dinner.

She was edging out of the doorway to collect her goods when

she saw the one in navy blue cashmere who had held Beaddie while they fed him Drano. He was standing three stores away, on Annie's side, watching the police lines, watching the copy center, watching the crowd. Watching for her. Picking at an ingrown hair on his chin.

She stepped back into the doorway. Behind her a voice said, "C'mon, lady, get the hell outta here, this's a place uhbizness." Then she felt a sharp poke in her spine.

She looked behind her, terrified. The owner of the haberdashery, a man wearing a bizarrely-cut gray pinstripe worsted with lapels that matched his ears, and a passion flame silk hankie spilling out of his breast pocket like a crimson afflatus, was jabbing her in the back with a wooden coat hanger. "Move it on, get moving," he said, in a tone that would have gotten his face slapped had he used it on a customer.

Annie said nothing. She *never* spoke to anyone on the street. Silence on the street. *We'll go, Alan; we're okay by ourselves. Don't cry, my baby.*

She stepped out of the doorway, trying to edge away. She heard a sharp, piercing whistle. The man in the cashmere topcoat had seen her; he was whistling and signalling up 51st Street to someone. As Annie hurried away, looking over her shoulder, she saw a dark blue Oldsmobile that had been double-parked pull forward. The cashmere topcoat was shoving through the pedestrians, coming for her like the number 5 uptown Lexington express.

Annie moved quickly, without thinking about it. Being poked in the back, and someone speaking directly to her . . . that was frightening: it meant coming out to respond to another human being. But moving down her streets, moving quickly, and being part of the flow, that was comfortable. She knew how to do that. It was just the way she was.

Instinctively, Annie made herself larger, more expansive, her raggedy arms away from her body, the dirty overcoats billowing, her gait more erratic: opening the way for her flight. Fastidious shoppers and suited businessmen shied away, gave a start as the dirty old black bag lady bore down on them, turned sidewise praying she would not brush a recently Martinized shoulder. The Red Sea parted miraculously permitting flight, then closed over instantly to impede navy blue cashmere. But the Olds came on quickly.

Annie turned left onto Madison, heading downtown. There was construction around 48th. There were good alleys on 46th. She knew a basement entrance just three doors off Madison on 47th. But the Olds came on quickly.

Behind her, the light changed. The Olds tried to rush the intersection, but this was Madison. Crowds were already crossing. The Olds stopped, the driver's window rolled down and a face peered out. Eyes tracked Annie's progress.

Then it began to rain.

Like black mushrooms sprouting instantly from concrete, Totes blossomed on the sidewalk. The speed of the flowing river of pedestrians increased, and in an instant Annie was gone. Cashmere rounded the corner, looked at the Olds, a frantic arm motioned to the left, and the man pulled up his collar and elbowed his way through the crowd, rushing down Madison.

Low places in the sidewalk had already filled with water. His wing-tip cordovans were quickly soaked.

He saw her turn into the alley behind the novelty sales shop *(Nothing over $1.10!!!)*; he *saw* her; turned right and ducked in fast; *saw* her, even through the rain and the crowd and half a block between them; *saw* it!

So where was she?

The alley was empty.

It was a short space, all brick, only deep enough for a big Dempsey Dumpster and a couple of dozen trash cans; the usual mounds of rubbish in the corners; no fire escape ladders low enough for an old bag lady to grab; no loading docks, no doorways that looked even remotely accessible, everything cemented over or faced with sheet steel; no basement entrances with concrete steps leading down; no manholes in the middle of the passage; no open windows or even broken windows at jumping height; no stacks of crates to hide behind.

The alley was empty.

Saw her come in here. *Knew* she had come in here, and couldn't get out. He'd been watching closely as he ran to the mouth of the alley. She was in here somewhere. Not too hard figuring out where. He took out the .38 Police Positive he liked to carry because he lived with the delusion that if he had to dump it, if it were used in the commission of a sort of kind of felony he couldn't get snowed on, and if it were traced, it would trace back to the cop in Teaneck, New Jersey, from whom it had been lifted as he lay drunk in the back room of a Polish social club three years earlier.

He swore he would take his time with her, this filthy old porch monkey. His navy blue cashmere already smelled like soaked dog. And the rain was not about to let up; it now came sheeting down, traveling in a curtain through the alley.

He moved deeper into the darkness, kicking the piles of trash, making sure the refuse bins were full. She was in here somewhere. Not too hard figuring out where.

Warm. Annie felt warm. With the ruined baby doll under her chin, and her eyes closed, it was almost like the apartment at 101st and First Avenue, when the Human Resources lady came and tried to tell her strange things about Alan. Annie had not understood what the woman meant when she kept repeating *soft monkey, soft monkey,* a thing some scientist knew. It had made no sense to Annie, and she had continued rocking the baby.

Annie remained very still where she had hidden. Basking in the warmth. *Is it nice, Alan? Are we toasty; yes, we are. Will we be very still and the lady from the City will go away? Yes, we will.* She heard the crash of a garbage can being kicked over. *No one will find us. Shh, my baby.*

There was a pile of wooden slats that had been leaned against a wall. As he approached, the gun leveled, he realized they obscured a doorway. She was back in there, he knew it. Had to be. Not too hard figuring that out. It was the only place she could have hidden.

He moved in quickly, slammed the boards aside, and threw down on the dark opening. It was empty. Steel-plate door, locked.

Rain ran down his face, plastering his hair to his forehead. He could smell his coat, and his shoes, oh god, don't ask. He turned and looked. All that remained was the huge dumpster.

He approached it carefully, and noticed: the lid was still dry near the back side closest to the wall. The lid had been open just a short time ago. Someone had just lowered it.

He pocketed the gun, dragged two crates from the heap thrown down beside the Dempsey, and crawled up onto them. Now he stood above the dumpster, balancing on the crates with his knees at the level of the lid. With both hands bracing him, he leaned over to get his fingertips under the heavy lid. He flung the lid open, yanked out the gun, and leaned over. The dumpster was nearly full. Rain had turned the muck and garbage into a swimming porridge. He leaned over precariously to see what floated there in the murk. He leaned in to see. *Fuckin' porch monk—*

As a pair of redolent, dripping arms came up out of the muck, grasped his navy blue cashmere lapels, and dragged him head-first into the metal bin. He went down, into the slime, the gun going off, the shot spanging off the raised metal lid. The coat filled with garbage and water.

Annie felt him struggling beneath her. She held him down, her feet on his neck and back, pressing him face first deeper into the goo that filled the bin. She could hear him breathing garbage and fetid water. He thrashed, a big man, struggling to get out from under. She slipped, and braced herself against the side of the dumpster, regained her footing, and drove him deeper. A hand clawed out of the refuse, dripping lettuce and black slime. The hand was empty. The gun lay at the bottom of the bin. The thrashing intensified, his feet hitting the metal side of the container. Annie rose up and dropped her feet heavily on the back of his neck. He went flat beneath her, trying to swim up, unable to find purchase.

He grabbed her foot as an explosion of breath from down below forced a bubble of air to break on the surface. Annie stomped as hard as she could. Something snapped beneath her shoe, but she heard nothing.

It went on for a long time, for a time longer than Annie could think about. The rain filled the bin to overflowing. Movement under her feet lessened, then there was hysterical movement for an instant, then it was calm. She stood there for an even longer time, trembling and trying to remember other, warmer times.

Finally, she closed herself off, buttoned up tightly, climbed out dripping and went away from there, thinking of Alan, thinking of a time after this was done. After that long time standing there, no movement, no movement at all in the bog beneath her waist. She did not close the lid.

When she emerged from the alley, after hiding in the shadows and watching, the Oldsmobile was nowhere in sight. The foot traffic parted for her. The smell, the dripping filth, the frightened face, the ruined thing she held close to her.

She stumbled out onto the sidewalk, lost for a moment, then turned the right way and shuffled off.

The rain continued its march across the city.

No one tried to stop her as she gathered together her goods on 51st Street. The police thought she was a scavenger, the gawkers tried to avoid being brushed by her, the owner of the document copying center was relieved to see the filth cleaned up. Annie rescued everything she could, and hobbled away, hoping to be able to sell her aluminum for a place to dry out. It was not true that she was dirty; she had always been fastidious, even in the streets. A certain level of dishevelment was acceptable, but this was unclean.

And the blasted baby doll needed to be dried and brushed clean. There was a woman on East 60th near Second Avenue; a vegetarian who spoke with an accent, a white lady who sometimes let Annie sleep in the basement. She would ask her for a favor.

It was not a very big favor, but the white woman was not home, and that night Annie slept in the construction of the new Zeckendorf Towers, where S. Klein-On-The-Square used to be, down on 14th and Broadway.

The men from the stretch limo didn't find her again for almost a week.

She was salvaging newspapers from a wire basket on Madison near 44th when he grabbed her from behind. It was the one who had poured the liquor into Beaddie, and then made him drink the Drano. He threw an arm around her, pulled her around to face him, and she reacted instantly, the way she did when the kids tried to take her snap-purse.

She butted him full in the face with the top of her head, and drove him backward with both filthy hands. He stumbled into the street, and a cab swerved at the last instant to avoid running him down. He stood in the street, shaking his head, as Annie careened down 44th, looking for a place to hide. She was sorry she had left her cart again. This time, she knew, her goods weren't going to be there.

It was the day before Thanksgiving.

Four more black women had been found dead in midtown doorways.

Annie ran, the only way she knew how, into stores that had exits on other streets. Somewhere behind her, though she could not figure it out properly, there was trouble coming for her and the baby. It was so cold in the apartment. It was always so cold. The landlord cut off the heat, he always did it in early November, till the snow came. And she sat with the child, rocking him, trying to comfort him, trying to keep him warm. And when they came from Human Resources, from the city, to evict her, they found her still holding the child. When they took it away from her, so still and blue, Annie ran from them, into the streets; and she ran, she knew how to run, to keep running so she could live out here where they couldn't reach her and Alan. But she knew there was trouble behind her.

Now she came to an open place. She knew this. It was a new building they had put up, a new skyscraper, where there used to be shops that had good throwaway things in the cans and sometimes on the loading docks. It said Citicorp Mall and she ran inside. It was the day before Thanksgiving and there were many decorations. Annie rushed through into the central atrium, and looked around. There were escalators, and she dashed for one, climbing to a second story, and then a third. She kept moving. They would arrest her or throw her out if she slowed down.

At the railing, looking over, she saw the man in the court below. He didn't see her. He was standing, looking around.

Stories of mothers who lift wrecked cars off their children are legion.

When the police arrived, eyewitnesses swore it had been a stout, old black woman who had lifted the heavy potted tree in its terra-cotta urn, who had manhandled it up onto the railing and slid it along till she was standing above the poor dead man, and who had dropped it three storeys to crush his skull. They swore it was true, but beyond a vague description of old, and black, and dissolute looking, they could not be of assistance. Annie was gone.

On the front page of the *Post* she wore as lining in her right shoe, was a photo of four men who had been arraigned for the senseless murders of more than a dozen bag ladies over a period of several months. Annie did not read the article.

It was close to Christmas, and the weather had turned bitter, too bitter to believe. She lay propped in the doorway alcove of the post office on 43rd and Lexington. Her rug was drawn around her, the stocking cap pulled down to the bridge of her nose, the goods in the string bags around and under her. Snow was just beginning to come down.

A man in a Burberry and an elegant woman in a mink approached from 42nd Street, on their way to dinner. They were staying at the New York Helmsley. They were from Connecticut, in for three days to catch the shows and to celebrate their eleventh wedding anniversary.

As they came abreast of her, the man stopped and stared down into the doorway. "Oh, Christ, that's awful," he said to his wife. "On a night like this, Christ, that's just awful."

"Dennis, *please!*" the woman said.

"I can't just pass her by," he said. He pulled off a kid glove and reached into his pocket for his money clip.

"Dennis, they don't like to be bothered," the woman said, trying to pull him away. "They're very self-sufficient. Don't you remember that piece in the *Times?*"

"It's damned near Christmas, Lori," he said, taking a twenty dollar bill from the folded sheaf held by its clip. "It'll get her a bed for the night, at least. They can't make it out here by themselves. God knows, it's little enough to do." He pulled free of his wife's grasp and walked to the alcove.

He looked down at the woman swathed in the rug, and he could not see her face. Small puffs of breath were all that told him she was alive. "Ma'am," he said, leaning forward. "Ma'am, please take this." He held out the twenty.

Annie did not move. She never spoke on the street.

"Ma'am, please, let me do this. Go somewhere warm for the night, won't you . . . please?"

He stood for another minute, seeking to rouse her, at least for a *go away* that would free him, but the old woman did not move. Finally, he placed the twenty on what he presumed to be her lap, there in that shapeless mass, and allowed himself to be dragged away by his wife.

Three hours later, having completed a lovely dinner, and having decided it would be romantic to walk back to the Helmsley through the six inches of snow that had fallen, they passed the post office and saw the old woman had not moved. Nor had she taken the twenty dollars. He could not bring himself to look beneath the wrappings to see if she had frozen to death, and he had no intention of taking back the money. They walked on.

In her warm place, Annie held Alan close up under her chin, stroking him and feeling his tiny black fingers warm at her throat and cheeks. *It's all right, baby, it's all right. We're safe. Shh, my baby. No one can hurt you.*

BRIAN GARFIELD

KING'S X

Here's a lighthearted adventure with a pair of likable rogues named Vicky and Breck. It's almost as if the best of the early Saint stories had been transplanted to Southern California and Hawaii. Edgar-winning author Brian Garfield brings just the right touch to a form that's familiar yet rare on the current mystery scene. We can only hope it's the beginning of a series.

She found Breck on the garage floor, lying on his back with his knees up and his face hidden under the car. His striped coveralls were filthy. There was a dreadful din: he was banging on something with a tool. When there was a pause in the racket she said, "You look like a convict."

"Not this year." He slid out from under the car and blinked up at her. He looked as if he'd camouflaged his face for night maneuvers in a hostile jungle. He didn't seem surprised to see her. All he said was, "You look better than I do."

"Is that supposed to be some sort of compliment?"

"My dear, you look adorable. Beautiful. Magnificent. Ravishing." He smiled; evidently he had no idea what effect the action had on his appearance. "That better?"

"I wasn't fishing for reassurance. I need to talk to you."

He sat up. The smile crumbled; he said, "If it's anything like the last little talk we had, I'd just as soon—"

"I haven't forgotten the things we said to each other. But today's a truce. Time out, okay? King's X?"

"I'm a little busy right now, Vicky. I've got to get this car ready."

"It's important. It's serious."

"In the cosmic scheme of things how do you know it's any more important or serious than the exhaust system I'm fixing?"

She said, "It's Daddy. They've ruined him." She put her back to him and walked toward the sun. "Wash and come outside and talk. I can't stand the smell of grease."

The dusty yard was littered with odd-looking cars in varied conditions of disassembly. Some had numbers painted on their doors, and decal ads for automotive products. The garage was a cruddy cube of white stucco, uncompromisingly ugly.

Feeling the heat but not really minding it, she propped the rump of her jeans against the streetlight post and squinted into the California sunlight, watching pickups rattle past until Breck came out with half the oil smeared off his face. He was six four and hadn't gained an ounce since she'd last seen him three years ago: an endless long rail of a man with an angular El Greco face and bright brittle wedges of sky-blue glass for eyes.

"Shouldn't spend so much time in the sun," he said. "You'll get wrinkles."

"It's very kind of you to be concerned about my health."

"Anybody tell you lately how smashing you look?"

"Is that your devious way of asking if I'm going with some-one?"

"Forget it," he said. "What do you want, then?"

"Daddy's lost everything he had. He was going to retire on his savings and the pension—now he's probably going to have to file bankruptcy. You know what that'll do to him. His pride—his blood pressure. I'm afraid he might have another stroke."

He didn't speak; he only looked at her. The sun was in her eyes and she couldn't make out his expression. Stirred by unease she blurted: "Hey—Breck, I'm not asking for myself."

"How much does he need?"

"I don't know. To pay the lawyers and get back on his feet? I don't know. Maybe seventy-five thousand dollars."

He said, "That's a little bit of money."

"Is it," she said drily.

"I might have been more sympathetic once. But that would've been before your alimony lawyer got after me."

"You always loved Daddy. I'm asking you to help him. Not me. Him."

"What happened?"

"He was carrying diamonds and they arrested him. It was all

set up. He was framed by his own boss. He's sure it was an insurance scam. We can't prove anything but we know. We just know."

"Where is he?"

"Now? Here in town, at his place. The same old apartment."

"Why don't you give him the money yourself?"

"I could, of course. But then I'd just have to get it back from you, wouldn't I."

"You mean you haven't got that much left? What did you spend it on—aircraft carriers?"

"You have an inflated opinion of your own generosity, Breck." She smiled prettily.

He said, "I can't promise anything. But I'll talk to him. I'll finish up here about five. Tell him I'll drop by."

The old man blew his top. "I'm not some kind of charity case. I've been looking after myself for seventy-two years. Women. Can't even trust my own daughter to keep her nose out of my business. Breck, listen to me because I mean it now. I appreciate your intentions. I'm glad you came—always glad to see you. But I won't take a cent from you. Now that's all I've got to say on the subject. Finish your drink and let's talk about something less unpleasant."

The old man didn't look good. Sallow and dewlappy. His big hard voice was still vigorous but the shoulders drooped and there were sagging folds of flesh around his jaw. It had been, what, two years since Breck had seen him? The old man looked a decade older. He'd always been blustery and stubborn but you could see now by the evasiveness in his eyes that his heart wasn't in it.

Breck said, "I'm not offering you money out of my pocket. Maybe I can come up with an idea. Tell me about the man you think set you up. What's his name? Cushing?"

"Cushman. Henry Cushman."

"If he framed you for stealing the money, that suggests he's the one who actually got the money."

"Aagh," the old man said in disgust, dismissing it.

"Come on," Breck said. "Tell me about it."

"Nothing to tell. Listen—it was going to be my last run. I was

going to retire. Got myself a condo picked out right on the
beach down at Huntington. Buy my own little twenty-two-foot
inboard, play bridge, catch fish, behave like a normal human
being my age instead of flying all over the airline route maps. I
wanted a home to settle down in. What've I got? You see this
place? Mortgage up to here and they're going to take it away
from me in six weeks if I can't make the payments."

"Come on," Breck said. "Tell me about it."

"I worked courier for that whole group of diamond merchants. I had a gun and a permit, all that stuff. No more. They
took it all away. They never proved a damn thing against me
but they took it all away. I carried stones forty years and never
lost a one. Not even a chip. Forty years!"

Breck coaxed him: "What happened?"

"Hell. I picked up the stones in Amsterdam. I counted them
in the broker's presence. They weren't anything special. Half-
karat, one-karat, some chips. Three or four bigger stones but
nothing spectacular. You know. Neighborhood jewelry store
stuff. The amount of hijacking and armed robbery lately, they
don't like to load up a courier with too much value on a single
trip."

"How much were the stones worth altogether?"

"Not much. Four hundred thousand, give or take."

"To some people that's a lot."

The old man said, "It's an unattainable dream to me right
now but hell, there was a time I used to carry five million at a
crack. You know how much five million in really good diamonds
weighs? You could get it in your hip pocket."

"Go on."

"Amsterdam, okay, the last trip. We wrapped them and
packed them in the case—it's that same armored steel attaché
case, the one I've carried for fifteen years. I've still got it for all
the good it does. The inside's divided into small compartments
lined with felt, so things don't rattle around in there. I had it
made to my own design fifteen years ago. Cost me twelve
hundred dollars."

"Amsterdam," Breck said gently.

"Okay, okay. We locked the case—three witnesses in the
room—and we handcuffed it to my wrist and I took the noon

flight over the Pole to Los Angeles. Slept part of the way. Went through customs, showed them the stones, did all the formalities. Everything routine, everything up-and-up. Met Vicky at LAX for dinner, took the night flight to Honolulu. In the morning I delivered the shipment to Cushman. Unlocked the handcuffs, unlocked the attaché case, took the packets out, and put them on his desk. He unwrapped one or two of them, looked at the stones, counted the rest of the packets, said everything was fine, said thank you very much, never looked me in the eye, signed the receipt."

"And then?"

"Nothing. I went. Next thing I know the cops are banging on my door at the hotel. Seems Cushman swore out a warrant. He said he'd taken a closer look at the stones that morning and they were no good. He claimed I'd substituted paste stones. He said the whole shipment was fakes. Said I'd stolen four hundred thousand dollars' worth of diamonds. The cops put an inquiry through Interpol and they got depositions and affidavits and God knows what-all from the brokers in Amsterdam, attesting the stones they'd given me were genuine."

Breck said, "Let me ask you a straight question then."

"No, God help me, I did not steal the damn stones."

"That's not the question."

"Then what is?"

"How come you're not in jail?"

"They couldn't prove it. It was my word against Cushman's. I said I'd delivered the proper goods. He said I delivered fakes. He had the fakes to show for it, but he couldn't prove they hadn't been substituted by himself or somebody working for him."

"Did they investigate Cushman and his employees?"

"Sure. I don't think they did an enthusiastic job of it. They figured they already knew who the culprit was, so why waste energy? They went through the motions. They didn't find anything. Cushman stuck to his story. Far as I can tell, none of his employees had access to the stones during the period of time between when I delivered them and when Cushman showed the paste fakes to the cops. So I figure it must have been Cushman."

"Did the insurance pay off?"

"They had to. They couldn't prove he'd defrauded them. Their investigator offered me a hundred thousand dollars and no questions asked if I'd turn in the stones I stole. I told him he had five seconds to get out the door before I punched him in the nose. I was an amateur light heavyweight just out of high school, you know. Nineteen thirty-one. I can handle myself."

Right now, Breck thought, he didn't look as if he could hold his own against a five-year-old in a playpen. But what he said was, "What else do you know about Cushman?"

"Snob. I don't know where he hails from but he affects that clenched-teeth North Shore of Long Island society drawl. Mingles with the million-dollar Waikiki condominium set. I guess they're his best customers for baubles."

"What'd they do to you?"

"Revoked my bond. I can't work without it. I tried to sue for defamation, this and that, but you know how these lawyers are. The case is still pending. Could be years before it's settled. The other side knows how old I am—they know all they have to do is wait a few years."

Breck said, "Maybe I'll have a talk with this Cushman."

"What's the point?"

"Maybe I can persuade him to give you back what he owes you. Don't get your hopes up. He's never going to admit he framed you—he'd go to jail himself if he did that. The best you can hope for is to get enough money out of him to pay off your debts and set you up in that retirement you talked about. The condo, the boat, the bridge games. That much I may be able to persuade him he owes you."

"Aagh."

The shop was a pricey-looking storefront at 11858 Kalakaua Avenue; the sign beside the door was discreetly engraved on a small brass plaque: CUSHMAN INTERNATIONAL DIAMOND CO.

Inside, every inch a gent in nautical whites, Breck stood looking down at several enormous diamond rings spread across a velvet background.

"My fifth wedding anniversary. I want to give my wife the

most beautiful present I can find. You were recommended—they told me they were sure you'd have what I'm looking for."

The man across the counter was bald and amiable. He looked fit, as if he worked out regularly. He wore a dark suit and he'd had a manicure. "Thank you, sir. You're very kind."

"Are you Henry Cushman?"

"That's correct. May I ask who recommended me?"

"A couple of people at a party for the governor. Let me have a look at that one, will you? The emerald cut."

Cushman picked up the third ring. Breck gave him the benediction of his best smile. "Mind if I borrow your loupe?"

Clearly a trifle surprised, Cushman offered him the small magnifying glass. Screwing it into his eye, Breck examined the stone. "Very nice," he opined.

Cushman said softly, "It's flawless, sir. Excellent color. And there's not another one like it."

"How much?"

"Four hundred and fifty thousand dollars."

Breck examined the ring even more closely. Finally he said, "Make it four twenty."

"Oh, I wouldn't be at liberty to go that low, sir." The bald fellow was very smooth. "You see, diamonds at the moment—"

"Four thirty-five and that's it."

There was a considered pause before Cushman murmured, "I think I could accept that."

"I thought you could." Breck smiled again. And then, a bit amused by his own air of tremendous confidence, he went around to the proprietor's desk and took a checkbook and a gold pen from his pockets and began to write out a check. "I want it gift-wrapped—and I'll need it delivered to my suite at the Kahala Towers no later than seven o'clock tonight."

He beamed when he stood up and handed over the check, accompanied by a driver's license and a gold credit card; Cushman scribbled lengthy numbers across the top of the check and Breck didn't give the jeweler a chance to get a word in edgewise. "Of course my wife'll have to approve it, you understand. I don't want to spend this sort of money on a gift she doesn't really like. You know how women can be. But I don't really think it'll be a problem. She's a connoisseur of good stones." Then he was gone—right out the door.

He went two blocks to the beach and shoved his hands in his pockets and grinned at the ocean.

Henry Cushman stood momentarily immobilized before he came to his senses and reached for the telephone. The bank's telephone number was on the check in his hand but he didn't trust anything about that check and he looked up the bank in the directory. The telephone number was the same. He dialed it.

It was a frustrating conversation. A bank holiday, this particular Friday. "I know you're closed to the public but I've got to talk with an officer. It's important."

"I'm sorry, sir. This is the answering service. There's no one in the bank except security personnel."

Cushman hung up the phone and made a face and wasn't quite sure what to do. He paced the office for a moment, alternately pleased to have made the sale but disturbed by suspicion. Finally he picked up the telephone again.

The lobby bustled: people checking in, checking out—business people and tourists in flamboyant island colors. In this class of hotel in this high season you could estimate the fifty people in the lobby were worth approximately $20 million on the hoof. Mr. Fowler watched with satisfaction until the intercom interrupted. "Yes?"

"It's Mr. Henry Cushman, sir."

"Put him on."

"Jim?"

"How're you, Henry?"

"Puzzled. I've got a little problem."

"Jim Fowler laughed. "I told you not to bet on the Lakers. Can't say I didn't warn you."

"It's serious, Jim. Listen, I've just sold a very expensive diamond ring to . . . a Mr. F. Breckenridge Baldwin. I understand he's staying at your hotel."

"Baldwin? Yes, sure he's staying here." And by the sheerest of meaningless coincidences Fowler at that moment saw the ex-

traordinarily tall F. Breckenridge Baldwin enter through the
main entrance and stride across the vast marble foyer. In turn
Baldwin recognized Fowler and waved to him and Fowler
waved back as Baldwin entered an elevator.

"What's that, Henry? Hell, sure, he's reputable. He and his
wife have been here three weeks now. Royal Suite. They've
entertained two bishops and a Rockefeller."

"How long are they staying?"

"They'll be with us at least another week. She likes the beach.
I gather he has business deals in progress."

"What do you know about him? Any trouble?"

"Trouble? Absolutely not. In fact he's compulsive about keeping his account paid up."

"He gave me a damn big check on the Sugar Merchants Bank."

"If you're worried about it why don't you call Bill Yeager?
He's on the board of the bank."

"Good idea. I'll do that. Thanks, Jim."

"That's all right. You're certainly welcome."

It took Henry Cushman twenty minutes and as many phone
calls to find Bill Yeager. In the end he tracked him down at the
Nineteenth Hole Clubhouse. There was quite a bit of background racket: a ball game of some kind on the projection TV,
men's voices shouting encouragement from the bar. Yeager's
voice blatted out of the phone: "You'll have to talk louder,
Henry."

"Baldwin," he shouted. "F. Breckenridge Baldwin."

"Is that the big tall character, looks like Gary Cooper?"

"That's him."

"Met him the other night at a luau they threw for the senator.
Nice fellow, I thought. What about him?"

"What does he do?"

"Investments, I think. Real estate mostly."

"Does he have an account with Sugar Merchants?"

"How the hell would I know?"

"You're on the board of directors, aren't you?"

"Henry, for Pete's sake, I'm not some kind of bank teller."

"It's important, Bill. I'm sorry to bother you but I really need to find out. Can you give me a home number—somebody from the bank? Somebody who might know?"

"Let me think a minute . . ."

"That's right, Mr. Cushman, he's got an account with us. Opened it several weeks ago."

"What's the balance?"

"I can't give out that kind of information on the telephone, sir."

"Let me put it this way, then. He's given me a check for four hundred and thirty-five thousand dollars. I need to know if it's good."

"I see. Then you certainly have a legitimate interest . . . If Mr. Yeager gave you my name . . . Well, all right. Based on my knowledge of that account from a few days ago, I'd say the check should be perfectly good, sir. It's an interest-bearing account, money-market rate. He's been carrying a rather large balance—it would be more than adequate to cover a four hundred and thirty-five thousand dollar check."

"Thank you very much indeed." Hanging up the phone, Henry Cushman was perspiring a bit but exhaustedly relieved. It looked as if he'd made a good sale after all.

Breck's hand placed the immaculate ring onto the woman's slender finger. Vicky admired it, turning it this way and that to catch the light, enraptured.

"It's the loveliest present of all. My darling Breck—I worship you."

He gave her a sharp look—she was laying it on a bit thick—but she moved quickly into his embrace and kissed him, at length. There was nothing he could do but go along with it. Over her shoulder he glimpsed Henry Cushman, beaming rather like a clergyman at a wedding.

Politely, Cushman averted his glance and pretended interest in the decor of the Royal Suite. If you looked down from the twelfth-story window you could see guests splashing around the enormous pool, seals performing in the man-made pond beside it, lovers walking slowly along the beach, gentle white-caps catching the Hawaiian moonlight.

Finally she drew away and Breck turned to the room-service table; he reached for the iced champagne bottle and gestured toward Henry Cushman. "Like a drink before you go?"

"Oh, no. I'll leave you alone to enjoy your evening together. It's been a pleasure, sir. I hope we meet again."

As if at court the jeweler backed toward the door, then turned and left. Breck and Vicky stood smiling until he closed it. Then the smile disappeared from Breck's face and he walked away from her. He jerked his tie loose and flung off the evening jacket.

She said, "You might at least make an effort to be nice to me."

"Fire that alimony lawyer and let me have my money back and I'll be as nice as—"

"*Your* money? Breck, you're the most unrealistic stubborn stupid . . ."

He lifted the bottle out of the ice bucket and poured. "We're almost home with this thing. I'll keep the truce if you will. Time out? King's X?"

She lifted her champagne in toast. "King's X. To Daddy."

He drank to that. "Your turn tomorrow, ducks."

"And then what?"

"Just think about doing your job right now."

AVAKIAN JEWELRY—BY APPOINTMENT ONLY.

It was upstairs in an old building in Waikiki village. Patina of luxury; the carpet was thick and discreet. Past the desk and through the window you could see straight down the narrow street to a segment of beach and the Pacific beyond.

There were no display cases; it wasn't that sort of place. Just an office. Somewhere in another room there would be a massive safe.

The man's name was Clayton; he'd introduced himself on the telephone when she'd made the appointment. His voice on the phone was thin and asthmatically reedy; it had led her to expect a hollow-chested cadaverous man but Clayton in person was ruddy-cheeked and thirty pounds overweight and perspiring in a three-piece seersucker suit under the slowly turning overhead fan. He was the manager. She gathered from something he said that the owner had several shops in major cities around the world and rarely set foot in any of them.

Clayton was examining the ring. "Normally I don't come in on Saturdays." He'd already told her that on the phone; she'd dropped her voice half an octave and given him the pitch about how there was quite a bit of money involved.

He turned the ring in his hand, inspecting it under the high-intensity lamp. "I suppose it's a bit cool for the beach today anyhow." His talk was the sort that suggested he was afraid of silences: he had to keep filling them with unnecessary sounds. "Raining like the devil over on the windward side of the island today, did you know that?" It made her recall how one of the things she'd always admired about Breck was his comfort with silences. Sometimes his presence was a warmth in itself; sometimes when she caught his eye the glance was as good as a kiss.

But that was long ago, as he kept reminding her.

Presently Clayton took down the loupe and glanced furtively in her direction. "It's a beautiful stone . . . shame you have to part with it . . . How much did you have in mind?"

"I want a quick sale. And I need cash. A hundred and fifty thousand dollars."

He gave her a sharp look. He knew damn well it was worth more than that. He picked up the hinged satin-lined little box. "Why don't you take it back to Henry Cushman? They'd probably give you more."

"That's my business, isn't it?"

"I may not have that much cash on the premises."

She reached for the box. "If you don't want the ring, never mind—"

He said, "No, no," accepting the rebuff. "Of course it's your business. I'm sorry." He got to his feet. "I'll see what I've got in the safe. If you'll excuse me a moment?"

She gave him her sweetest smile and settled into a leather armchair while the man slipped out of the office. He left the ring and the box on the desk as if to show how trustworthy he was.

She knew where he was going: a telephone somewhere. She could imagine the conversation. She wished she could see

Henry Cushman's face. "That's my ring all right. What's the woman look like?"

And the manager Clayton describing her: this tall elegant auburn-haired woman who looked like Morristown gentry from the horsey fox-hunting set. In her fantasy she could hear Cushman's pretentious lockjaw drawl: "That's the woman. I saw him put the ring on her finger. That's her. Wait—let me think this out . . ."

She waited on. *Patient, ever patient, and Joy shall be thy share.*

Henry Cushman would be working it out in his mind—suspicion first, then certainty: by now he'd be realizing he'd been had. "They set it up. They've stuck me with a bum check."

She pictured his alarm—a deep red flush suffusing his bald head. "They must have emptied out his bank account Thursday evening just before the bank closed. They knew I'd inquire about the account. But the check's no good, don't you see? I've given them one of the best stones in the islands and they've got to get rid of it before the bank opens. If you let her get away . . . by Monday morning they'll be in Hong Kong or Caracas, setting up the same scam all over again. For God's sake stall her. Just hold her right there."

She smiled when Clayton returned.

He said in an avuncular wheeze. "I'm afraid this is going to take a few minutes, madame."

"Take your time. I don't mind."

Breck sat in the back seat of a parked taxi, watching the building. He saw the police car draw up.

Two uniformed officers got out of the car. They went to the glass door of the building and pressed a button. After a moment the door was unlocked to permit them to enter.

After that it took not more than five or six minutes before Breck saw Vicky emerge from the shop, escorted by a cop on either side of her. She was shouting at them, struggling, forcing them to manhandle her. With effort the cops hustled her into the police car. It drove off.

In the taxi, Breck settled back. "We can go now."

Henry Cushman looked up at him. Cushman's eyes were a little wild. The smooth surface of his head glistened with sweat.

"A terrible blunder, Mr. Baldwin, and I can only offer my most humble apologies. I'm so *awfully* embarrassed . . ."

On the desk were the diamond ring and Breck's check.

Breck impaled him on his icy stare. With virulent sarcasm he mimicked Cushman's phony accent:

"Your *awful* embarrassment, Mr. Cushman, hardly compensates for the insult and injury you've done to my wife and myself."

The quiet calm of his voice seemed nearly to shatter Cushman; the man seemed hardly able to reply. Finally he managed a whisper:

"Quite right, sir."

Breck stood in front of the desk, leaning forward, the heels of both hands against its edge; from his great height he loomed over the jeweler.

"Now let's get this straight. You called the bank this morning . . ."

"Yes, sir."

"And you found out my check's good." He pointed to it. "*Isn't* it. The money's in the bank to cover it."

Henry Cushman all but cringed. "Yes, sir."

"But because of your impulsive stupidity, my wife was *arrested* . . . Do you have any idea what it's like for a woman of Mrs. Baldwin's breeding to spend a whole night locked up in whatever you call your local louse-infested women's house of detention?"

Cushman, squirming, was speechless.

Breck was very calm and serious. "I guess we haven't got anything more to say to each other, Mr. Cushman." He wheeled slowly and with dignity toward the door. "You'll be hearing from my lawyers."

"Please—please, Mr. Baldwin."

He stopped with his back to the jeweler, waiting.

"Mr. Baldwin, let's not be hasty. I feel sure we can find a solution to this without the expense of public litigation. . . ."

With visible reluctance Breck turned to face him. Very cold now: "What do you suggest?"

"No, sir. What do *you* suggest."

Breck gave it a great deal of visible thought. He regarded the check, then the ring. Finally he picked up the ring and squinted at it.

"For openers—this belongs to me."

He saw the Adam's apple go up and down inside Cushman's shirt collar. Cushman said, "Yes, sir."

"And I can see you haven't deposited my check yet. So here's my suggestion. You listening?"

"Yes, sir."

"I keep the ring—and you tear up that check."

Cushman stared at him. Breck loomed. "It's little enough for the insults we've had to suffer."

In acute and obvious discomfort, Cushman struggled but finally accepted defeat. Slowly, with a sickly smile, he tore up the check.

It earned the approval of Breck's cool smile. "You've made a sensible decision. Saved yourself a lot of trouble. Consider yourself lucky."

And he went.

She said, "Don't you think we make a good team?" She said it wistfully, with moonlight in her eyes and Remy Martin on her breath. "Don't you remember the time we sold the same Rembrandt three times for a million and a half each? I remember the Texan and the Iranian in Switzerland, but who was the third one?"

"Watanabe in Kyoto."

"Oh, yes. How could I have forgotten. The one with all the airplanes and the pagoda in his yard."

A breeze rattled the palm fronds overhead. He looked down into her upturned face. "I've got a race next week in Palm Springs, which means I've only got a few days to get the car in shape. Besides, you still need to learn a man doesn't like paying alimony. It feels like buying gas for a junked car."

"Don't talk to me about that. Talk to my lawyer," she said. "Are you going to kiss me or something?"

"I don't know. I seem to remember I tried that once. As I

recall it didn't work out too well. Turned out kind of costly."
He began to walk away.
"Hey. Breck."
Her voice pulled him around.
She said, "King's X?"
He threw up both arms: his eyes rolled upward as if seeking inspiration from the sky. And shaking his head like a man who ought to know better, he began to laugh.

PAULA GOSLING

MR. FELIX

Paula Gosling is another writer making her first appearance in this annual. Ms. Gosling, who resides in Bath, England, is one of the newer British crime writers and already one of the most honored. Her sixth book, Monkey Puzzle *(1985), won the Gold Dagger award as best novel of the year from the Crime Writers Association, and the story that follows was a nominee for this year's MWA Edgar award.*

Edward Felix stood in the doorway of the Leaker's Lounge and glared at the inhabitants. Officially it was the Yellow Lounge, of course, but anybody with half a nose could figure out why those particular people were in that particular place, across from the loos. Since most of them needed frames to walk even that distance, accidents would happen, and had been happening for a long time. The roses on the table weren't much competition. Thank God incontinence wasn't one of his problems. Not yet, anyway, fingers crossed.

"Come along, Mr. Felix," came the determinedly cheerful tones of one of the Care Assistants. "Time for dinner."

Mr. Felix grunted and stepped out of the doorway, transferring his glare to the pretty, good-natured face of Debbie. When he saw who it was, his expression softened. Debbie wasn't as bad as some of them. "I'll fetch a wheelchair for Mabel," he offered. "She needs a chair."

"That's very nice of you," Debbie said, beaming at him as if he were some idiot child who had just buttoned his own coat.

Mr. Felix walked down the long hall to the place where the wheelchairs were kept folded, like collapsed bicycles, against the wall. He chose the least battered and snapped it open, trundling it over to the Green Lounge, where Mabel Tucker greeted his appearance with a crow of delight. Mabel knew what was what, although she couldn't say so, for a stroke had left her wordless, if not soundless. She didn't really belong here, he thought, as he helped her into the chair. She wasn't like the rest. But there was nowhere else for her to go. No family left. No friends, either, until Mr. Felix had come along.

In the beginning, he hadn't intended to stay at Eastberry, but once he got to know Mabel he changed his mind. It didn't matter to him that Mabel couldn't talk. He understood her well enough. She had spirit, despite her problems. Mr. Felix admired that. There wasn't much spirit in evidence at the Eastberry Residence for the Elderly. Most of the residents were exhausted by their years of living, and were beyond showing simple signs of sentient life more than once or twice a day. They sat in their chairs, gray heads hung down like faded flowers on tired stalks, fumbling with the buttons of their cardigans and having their poor noses wiped by the staff. Some caused trouble, most just existed.

Mr. Felix viewed the Leakers and the Babblers and the Whiners with resignation, waking up every morning wondering if he had become one of them—and, if so, which kind. So far he'd managed to keep his faculties, if not his hearth and health. This was home now, and he supposed he was lucky to be here: lovely building, lovely view, lovely room, lovely food, lovely staff, lovely.

Really.

It was the council tearing down the street where he and Alice had lived for so long, so happily, and the arthritis tearing down his joints that had combined to bring Mr. Felix to Eastberry. At first he had fought, but by the time the moment arrived to close his old front door for the last time, he didn't really mind. The children were long gone to America and Australia, and Alice to her eternal rest, so what was the point to clinging to the past? His time was over.

Every day he was a little more stiff. Every day he put on a little more weight. Every day it was harder to get out of bed, to rise from a chair even, much less find the ambition to do more.

On the record card in the files of the Eastberry Residence for the Elderly, Mr. Felix's previous occupation was listed as "jewelry repairer," and indeed that was what he had been. For the record.

But, unknown to the staff at Eastberry, or any other living soul for that matter, Mr. Felix had practiced a sideline. He had also been a thief—a very successful thief, with a great deal of money in various building societies and banks (under the name of Braithwaite), and never caught.

Never even *suspected.* Not once.

Well, who would notice an ordinary chap like Edward Felix, small and thin and going bald, living queitly, nothing fancy to show, a nice little job, with one month's holiday a year his only perk?

"Off to Cornwall again, Mr. Felix?" the girls in the shop used to ask.

"Oh, yes, indeed," he'd nod. "Cornwall again, visiting my wife's sister."

The sister didn't exist, and, for that month at least, Alice and Edward didn't exist, either. The fact that a certain Mr. and Mrs. Braithwaite spent the same month in Acapulco or Rio or Florence, staying at the most expensive hotels, wearing beautiful clothes, and driving an expensive rented car was merely coincidence. There was no reason to connect them at all. He'd made sure of that.

"We're quiet folk," Alice used to say, when they'd return to their little terraced house in Cornmarket Street, having changed clothes, suitcases, and personalities in another town. Always a different town. Always a different storage for the Braithwaite effects. Always a store of memories—and great relief when it was over.

The simple fact was, a month was about as much as Edward and Alice Felix could stand of being the Braithwaites and living the Braithwaite life. Unfortunately, it was the only safe way they could think of to get rid of the money.

For while some men put ships in bottles of an evening, and some built shelves or chairs, and some got drunk in front of the television, and some went for walks with the dog, Mr. Felix spent his leisure hours planning and carrying out one splendid jewelry theft a year. He took his time looking for the target, planning his moves, doing the job, and then fencing the results.

Alice helped, especially when it came to selling the stuff, for in her cloth coat and little hat and flat shoes she looked like the most innocuous day-tripper that ever crossed on a ferry to Dieppe. It was just the money that was difficult.

For if they had lived beyond their means, or drawn attention to themselves in any way, Mr. Felix might have been caught, and that would have spoiled everything.

He didn't *do* it for the money, after all was said and done. It was the *challenge* of the thing that drew him. And knowing the secret, sharing the secret, with Alice. That was the best part.

"Why, it's the finest hobby a man ever had," Alice would say.

"Oh, yes," Mr. Felix would agree. "I'd recommend it to anyone!" And they would laugh and laugh.

Even after he'd retired from the jewelry trade, he kept on, dropping in on his old boss from time to time for a chat, subscribing to the trade journals, keeping in touch. Although he had more time on his hands, he still kept to just one theft a year. No sense being greedy, he and Alice had agreed. Better to take the time to make a better job of it.

But it had all stopped when Alice died. After her death, he'd gone abroad once as Mr. Braithwaite but had come back after two weeks, dispirited and sad. It was no fun without someone to share the secret. He'd put the cases and the false passports into storage for the last time, arranging to pay by the year as usual. He'd sent off a check again only last week, for old time's sake, for Alice's sake. The books and statements for the Braithwaite accounts were in the locked suitcase on the top of the cupboard in his room at Eastberry. Practically the only pleasure left to him was the thought of the confusion they and the other things would cause after his death.

Or it *had* been the only pleasure left to him until a month ago, when he had been returning from the dentist, taken a turn down the street, seen that sign, and remembered the name and what it stood for.

Midden and Warren, Ltd., Wholesale Jewelers. So they'd extended themselves to yet another branch office, had they? How enterprising of them. Business must be as good as ever. Such a discreet new brass plate by the door of the old Georgian house converted to business offices, such innocuous curtains at the windows overlooking the street, such a nondescript facade. They had no need to advertise themselves for passing trade. Every time he thought of it, his mouth went dry. Emeralds, diamonds, rubies. In handfuls. Just lying there. Waiting for him.

"Come along, Mr. Felix," said one of the Care Assistants, startling him from his reverie. "Come along, now. It's roast chicken today."

"Surely you're not going to leave all that, Mr. Felix?" Debbie said in dismay, looking down at his plate. "There's those starving in Africa would be glad of that."

"Then get me some brown paper and a bit of string and I'll post it to 'em," Mr. Felix said, with a wink at Mabel. "I've had my fill, thank you."

Debbie looked at him carefully. "You're feeling all right, are you? Tummy not upset, anything like that?"

"I'm right as rain," Mr. Felix assured her. And still too fat to get through a window, he added to himself. I'll need another three pounds off before that window will be open to me. He stood up and pushed his chair back resolutely. "Come on, Mabel, we can have a game of rummy before that serial of yours comes on the telly."

Mabel babbled her agreement cheerfully, and they returned to their corner of the Green Lounge and the little card table tucked away behind a pillar.

That night, Mr. Felix looked at the plans again. He was tired and it was hard to summon the energy to get the locked suitcase down from the top of the cupboard. The worst part was the rigmarole of checking the hall and steadying the chair, all the while mentally bracing himself against the possible shriek from the doorway of "Mr. Felix, whatever can you be thinking of, climbing up there like that?"

But when his strength faltered, his mind began its own shouting—"What a setup, Ted, what a dream of a chance! One chance, the last chance, the best chance of all! It's a gift—a gift!"

And so it was.

Because Mr. Felix was healthy if not hale, he was allowed to go out of Eastberry for a stroll whenever he liked. Some days a stroll was the last thing he felt like doing, but he forced himself out so as to establish a routine. More than anything else, a routine was the best disguise. People didn't notice what they saw every day, people didn't question why an old man would walk half a mile for a packet of sweets or cigarettes from the shop at the corner of a particular street, because they didn't *know* he came half a mile, and they didn't know where he returned when he left the shop. He was just another "regular," a little slow and vague, someone to be indulged, and perhaps smiled about behind his back.

But every time Mr. Felix "stopped to catch his breath" he was watching something. The people who came and went through the unimpressive doorway of Midden and Warren, Ltd. The alleyway behind the building. The height of this, the depth of that, the breadth of the other. Wires leading in and out. Alarms? What kind? Real or fake? (There was more than one firm he'd known that thought an empty box ostentatiously marked ALARM would do the trick—more fools, they.) Windows—ah, windows were very important. Who could see what through each one, and who was apt to be behind them to look out at night? Which led to what? Did that small window he'd chosen open into a lavatory or a hall? How far, how long, how much time, when, where?

There was such a lot to keep in mind.

The last regular "round" they made at Eastberry was at eleven, and they didn't bring the morning tea until seven. The nights were drawing in now, which gave him more darkness for cover, but they were also getting colder. He couldn't wait much longer. Eight hours to get out, to do the job, to get back.

He knew he could do it.

He wanted to do it.

It had been an unusually warm October day, probably the last before the frosts came, and light had lingered long in the sky. Too long for Mr. Felix's peace of mind. At last, however, the querulous voices of his fellow residents had stilled and the last of the bedroom doors had closed. He could hear the staff down in the kitchen, no doubt having a cup of tea after the rigors of getting forty-five elderly babies into bed and tucked up for the night.

He rose from his bed and rearranged it in lumps and bumps sufficient to satisfy a casual glance from the doorway. He was dressed twice over—beneath loose-fitting street clothes for getting there and back, he wore the black trousers and pullover he'd always used on his "special jobs." They were very tight, even though he had lost as much weight as he could and done surreptitious exercises morning and night to loosen his uncooperative joints.

His room at Eastberry was on the ground floor, so getting out was no problem. Getting across the lawn unseen was more difficult, and he had a nasty moment or two when Debbie, who was on night duty this week, came to stand beside the open kitchen window with a cup of tea in her hand. Debbie was a bit of a dreamer. He stood pressed hard back against a rose bush, grinding his teeth, watching her gaze up at the night sky.

Then she turned away as someone spoke to her and he was able to continue his flight from tree to tree and thus to freedom beyond the walls. A glance at his watch under a streetlight told him he had wasted twenty minutes getting past Debbie and her dreams, and he walked a little faster, the tools in the special pockets of his clothes bumping against his body.

The alleyway behind Midden and Warren was a narrow one, and much cluttered with rubbish and bins. The entire street was made up of converted Georgian terraces, their stepped rear aspects a gift to an agile man but a nightmare to Mr. Felix.

There was one moment, as he hung from a rotting windowsill, his rubber-soled feet scrabbling at the stonework, that he actually considered giving the whole thing a miss. But then he found a foothole, hauled himself up, and lay on the sticky tar of the roof, staring up at the stars.

They twinkled like diamonds, cold and far. Not exactly an inspiration—more of a challenge. They didn't give a damn for him, an ant on a rock hung in space, swinging between constellations. After a while he got enough breath back to curse their disdain in a careful whisper, then got painfully to his feet to face the little window.

God bless the human bladder, he thought, not for the first

time. If it weren't for the fact that people had to empty it regularly, offices wouldn't need little rooms with little windows that hardly ever had adequate locks. And little men, like me, would be out of business.

But Midden and Warren, Ltd. were more cautious than he'd thought. There was a lock on the window, a good one, and wires to an alarm too. Another hour gone. Thank God there were no flats overlooking the roof where he stood. Finally, he slipped through into the dark stillness inside. He sat down and rested on a toilet until he was calm again. The night was cool, but he was perspiring heavily. As he'd come through the window, one of his tools had caught on the windowsill and he'd had to rip his trousers to get free. A cold draft came through the tear and made the muscles of his thigh flutter and shiver.

He got out his pencil torch and looked at his watch. (Never a luminous watch—fancy trying to hide in a dark corner with your watch screaming out like a neon sign? No thank you.) Two-thirty, and he wasn't even in the office yet. Damn.

He slipped out of the lavatory, the acrid odor of disinfectant clinging to him, and into the offices beyond. He'd come to the offices one afternoon a few weeks back, pretending confusion, in order to get a general idea of the layout. The receptionist had been kind at first, then exasperated as he'd wandered about, murmuring about how he'd lived here as a boy, and wasn't it all changed, and what's your name, my dear? He wouldn't have gotten away with that little number years ago.

He tried a door and smiled to himself. As he'd thought—the windows were wired, but the offices within were wide open, and no money wasted on inner locks. Another forty minutes to find the safe (somebody wasn't so clever), another hour to open it.

The trays of uncut gems were on top, the stones in settings in boxes below. So simple, wholesale jewelry. Such a nice, old-fashioned firm, Midden and Warren, Ltd. So reputable, so very, very reliable.

He removed the trays and boxes and set them aside. Beneath, in a rather battered box-file, he found what he was looking for. The stones that *weren't* on the inventory, or the files, or the insurance forms. Some of them might even be from the last job he'd pulled before Alice died—that big pigeon's-blood ruby looked a bit familiar. Good old Midden and Warren—they only fenced and smuggled the best.

He slipped the contents of the box-file into the long narrow pockets along the seams of his trousers, working as quickly as he could in the tight gloves. His fingers had grown so stiff in the past year. He found himself crying the easy tears of age as frustration made him fumble.

At last it was done. He replaced the box-file, the boxes, the trays, and closed the safe once more. He'd done it, he'd really done it. He wasn't old, not yet—or past it, either. Planned and executed, neat as you please, just like old times. Alice would have been proud. Now just ten minutes' rest and he'd be on his way. Plenty of time now.

When he awoke it was eight-thirty. Sunlight was pouring in the windows and he could hear traffic in the street below, people talking, a milk-cart clanking. For a moment he didn't know where he was, and then panic struck through him like a short circuit, galvanizing every aching muscle. He cried out, briefly, at the pain in his body, bones and flesh protesting their unaccustomed efforts of the night before.

Eight-thirty! He'd have long since been missed at Eastberry. And soon the office staff would be arriving here. They might walk in any minute, in fact. He couldn't climb back out the way he'd come in, someone might see him. He was trapped. Trapped!

"Come along, Mr. Felix." The young policeman had a firm hold on his upper arm and propelled him toward the doors, which swung open and then crashed shut behind them with a terrible finality.

"Oh, Mr. Felix, we've been so worried!" Debbie cried, coming out of the office. "What on earth . . . what on earth . . ."

The young policeman smiled. "We found him asleep in a doorway in town," he said. "Fortunately, it wasn't cold last night, so I don't think he'll be too bad off. The receptionist told us he'd been in there once before, a few weeks ago. Told her he'd lived in the building as a boy. We get that now and again.

Seems when they start to wander, they go back in their minds, like. Probably when he felt lost he just found his old way home, sort of like a lost kiddie would. No harm done."

"You're a bad boy, Mr. Felix, scaring us like that," Debbie scolded, but he knew she didn't mean it.

"I'm tired," he said plaintively. "Can I go to bed?"

"I expect you *are* tired, wandering around all night," Debbie said. "I don't know what you must have been thinking of, sneaking out like that. I never would have thought it of you." Mr. Felix hung his head and sighed.

Debbie touched him on the shoulder. "Go on, then. Do you want any help getting undressed?"

"I'm not that bad off yet," he said grumpily and stalked down the hall to his room. Debbie and the policeman exchanged a not disinterested glance.

"I expect he's a bit of a handful," the young constable said admiringly. She was a young girl to be working here among all these old fogeys, he thought. Pretty too.

"Oh, not at all. He'd never done anything like this before. I hope it's not a bad sign," Debbie said, gazing with concern after Mr. Felix, who was walking stiffly away, injured pride evidently the only thing keeping him upright. She seemed to mentally cross her fingers, and then braced her shoulders with a smile. "I expect he just had a dream or something and forgot where he was. I'll mention it to the doctor when he comes round. He's really a very sweet old man, is Mr. Felix. Never any trouble to anyone." She smiled up at the handsome young constable, who was obviously in no hurry. "Would you like a cup of tea?"

Mr. Felix hung up his outer clothes—rescued from beneath the little window with the aid of a broom handle and a wire coat-hanger—and carefully stripped off his dark underclothing. It was agony to drag the chair over, get down the locked suitcase, and put everything away, but he managed.

He put on his pajamas and lay down gratefully on his bed. Getting out the front door and curling up in the entryway of Midden and Warren had been even harder than getting in through the little lavatory window the previous night. He'd only been settled for a few minutes when the receptionist arrived and found him.

He wondered if they'd opened the empty box-file yet. He smiled a little, thinking of their rage, their suspicions, and their inability to do a damn thing about either one, because who does a thief complain to when *he's* been robbed? He thought of the jewels he'd take out and count later on, and of the bank-books, and of the Braithwaites in hibernation. And then he fell asleep.

They took him in to supper that evening in a wheelchair—special treatment, because he was so stiff and sore.

"Serves you right, you wicked man," said Debbie, smiling down at him. "Gallivanting around at all hours."

After dinner she parked him beside Mabel in the Green Lounge. Mabel smiled at him. Nobody said anything, nobody paid the least attention to the two of them. Nobody ever had. Those who weren't asleep were watching *Dallas*. After a moment, he leaned over and took Mabel's hand.

"Here, my dear," he whispered. "Ever been to Rio?"

JOYCE HARRINGTON
THE AU PAIR GIRL

Edgar-winning short story writer and novelist Joyce Harrington had a busy year in 1987, publishing her third novel, Dreemz of the Night *(St. Martin's Press), and serving a term as executive vice president of the Mystery Writers of America—all while holding down a full-time job in public relations. Somehow she also managed to produce this memorable novelette of New York life as seen by a newcomer to that city. It was another nominee for this year's Edgar award.*

I never thought, when I came to New York to be an actress, that I'd wind up being a nursemaid. That's what it amounts to, even though Carl and Stacy insist on referring to me as "the au pair girl." To tell you the truth, I had to look it up to find out what it meant, and I'm still not sure. It sounds as if there ought to be two of me, both tiny and dark-haired, one to change the diapers and the other to teach French. I can change the diapers all right. I've had lots of experience at that, babysitting for small change and taking care of each new kid my mother seemed to produce while she was thinking about something else, but I was never good at French or anything else in school. I guess my mind was too occupied with trying to figure out how to get out of Mudville. And tiny and dark, I'm not. Five foot eleven and a half, you might as well say six foot, and naturally blonde all over. Even my eyebrows.

My hometown's not really called Mudville. I just call it that because it fits, and because I wouldn't want anybody there to know about what's been going on here. I changed my name too, but I did that when I left home, to something a little more suitable to my new life. And I don't mean my life as an au pair girl. I still intend to see Nadya Nystrom up in lights on Broadway, although between you and me I would gladly settle for off-

Broadway or off-off, or even a New Jersey car dealer commercial in sequins and smiles, just to get started.

Stacy says that Nadya Nystrom is a perfect name for an au pair girl. Sometimes she's so insensitive. She tells her snooty friends that she brought me over from a tiny village in Sweden where the only thing I could look forward to was marrying a local boy and getting old before my time. Sounds pretty much like Mudville to me, so I don't argue with her. I even put on a fake Swedish accent whenever any of her friends come over. I figure it's good training in case I ever have to play that sort of role on stage.

Stacy and Carl have had a Major Tragedy in their lives, even though they're rich and young. I don't know exactly how rich they are, but they pay me more than I could make waiting tables, even with tips, and they live in this absolutely gorgeous duplex penthouse apartment with a view of the whole city— the sort of place I'm going to have some day. I live here too, of course, so I can take care of the baby. Stacy can't take care of her because she's too nervous. Stacy, I mean. Not the baby. Everything, every little thing, upsets her. And how I know how old she is, is because that upsets her most of all. The fact that she'll be thirty in a couple of years. You'd think her life was coming to an end, when I know for a fact that my mother is well over forty and she gets more fun out of a night at the bowling alley than Stacy ever had in a year of whatever it is she does with her time. Carl's already thirty. I came to work here the day after his thirtieth birthday party, and that was the first thing I had to do. Clean up the morning-after mess. I would have walked out on the spot, except the baby was a mess too, and Stacy was flaked out in bed with one of those blue cold-pack masks over her eyes. And anyway, like I said, the pay's good and I have my own room and whenever I have to go to an audition, Stacy gets a babysitter.

She says she likes to think she's helping out a future star. I don't argue with her.

But I was going to tell you about their Major Tragedy. This baby they have now, Alyssa Morgana Winston, is adopted. And the reason she's adopted is that Stacy can't have any more kids. She's had two already, and they both died. Crib death. One right after the other. They were twins, and they both died in the same month, October, almost two years ago. So you can understand how come Stacy's a nervous wreck. Carl told me once that right after it happened he was afraid he was going to lose her too. You know what I mean. The Big S. Suicide. I think Carl likes me a little.

Well. Now that you know a little of the background, I guess I'd better fill you in on the foreground. The stuff I wouldn't want making the rounds of all the breakfast nooks and back porches of Mudville, U.S.A. Not that I ever intend to go back there, but one never knows, do one?

What I said a little while back, about how I think Carl likes me a little? That was just a slight misunderstatement. Carl likes me a lot. So much, in fact, that he's been helping me with this scene I have to do for my acting class. It's a scene from *A Streetcar Named Desire*. You know the one, where Stanley and Blanche? and lah-di-dah and so forth. I do a pretty good Southern accent too. But Carl trying to be mean and sexy is pretty laughable. Not that he's not handsome and all that, but it's such a clean kind of handsome. I don't think his alligator polo shirts know the meaning of the word "sweat." I got the giggles so bad, his feelings were hurt, so of course I had to make it up to him. And one thing led to another, and there we were.

I should say, "and there we are." Because that was a week ago, and since then, every night, Josephine, he's in my room. My room is downstairs, along with the kitchen and the laundry and Alyssa Morgana's room and things like that. And Carl's den. The room he calls his "home office" on his income tax return, and how I know that is, he told me. He tells me lots of things. Sometimes he comes to my room just to talk. It's as if he never had anybody to talk to in his whole life. Well, I'll admit it's a little hard to get a word in edgewise with Stacy, the way she goes on. So I listen. I listen to him and I listen to her, and little by little I guess I know more about both of them than they know about each other.

I think it'll come in handy in my acting career. You can never know too much about people if you're going to be a great actress.

So now we're up to yesterday when the weirdest thing happened. I'd just come back from the park with Alyssa Morgana in her pram. That's short for perambulator, which is a fancy English way of saying baby carriage. I write things like that down in my notebook because you never know when you're going to need them. Anyway, we got off the elevator, which opens right into the apartment, and I took Alyssa Morgana into her room to change her diaper. And guess what? There was Stacy, all curled up in Alyssa Morgana's crib, sucking on her thumb.

Well, I'd seen that old movie, *Baby Doll,* where Carroll Baker does that. I just love Tennessee Williams, don't you? He's so weird. So I said, "Hi, there, Baby Doll. Rise and shine."

That's what my mother always said to me whenever I was trying to get a few minutes' extra sleep. "Rise and shine." Only she didn't call me Baby Doll. She called me a lot of other things that don't bear repeating, but never anything remotely decent. My mother's mouth could singe the hide off an alligator, but she goes to church and sings hymns as if sweetness and light was all that ever passed her lips.

Stacy rolled over and buried her face in Alyssa Morgana's Cabbage Patch Kid and let out a howl that sounded like *The Night of the Living Dead.* Alyssa Morgana started crying too, so I really had my hands full.

I put Alyssa Morgana down on her dressing table but I couldn't leave her there because she's old enough to wiggle right off but not old enough to know she'd fall on the floor and break her neck if she did. So I held onto her and changed her and powdered her and tickled her and pretty soon she was laughing.

But Stacy was still howling. In between the shrieks and the moans and the groans, there were words. I started listening. I couldn't help it. She wasn't whispering or trying to keep anything a secret. I started hearing things like "wish I were dead" and "he doesn't care about me" and worst of all, "send the baby back where she came from."

Well. Without Alyssa Morgana, I'd be out of a job and a nice place to live. Not to mention that I doubted very much if Carl would take the trouble to visit my room if my room was a dingy two-by-four in a fleabag hotel, which is all I could afford if I went back to waitressing, which I never want to do again in all my life.

So I thought about that. And about how tough it was turning out to be to even get started being a great actress. There are only about two million girls from Mudvilles all over the country here in New York trying to be great actresses. The other two million are out in Hollywood. And out of those four million, maybe three—count 'em, three—get to be really big stars. And even that could be an exaggeration.

On the other hand, here was Stacy Winston with no ambition to be anything, miserable and whining like a baby in spite of having everything handed to her. So she wished she were dead. Not a bad idea. So Carl didn't care about her. Well, I'd sort of caught on to that little moment of truth quite some time ago, without any help from her. But send Alyssa Morgana back where she came from? Over my dead body!

Or Stacy's.

Now that was a thought to be thought about. There she was in her crib just asking to be put out of her misery. Not the same crib, let me assure you, in which those poor twin baby boys died of crib death. Actually, there'd been two cribs, and Carl told me they'd both been donated to one of those ritzy thrift shops on Third Avenue. So, some other babies are sleeping in them now, and Alyssa Morgana's crib is a brand-new one, very modern and expensive looking. From Bloomingdale's. Stacy told me that.

However. It was hard to think about anything, especially how to make Stacy's wish come true, with all that screeching going on. I put Alyssa Morgana into her playpen and gave her a teething biscuit to gnaw on, and went over to the crib for a closer look at Stacy.

She was wearing her dove gray designer sweatsuit, so she must have been doing her physical jerks when the fit came on. She has a real thing about keeping in shape, even though she weighs about ninety-nine pounds fully decked out in one of her five fur coats. In case you're wondering, two of them are mink for everyday use, one's Russian sable for evening wear, one's an outrageous Canadian lynx that I'd kill for if it wasn't too small for me, and then there's the old sheared beaver left over from her college days that she never wears anymore.

My winter coat is a leftover too. From high school. My mother picked it out. It's orange, green, and purple plaid, and about the only good thing you can say about it is, it's warm and I think it scares muggers.

Stacy's face was red and wet. The shape she was in, not even those five fur coats could make her look like anything but a mess. I said, "Stacy, what's the matter, honey?"

She bawled some more, but the volume was lower. Maybe she was losing her voice.

I said, "Come on, Stacy. Alyssa Morgana needs to take her nap."

You may be wondering why I call her Stacy and not Mrs. Winston like a real servant person should. That's the way she wants it. She told me I shouldn't be made to feel like a servant since I was really an actress, and anyway she was far too democratic to expect people to treat her as anything but an equal. The cook calls her Stacy to her face and Mrs. Flintstone behind her back.

"Oh," she whimpered, "the baby. Where is she?"

"Right over there in her playpen," I told her. "You just about scared her into convulsions with all your screeching."

"I'm just not cut out to be a mother," she whimpered some more. There's nothing like a little self-pity to brighten up your day.

"Well, I told her, "not many people are. My own mother never got the hang of it, but that didn't stop her from popping out six of us at last count and for all I know there may be seven by now."

I said the wrong thing. That set her off again about how she was useless and worthless because she could never have a child of her own. I ask you. In this day and age. There were only about ten zillion things she could do with her time and her money, and there was even Alyssa Morgana, who was pretty sweet and cute as babies go, but no, Stacy just wasn't interested.

Alberta, the cook, poked her head in the door about then to ask what Stacy wanted to have for dinner, but really to find out what was going on. I said, "Stacy's sick so maybe she should

just have some tea and a poached egg, but I think Carl would
like to have grilled swordfish and spinach soufflé." He'd told me
the night before that he liked those two things best in the world
and they never had them at home.

"Oh, you do, do you?" said Alberta, getting all puffed up and
huffy. "Well, he's gonna get chicken and dumplings and boiled
carrots. I've already done the shopping." Alberta is very inde-
pendent. That's what comes from Stacy encouraging all this
democracy.

"If you already knew, why did you bother to ask?"

"Because she always tells me to cook whatever I want. And
that's what I want. So don't you go getting any ideas. What's the
matter with her?"

It was now or never. I already had the thought. Now I had to
plant the seed. "I don't know," I said in my meekest possible
tiny voice so only Alberta could hear me. "I came home from
the park with Alyssa Morgana, and there she was in the crib,
yelling that she wanted to kill herself."

"Oh, sure," said Alberta. "We've been through that before
with her. She doesn't mean it. She just wants attention. Don't
give it to her. It just makes her worse."

"But somebody should pay attention," I protested. "What if
she really does it?"

"She won't," said Alberta scornfully. "She's too chicken."

"But what if she does?" I persisted.

"Oh, you are just too young and too dumb." Alberta doesn't
like me much. But that's okay with me. I would hate to have
her liking me and wanting to talk to me over cups of her awful
coffee in the kitchen. She huffed off down the hall to tend to
her chicken and dumplings. It may sound ungrateful, but the
food here is worse than Mudville, and that's saying a lot.

So back I went to the crib. Stacy had quieted down a bit and
had her thumb back in her mouth. She stared up at me with
those big frightened eyes of hers. What does she have to be
frightened of, I asked myself. She's got everything and I've got
nothing. Nothing but my hopes and dreams and every day I see
them turning into cow chips before my eyes. Like the time I
went to an audition, so-called, and this guy, I don't know who
he was but he sure wasn't the director, maybe the stage

manager or the janitor, said I was perfect for the part but would I mind trying on one of these costumes because they bought the whole show and the costumes came with it. So I said, "Okay, where's the dressing room?" And he said, "Sorry, there isn't one but you can just change right here." And I said, "What are you, a leg man or a fanny man or a titty man? What do you want me to take off first?" And would you believe it, he said, "Take everything off, real slow, and then start in on me." He must have thought I was a real turkey. What I did was, I started in on him. I took his tie, greasy as it was, and yanked it right off his scrawny neck and then I wrapped it back around twice and pulled real hard. I'm kind of strong for a girl. I said, "Do you still want me to take it off real slow?" He didn't say a word, just turned red in the face. I let go before he turned blue.

I didn't get the part.

Six months in New York City and I haven't got a single part yet. All I've got is this au pair girl thing, and Alyssa Morgana, who really likes me. And then there's Carl. I don't know what to do.

Yes, I do. But I guess I don't know how to do it. I've never done anything like this before, even though I've felt like it about a trillion times.

"What do you want, Stacy?" I asked. I didn't expect her to answer me, but she did.

"Sleep," she moaned. "I can't sleep."

"How about some hot Ovaltine?" I said. That's what my mother used to make us drink when we got too hyper. I hate hot Ovaltine.

Stacy did too, I guess. She made disgusting throw-up noises.

"Well, what *do* you want?" I asked her again.

"Pills," she whispered. "Don't tell Carl."

"What pills?" I asked. As if I didn't know. Carl told me he kept them locked up in his desk and only gave them to her once in a while, one at a time, because one time she took a whole fistful of them and had to have her stomach pumped out.

"Sleeping pills!" she screeched. "God! Are you stupid!"

I'm not stupid, but it's okay with me if she wants to think I am. I won't argue with her. Carl doesn't think I'm stupid. He thinks I'm pretty smart and pretty pretty. He said so. He said,

"What's a smart pretty girl like you doing alone in New York without a boyfriend?"

He laughed when I told him, "There aren't any guys smart enough or pretty enough for me."

"You just haven't found the right one yet," he said, and then he smiled in that wise way he has as if he knew something you didn't know, but if you play your cards right he might just tell you.

I didn't push him on it, but I think I know what he meant. But back to Stacy and her sleeping pills. "Where are they?" I asked, all innocent and eager to help. I really am a good actress. "I'll get them for you."

"I don't know," she wailed. "They're somewhere in Carl's den. I was looking for them, but I couldn't find them. You go look."

"Okay," I said. "But you mind the baby."

She gave me a look as if I was the crazy one. I'm afraid she really doesn't like Alyssa Morgana much. Beats me why she adopted her. My own mother all over again, only my mother at least had the fun and the pleasure of knowing we were all her own. When I got old enough I asked my mother one time why she didn't take the Pill or at least use something. She said she never could remember and anyway wasn't I glad she didn't. I guess I am, but if I'd never been born I don't think I'd have known the difference.

I went over to the playpen to see how Alyssa Morgana was doing. She smiled up at me, her face all smeared with gooey teething biscuit mixed with spit, and held up her arms so I would pick her up.

"Not now, piglet," I told her. "I'll be right back. Be a good girl and take care of your mother. She's a mess."

Alyssa Morgana nodded as if she knew what I was talking about. And I went off to Carl's den to see what I could find.

Stacy'd really done a job, trying to find her pills. All the books from the bookshelves were on the floor, some of them ripped as if she thought the pills could be hiding inside the pages. Carl had a row of tobacco humidors sitting in a row on the fireplace mantel; they were all dumped out and scattered around the floor. One of them, a blue and white china number, was broken, and there was pipe tobacco all over the place. And that's just a hint of the wreckage dear little Stacy had created. Somebody'd have to clean it up, but not me. That doesn't go with the au pair territory.

But she hadn't found the pills. I saw where she'd attacked the desk drawers with a letter opener. Carl wouldn't like it so much that his mahogany was all scratched and chipped. Stacy was so dumb. That was no way to open a lock, especially if you don't want anybody to know you'd opened it.

Over the years, since I was a little kid, I've been collecting mystery keys. You know what I mean—keys that you don't know what they're for. I had about two hundred of them tucked away in my dresser drawer, all sorted by size and shape and so forth. You never know when something like that might come in handy. Like right now.

I zipped into my room and groped under my underwear for the Whitman's Sampler candy box where I kept my collection. Right enough. There was a key ring that had about fifteen or twenty little-bitty keys on it. The kind that open desk drawers.

Stacy was still moaning and sobbing. Not real loud, but loud enough so I could hear her. Alberta wouldn't come snooping around to see what was going on. She'd already done that once, and I knew she didn't want to get mixed up with Stacy's fits. She'd stay in the kitchen, boiling her stupid carrots and glopping up her cannonball dumplings. The coast was clear for what I thought I ought to do.

I went back to Carl's den, stepping over the spilled tobacco as best I could. I reminded myself that after it was all over I'd better clean off my shoes real good so no one could find any tobacco shreds on them. The rest of it was so simple. I unlocked the desk after only five or six tries and found the pill bottle way in the back of the top drawer. It was almost full. I don't know what I'd have done if it had been almost empty. Well, it was about time I got lucky, don't you think?

Alyssa Morgana's room had its own bathroom, which was my bathroom too, with two doors, one into her bedroom and one into mine. Another stroke of luck. I'd probably need lots of glasses of water. I went in there and filled the first one, and then I went over to Stacy in the crib.

"Here, honey," I said. "Sit up now. I found your pills and I'm going to let you have just one."

She sat up and goggled at me. Red eyes, red nose, and all her makeup smeared. I'd really hate for anybody to see me in that shape. "Two," she begged. "I can't get to sleep without at least two."

"Well, I don't know." It was delicious, teasing her like that. "How many would Carl give you?"

"Oh, Carl," she groaned. "He doesn't want me to have any. Please. Two. I'm so tired."

"Well, okay. But that's all. If that doesn't work, you can't have any more."

She held out her hand for the glass of water, and I opened the pill bottle and shook out two capsules into the palm of my hand. A third one slid out of the bottle sort of by accident. Before I could put it back, Stacy snatched all three and popped them into her mouth.

I didn't say anything, just stood there with the open bottle in my hand.

She gulped them down and drank the whole glass of water. Then she smiled at me. "Thanks," she said.

"You're welcome," I said.

She held the empty glass out to me. "I'm so thirsty," she said. "Would you mind?"

"Oh, sure." I took the glass, put the open pill bottle down on top of the dresser next to the crib right in front of Alyssa Morgana's duck lamp and went back to the bathroom. When I came back with the glass of water, the pill bottle wasn't exactly where I'd put it, and Stacy had a kind of squirrelly look about her face, like she had acorns or something stuffed in her cheeks. She grabbed the glass of water and gulped it down, dribbling all over her chin and practically choking on it.

I didn't think she was going to be so cooperative about it, but *c'est la vie,* as they say.

The pill bottle wasn't quite empty. I picked it up and made as if to put the lid back on. "Guess I better put this back where I got it," I said.

"Wait a minute," she said. "What would you do if you couldn't stand to live with yourself?"

"I can't imagine that ever happening," I said. "But if it ever happened, I guess I'd blow my brains out or go jump in front of a subway train."

She shuddered. "You don't really understand," she said. "You've never done something so bad it'll haunt you all your life."

I had to agree with her. I wasn't the easily haunted type. But she was getting at something, and I wanted to know what it was. "Have you?" I asked.

She nodded, drooping all over herself. "I have to tell somebody. It's driving me crazy. I can't sleep. I can't do anything. It's always on my mind. I think Carl knows, but he doesn't *want* to know, so he won't talk about it and he won't listen. He just wants to pretend that everything is normal and I'll snap out of it after a while. But I won't. I know I won't. Can I tell you?"

"Sure. Why not?" I was all ears.

"It's so hard to say it. You'll think I'm some kind of monster."

"No, I won't."

"Whether you do or not, it doesn't matter. Pretty soon, nothing will matter. Listen."

"I'm listening."

All of a sudden, Alyssa Morgana started crying. She'd been playing quietly in her playpen, and I'd almost forgotten about her. It was past time for her nap, and she was getting cranky. She'd quiet down if she had her bottle, but I couldn't leave right in the midst of things to go to the kitchen to get it. I picked her up and carried her over to the crib.

Stacy glared at her and snarled, "Get her out of here."

"How can I?" I asked, all sweet reason. "You're in her crib and she wants to take a nap."

"I never wanted her in the first place. That's what I'm trying to tell you. It was all his idea." Stacy's words were beginning to slur and her eyes were getting a weird kind of glassy look. "She was supposed to make me forget, but she only makes me remember. I'm afraid."

"Of what?" I asked. Alyssa Morgana put her head down on my shoulder and started sucking on a strand of my hair.

"Oh, God!"

The way she said it sent shivers up and down my spine. It

dawned on me that maybe there was more going on here than just a spoiled rich bitch having a tantrum.

"It can't be all that bad," I said. "Tell me what you're afraid of."

She took a deep breath and then blurted it out. "I'm afraid I'll do the same thing to her that I did to them."

I was still in the dark, but I was beginning to see a little spark of light. I didn't much like what I thought that light might show up, but it was too late to stop finding things out. I had to know the whole story.

"What did you do?" I asked.

I knew before she spoke what she was going to say, but I kept hoping it would turn out to be something else. I know I'm no prize package, but I'd never do anything as awful as that. Even what I was doing right at that moment wasn't that bad.

"I killed them," she said. "I held a pillow over their little faces until they stopped breathing. First one, and then a few days later, the other one. Don't ask me why. I can't tell my shrink, so I can't find out."

"Does Carl know?"

"I don't know what he knows. The way he looks at me sometimes, I think he does. But if he knew, why would he have insisted on adopting her?" She grimaced at the baby and then let herself fall back in the crib. She lay there, staring at the ceiling. No more tears, no more moaning. She was quiet. "I'm so tired," she murmured.

"Want some more water?" I didn't know what else to suggest. If she was determined to off herself, I might as well help her. It wouldn't be murder, which is what I originally had in mind. More like justice. How could a mother kill her own kids? As flaky as my own mother was, she loved each one of us in her own way. But I believed what Stacy told me. It accounted for so much, even for Carl coming to my room every night. I might as well take advantage of the situation, I thought.

"More water?" she asked. Her voice was really faint and far away. "Yes. That would be nice. I'm very thirsty."

I put Alyssa Morgana back in her playpen where she just curled up and went to sleep. Poor kid. She'll never know what could have happened to her if I hadn't been around to save her.

I had to hold Stacy up and feed her the rest of the capsules one by one. She was so groggy she could hardly swallow, but she managed to get them all down. Then I let her down gently and covered her up with Alyssa Morgana's bunny rabbit quilt. Except for the smeared makeup, she looked like a sleeping baby. Peaceful and innocent. I cleaned off her face so no one would find her looking like a dead clown. Then I wiped off the empty pill bottle and stuck it under the crib mattress, and I took the water glass back to the bathroom and washed it off and dried it and put it into Stacy's hand. It just flopped over but that was okay. It was empty.

I carried Alyssa Morgana into my room and put her in my bed. She whimpered a little and almost woke up. I didn't like to leave her there alone in case she might roll over and fall off the bed, but I thought I'd better make an appearance for Alberta.

There were horrible cooking smells drifting down the hallway when I headed for the kitchen, hoping Alberta wouldn't be able to read my mind and figure out what I'd been up to.

She was sitting at the kitchen table, eating a huge chunk of chocolate cake. That was one thing she did do pretty well, eat, but she didn't offer me any. "Stacy's gone to sleep," I told her. "I couldn't get her out of the crib, so I put the baby in my bed."

"If she wets it, you'll have to change it yourself," Alberta grumped.

"I don't mind." I went about warming up a bottle of milk just as I always did for Alyssa Morgana's nap. I wanted everything to be just as normal as possible. "Do you really think she's only trying to get attention? I'd hate it if she really did something to herself."

"Mrs. Flintstone? Hah! If you ask me, she'd be a lot better off if she took care of that baby herself. Of course, that'd put you out of a job, but that might not be such a bad idea either. I've seen him looking at you. Don't let yourself be taken in by that moony look of his. He's got other things in mind."

"Who? Carl?" I'm afraid my innocent façade developed a great big crack right then, and I hoped Alberta didn't notice. Nothing much gets past Alberta. "Looking at me?" I'm embarrassed to say my voice squeaked.

"Yes, you. The same way he's looked at all the girls who came before you, and all the pretty young nurses who've been here to take care of Her Majesty. And they all went off with nothing but a week's severance. That's the way he does it. Once he gets them into bed, it's only a matter of time, poor things. They all thought he was gonna get rid of her and marry them. What they didn't know was that if he ever does get rid of her, he's got the next Mrs. Winston all picked out."

"Is that a fact?" I said, pouring milk into Alyssa Morgana's bottle. "Well, I think that's terrible. Those girls got just what they deserve. Imagine trying to come between husband and wife. I don't think I'll ever get used to New York City ways." I sure didn't want Alberta to stop talking right then, and the surest way to keep her talking was to ignore the juiciest part of what she had to say.

"Well, just listen to her, will you?" Alberta mouthed around a gross mouthful of chocolate cake. "Little Miss Goody Two-Shoes. Thinks I can't see what's going on right under my nose." What was under her nose right then was a big smear of cake frosting. It was all over her teeth and in her throat too, and it made her voice all thick and brown and slimy. It was time for me to do the best acting job of my career.

"Oh, Alberta," I whispered, "please tell me what to do. I've got nobody to turn to and if I lose this job, I'll be out on the streets. I'm scared." I tried not to overplay it but I figured the way Alberta loved her soap operas, there wasn't much danger of that.

"And well you should be." Alberta had cornered the market on sanctimonious. That's a word I looked up because I like the sound of it, and there's an awful lot of it going around these days. "I'd hate to think you were carrying on with him, and you so young and all. Them others were older and should have been wiser, but I just know in my heart that you're just young and a little bit stupid."

Did you ever want to smack somebody right in her fat mouth? But there was no stopping her now. I put Alyssa Morgana's bottle in a pot of water to heat on the stove.

"I hope it hasn't gone any further than looks," she said. "Don't ever let him into your room at night, though. He can't be trusted. You can't trust any of them." The chocolate cake was disappearing as fast as the smirky words oozed past it on the way to my ears. "Some day she'll walk in on you, and then it'll be the same old story all over again. I'm just glad I've got my own place to go home to at night. I couldn't be responsible for what I'd do if he ever tried his silliness on me."

It was all I could do to keep from laughing out loud. Alberta certainly had a high opinion of herself. But then it dawned on me. She was jealous. She'd give anything if Carl *would* pay some attention to her, fat and forty as she was, and that's why she was trying to turn me against him.

"Just supposing something did happen to Stacy," I said, "who's the lucky lady he's got in mind to take her place?"

"Wouldn't you like to know?" she bleated. "You'll just have to take my word for it and don't get your hopes up. I've been keeping an eye on things here for a long time. He'd divorce her if she wasn't such a pitiful mess. Besides, where do you think all the money comes from? He's not going to give that up in a hurry. Isn't that milk getting a little too hot?"

It was, and I didn't want to seem too eager to know more. I said, "Thanks for the advice, Alberta. I really appreciate your taking an interest in my welfare. I had no idea."

"Any time," she said. "Come and have a cup of coffee with me whenever you feel like it. I could tell you plenty more. You're a nice kid, but you need to smarten up."

I got out of there without letting her know how disgusting I thought she was. But she'd certainly given me plenty to think about. If what she'd said was true, I'd done Carl a big favor and I wasn't likely to get anything in return except maybe an invitation to the wedding.

I peeked into Alyssa Morgana's room. Everything was quiet. Stacy hadn't moved from where I'd left her. In a way, I wished I could wake her up and ask her a few things, just to be sure about what I should do next. Carl would be getting home in a few hours. I could wait around and see how he took the news. Or Nadya Nystrom could just disappear off the face of the earth, and I could get the first bus back to Mudville, which wouldn't make me or my mother very happy. Or I could suddenly "discover" that Stacy had scarfed down all those pills and raise the alarm. But that wouldn't change my situation one way or the other.

I hated to admit it, but I really hadn't thought this thing through beyond taking advantage of an opportunity that was right under *my* nose.

Back in my own room, Alyssa Morgana was sleeping in the middle of my bed. I'd really miss her if I went away. I felt more like her mother than Stacy ever pretended to feel. And it was true that I'd entertained the notion of really *being* her mother if Stacy wasn't around anymore. Alberta wasn't wrong about that. So she probably wasn't wrong about all the other garbage she'd told me. Especially the part about Carl having the next Mrs. Winston all picked out.

I sat down on the edge of the bed and tried to think. But the more I thought, the madder I got. And the madder I got, the more I realized that I no more wanted to marry a wimp like Carl than I wanted a bad case of poison ivy. Wasn't he letting me do all the dirty work while he got all the benefit of getting rid of Stacy and being free to do as he pleased?

It was beginning to look like I'd have to do something about *him* too. But what? I lay down next to Alyssa Morgana to do some heavy thinking.

Well, of course, I fell asleep. Thinking is very exhausting, and I'd been doing a lot of it. When I woke up, the late afternoon sun was blazing right into my eyes and Alyssa Morgana was bouncing up and down on my stomach. "Hi, piglet," I said. "What'll we do now?"

She gurgled and gave me a gummy grin. Nice, but no help at all. I rolled off the bed with her in my arms and went and looked at the two of us in the mirror. We really did look alike, both blonde, both blue-eyed, both of us pretty, if I say so myself. But we both needed a bath. Carl liked to spend twenty minutes or so playing with Alyssa Morgana when he got home from the office, and I liked to be looking my best while he was doing that.

With Alyssa Morgana in my arms, I tiptoed through the bathroom and back into her room. Everything was quiet in there. I didn't want to look at the crib, but I couldn't help it. Stacy hadn't moved. The bunny rabbit quilt didn't move. I didn't go close enough to find out if that was because she wasn't breathing. Quick as a bunny, I gathered up a change of clothes for Alyssa Morgana and went back into the bathroom. Closed the door.

Alyssa Morgana and I had fun in the bathtub. We always did. We played submarine and put bubbles on each other's faces so we looked like Santa Claus, both of us giggling like a couple of loonies. But all the while, in the back of my mind, I was thinking about what I would do when Carl got home and it was time to find Stacy. When we were all dried off, I took Alyssa Morgana back into my room to get dressed. No way did I want to disturb Stacy or even look at her.

I dressed Alyssa Morgana in her blue smocked pinafore and put her down on the floor where she crawled around on the rug while I put on the dress I always wore to auditions for sweet young thing parts, a white number with little blue spriggy flowers all over it and a lacy collar. No makeup except for a little blusher because I was looking pale, and some pink lipstick. I let my hair hang loose, with only a thin blue ribbon tied on top of my head. I looked pretty good, like Alice in Wonderland, but I still hadn't come to any conclusions. I'd just have to improvise, like we did in acting class.

When we were all ready, I carried Alyssa Morgana into the kitchen to see if Alberta had done any snooping while we were asleep. She was brooding over the stove. Probably things weren't overcooked enough to suit her.

"Smells real good," I said, hoping the lie didn't choke me before the dumpling fumes did. "I can't wait till dinner. I'm starving."

"It's my mother's recipe," said Alberta, reverently. "She brought it over from the Old Country."

"Which old country was that?" I asked.

"Bohemia," she said. "I'm a Bohemian. There aren't many of us left. By the way, there was a phone call for you. I told him you were sleeping." She frowned at me as if sleeping on the job was worth a firing squad at dawn.

"Oh?" I said, indifferently. "Who was it?"

"I don't know. Somebody about a show." Again, the frown, as if shows got you hung, drawn, and quartered.

"Oh, well," I said. "It's probably another thanks-but-no-thanks." But I didn't believe that for a minute. Nobody in New York was polite enough to call you up to say that. "Didn't happen to leave a number, I suppose."

"Yes, well, he did. If I can remember where I put it."

Did you ever want to boil somebody alive in her own chicken stewpot? And then feed the remains to the dogs?

She finally found the number, scribbled on a piece torn off of a page of *Soap Opera Digest,* right there in her apron pocket where she knew it was all along. "I'm not sure I got the name right," she said. "He sounded like he was on drugs or something. Hervy Scurvy's what it sounded like to me." She handed me the scrap of paper as if it was a death sentence.

Harvey Scovill! Oh, my God! Harvey Scovill calling me! He was only the director of the play I'd auditioned for almost two weeks ago. I'd given up hoping. It was a part to die for. True, it was by an unknown playwright, and true, it was way off-Broadway. But also true, it was about a young girl who lived in a small midwestern town and wanted to write poetry but didn't have anything to write about except the ladies who came into the beauty parlor where she worked as a manicurist. It was called *Fingers.* And *Fingers* was the name of the book of poetry she'd written. And it was goofy and funny and sad, because in the end she kills herself by drinking nail polish remover. And I don't care how awful the play was, it was the *lead* role. And Harvey Scovill was calling *me!*

"Would you please mind Alyssa Morgana for a few minutes?" I said.

"Well, I don't know," said Alberta. "Why don't you leave her with Mrs. Flintstone? I've got to tend to the dinner."

It was on the tip of my tongue to say I couldn't very well leave the baby with a corpse, but I caught myself in the nick of time. I shoved Alyssa Morgana into Alberta's arms and ran to the phone in Carl's den. All the way down the hall, I heard Alyssa Morgana crying and Alberta yelling about how it wasn't fair that she had to do two people's work. I closed the door and picked my way through the debris on the floor to the desk.

It felt good, sitting at that big, important desk, picking up the phone to make the most important call of my life. I dialed the number. The phone rang. And rang, and rang, and rang. When it was finally answered, it wasn't by Harvey Scovill.

"Yello," said a bored woman's voice.

"Is Mr. Scovill there?" I asked.

"Yais. But he cahn't come to the phone. He's with his reflexologist."

I remembered a tall, scrawny woman who'd sat next to Harvey Scovill at the audition and scribbled notes on a clipboard when she wasn't whispering in his ear. She'd whispered throughout my reading and almost destroyed my concentration. I hated her for that. "I'm Nadya Nystrom," I told her. "Mr. Scovill called me this afternoon."

"Oh, yais. We'd like you to come back for a second reading. Ten o'clock tomorrow morning. Can you make it?"

"Yais," I said, and caught myself before I unconsciously mimicked her any further. "I'll be there," I added briskly. "Same place?"

"Yais."

"What's a reflexologist?" I asked. But she'd hung up. I hoped she wasn't mad at me for imitating her peculiar accent. It was something I did automatically. I'd have to watch it tomorrow morning.

When I hung up the phone, Alberta was standing in the doorway, leaning against the open door and looking shocked. She didn't even notice that the room was a mess.

"What's the matter?" I cried, rushing over to her and steering her back out into the hall before she had a chance to come to her senses and start crabbing at me.

"She's really done it this time!" she gasped. "Call the doctor! Call the police!" She sagged against the wall and I had a hard time holding her up. "Oh, my nerves!" she whimpered. "I can't stand this. It'll be the death of me."

"Done what?" I asked. "Where's Alyssa Morgana?"

"In her room," Alberta groaned. "I had to put her down because the carrots were boiling over. You shouldn't have left her with me. You know that's not my job."

I let go of her and she slid down the wall and just sat there like a beached whale with her huge lumpy legs spread out in front of her.

I ran down the hall to Alyssa Morgana's room. Alberta had left the door wide open. Alyssa Morgana was there in her playpen, googling at me and wanting to be picked up. But first I went over to the crib.

The bunny rabbit quilt had been thrown back. Alberta the Busybody's doing, no doubt. She'd probably tried to wake Stacy up. But it would take more than Alberta screeching at her to rouse her from this nap. Even I could see that. I touched her cheek. It wasn't cold, but it wasn't exactly warm either. As far as I could tell, she wasn't breathing. Well, now.

I picked up Alyssa Morgana. She hugged my neck, and I hugged her warm little body. It was good to have something warm to hang onto. "Piglet," I said, "there's going to be a scene or two around here pretty soon. Wish me luck."

She tried to bite my nose.

Back in the hall, Alberta was still foundered on the floor with her eyes closed and her mouth open. But at least she was breathing. I could hear her from ten feet away.

"Alberta!" I yelled at her. "Do something! Stacy's sick!"

She blinked and rolled her head around on her fat neck. "*You* do something," she muttered. "Can't you see I'm having an attack? What if it's a *heart* attack? Call the doctor. Turn the stove off. If I live through this, I'm quitting."

"What's going on here?" It was Carl. I hadn't heard the elevator door open, but there he was, staring at Alberta and then at me, his handsome face trying to decide whether to be angry or sympathetic. "Has she been at the brandy again?" he asked.

"No. I don't think so," I said uncertainly. But if she had, it would be a darn good thing. "It's Stacy . . ." And then I burst into tears. It was a major asset, being able to do that at a moment's notice. I pointed, with a shaky hand, toward Alyssa Morgana's room.

He dashed past me and ran into the room. Alberta was eyeing me fiercely. "You could have sounded a little more positive," she snarled. "I've never been drunk on the job yet." She lumbered to her feet and staggered away back to the kitchen. I thought she muttered something like "Good riddance."

I tiptoed over to the door to Alyssa Morgana's room and

peeked in. Carl was bending over the crib, just staring down at his wife. I'd have given anything to know what was going on in his mind at that moment. Alyssa Morgana chose that moment to say her one word. "Da!"

Wearily, Carl turned his head. His eyes met mine and I made mine well up with tears again. He sighed and then reached down to cover Stacy once again with the child's quilt. "Well," he said. "She's finally done it. Although how she could have done it with both you and Alberta in the house is beyond me."

I blinked away my tears and took a good hard look at his face. There was nothing in it for me. So Alberta'd been right. Well, well. All I could do for the moment was to keep on looking sorry and pitiful. "Should I call the doctor?" I whispered.

"He can't do anything for her this time. But I suppose we have to have him. It looks like sleeping pills again. But how did she get at them? I had them locked up."

"Just take a look at your den," I suggested.

I trailed along behind him as he mooched along to his den. I didn't want to miss a single moment of his reaction to the mess in there. I needed to know whether or not he was completely sold on suicide. It meant a lot to my future.

He opened the door to his den and just stood there, staring in at the wreckage. Finally, he said, "I guess anybody *that* determined is entitled to get what she wants." And then he turned to me. "Nadya," he said, "I hope this won't drive you away. I need you now."

I didn't say a word, but something like satisfaction began to lighten up the heaviness in my heart. Maybe Alberta was wrong, after all. Maybe I *wouldn't* have to do something about Carl. I tried on a tremulous smile, but the lightness didn't last very long.

"Alyssa Morgana needs you," he went on, "at least until I can straighten things out around here. Stacy wasn't much of a mother—or much of a wife, for that matter. I'd be lying if I said I am sorry she's gone. We haven't been truly husband and wife for a long time. But I guess you know that."

I nodded, waiting for him to continue to dig his own grave.

"I'm going to call the doctor now. And I'll probably have to call in the police. But before I do, I'm going to call a friend of mine. She's a good, kind, sensible woman, and she'll be a big help to all of us. I'd appreciate it if you'd do whatever she asks you to do."

"Okay," I said. And then I couldn't help asking, "Is she *that* good a friend?"

"What?" he said, startled. "Oh, I see what you mean. Well, yes, I guess she is. Only it's a little too soon to think about what might happen six months or a year from now. Nadya, don't think I'm not grateful for the evenings I've spent with you. I was lonely, and you were sweet. I'll never forget that. And you won't be sorry. I'll make it up to you. I hope we'll always be friends."

But not *that* good a friend, I said to myself. "Sure," I told him. "For as long as we both shall live."

He gave me a puzzled look, but then shrugged it off and went into his den and closed the door.

I opened it and said, "I've got an audition in the morning. Is it okay if I get a babysitter? That's what Stacy always did."

"Of course," he said, staring down at his desk drawer and fingering the marks of the letter opener. "You've got your career to think of. Good luck." He picked up the phone and started dialing.

I closed the door and snuggled my face into Alyssa Morgana's sweet baby-powder smell. "It'll have to be soon," I whispered to her. "It'll be something like this. He couldn't live without her. I don't know yet how it'll happen. Maybe he'll jump out a window. Or drink poison in his Tequila Sunrise. Poor guy. He was just so upset and depressed. Blamed himself for what happened. Don't worry. I'll figure it out. If there's one thing an au pair girl has to be, it's resourceful."

Alyssa Morgana gurgled and pulled the blue ribbon off my head. I didn't mind. This particular costume had served its purpose.

And to tell the truth, Stacy'd given me a few ideas about how to play the suicide scene at the audition tomorrow morning. She always said she wanted to help out a future star.

ERIC M. HEIDEMAN

ROGER, MR. WHILKIE!

We welcome Eric M. Heideman to these pages with his first published story, winner of this year's Robert L. Fish Award, given annually by MWA in recognition of the best story by a new writer. We hope we'll be hearing more from the talented Mr. Heideman.

Mr. Whilkie had just passed his forty-seventh birthday, after twenty-one years of marriage and twenty-four of faithful labor in the Government Printing Office, when he became certain that someone was trying to kill him.

The discovery was gradual in terms of evidences accumulated, but his realization that those evidences led—could only lead—in one direction came quite suddenly, at 4:22 P.M. on a Wednesday in mid-July. Mr. Whilkie drew a red slash mark through the last *k* in "two pairs shorts—khakki," then looked up, sniffing rabbit-fashion as he was sometimes wont when trying to recapture a thought.

Something, he could almost sense through his pores, something was out of place on his desk . . . yes, the white-out. He reached into the top left drawer where it had predictably rested since he had been advanced to this desk eight years ago, but there was no white-out to be found.

It had been a quiet, uneventful day, as were nearly all of Mr. Whilkie's days, from his rising at 6:15 A.M., eating oatmeal and English muffins while reading the *Post,* and walking out his door at 7:22, through hours of carefully examined words and punctuation, until this moment when everything fell off kilter. Vanishing bottles of white-out were simply not among the factors with which one had to contend in one's life.

Mrs. Sylverman, waiting patiently, said, "Did you lose something, Mr. Whilkie?"

"I—no. Here it is." (But in the *wrong drawer!*) He read her the next sentence . . .

. . . and heard Miss Gurney and Mr. Otani conversing on the other side of the room: "How long do you figure the old bozo will hang on?" "Oh, he'll be out after November, for sure." Their words became inaudible as Mr. Whilkie's efficient hands were discovering other things out of their proper places: scissors, masking tape, even the roll of Life Savers. *Someone else* had been in this desk. He continued reading to Mrs. Sylverman, fairly sure that his voice betrayed no further sign that something was wrong.

Mr. Brubbage walked up to his desk. "Hello there, Roger. Keeping up the fort?" Mr. Whilkie attempted to smile politely. "You know, we'd like you to give a testimonial for old Wortlandt two months from now when he retires. Think you can do that?"

It had been many years since it had occurred to Mr. Whilkie that he could say no to a superior. He said yes. "Knew we could count on you." Brubbage gave his hand three shakes. "You're a good man, Roger. You can't find so many first class workers these days, people like Wortlandt and Carcastle." He nodded significantly. "We're looking to you to fill their shoes."

Mr. Whilkie allowed himself a silent sigh. Everything going wrong all at once. Brubbage knew he was no speaker, why pick *him* to give a testimonial? Something about . . . fill their shoes . . . Carcastle. *Car*castle!

Suddenly there was no confusion, no vague uneasiness that something might be wrong. Suddenly he *knew.* And, knowing, he froze the thought off altogether and went back to his proofreading.

Promptly at 5:00 P.M. Mr. Whilkie straightened his desk and got up to catch the bus to Rockville. On his way out the door his left foot connected with a misplaced wastebasket, almost toppling him. He was quite sure the basket had never been placed there before.

He saw, on his way out of the building, that the Printing Office bookstore was as usual drawing a steady flow of business. A strategic removal and wiping of his gray-framed glasses afforded him opportunity to see that to the left of two bored-looking cashiers, a man in a knee-length white coat was, in fact, hunched up in concentration before a shelf of pamphlets.

At the corner of the block where he was to catch his bus Mr.

Whilkie observed that the lid to a manhole was slightly, but definitely, ajar. A heedless footfall in the wrong spot and . . .

The bus arrived and people surged into it, Mr. Whilkie waiting, as always, until nearly last. And when he had seated himself in the one remaining window seat, mopped his forehead with his handkerchief, and commenced looking out at the ever-bustling scenery, then, and then only, did he allow himself to think over the train of events, and the burst of intuition linking them together, that he had flash-frozen in his mind for the past hour, not permitting them, by a supreme effort of will, to interfere with the ordered carrying out of his duties.

Now that he felt free to look hard and clear at his discovery, he realized that it had shaken him to the very core of his quiet being.

Lest he be mistaken about something so vitally important, he followed the train backward through the manhole cover and the wastebasket to the man with the coat, the chatter in the office that afternoon (just which old bozo was that?), the invasion of his desk—and, yes, that damnable invitation from Brubbage. Fill Carcastle's shoes . . .

Mr. Whilkie shook his head from side to side at the wonder of it all. He was a fastidious worker whose regular habits—never a day's sick-leave—had drawn warm praise from his superiors, but it seemed to him that his life had otherwise been totally unexceptional.

He had, to his knowledge, no friends of odd political leanings and, beyond an occasional glass of brandy and a craving for mystery novels (and, in his younger days, for movies), he was without vices. Yet, now, this new thing had entered into his life, and everything that had gone before stood transformed. Fill old Carcastle's shoes. The moment Brubbage had said that, he'd realized that Carcastle was gone, had been gone from the office for well over a year, simply vanished. Because no one had mentioned his absence, it had never occurred to Mr. Whilkie to think about it.

Still—be methodical. This much could be explained away. Review the other evidences:

*In March, driving home from Connecticut, he had turned a corner and found himself bearing down on not one but *two* garbage cans and their former contents. Fortunately he had learned, driving a jeep in the army, how to bring an automobile to a quick stop.

*He had known to look for the man in the white overcoat because for the past three weeks, whenever he had left for the day, he had seen a man browsing in the bookstore, wearing a white overcoat. There were, so far as he could discern from behind, three different men, but each of them wore a nearly identical coat. In Washington. In July. There was more: six times during those three weeks, while eating lunch in Union Station, he had spied one or another of those men dialing number after number on a pay phone.

*Eight evenings ago (things were accelerating!), as he sat alone in his living room, Mr. Whilkie's attention had been jerked from the book he was reading by the *thwacking* impact of a bird against the window. He hurried outside, and saw—he was prepared to swear to it, although he told no one—a passenger pigeon, dead. A *passenger* pigeon, presumed extinct all these years, but really nurtured in some secret place so that it could kill itself against *his* window. Quickly, before his wife could return from her auxiliary meeting, he had fetched a shovel from the garage and buried the bird in the yard.

And, of course, that was far from all. He had vaguely known for months that all was not well—little things, an infinitude of little things, no two of them, till now, connected by a discernible thread. He closed his eyes and conjured up an image of himself the previous Saturday sitting up late to watch the World War II picture. As he sat nodding, in his bathrobe, the pilot turned from his control panel to the screen and said in a different, sharper voice. "Roger Willco." "That's Whilkie. R. W. Whilkie," he replied before catching himself. Now, days later, he knew the message *had* been for him. Somewhere in the television industry he had a friend, someone who had tried to warn him.

Amazing as it was, the evidence did seem to point clearly in this one direction. Someone meant to kill him.

It was singular—the most singular situation, he quickly realized, that he had ever been in. How had it come about? What had he done, to acquire such committed enemies?

Mr. Whilkie began to enumerate his accumulation of sins. It was not, he realized with mingled pride, pique, and modesty, an extensive list. He passed over such college indiscretions as a loud song and a drink too many or keeping a young lady past her curfew, and passed too the early, idealistic years in Washington. This thing would almost surely have had its beginnings in more recent times.

Six years ago, before his car was stolen and Mrs. Whilkie dissuaded him from driving the new car to and from work, he had backed into the right fender of a parked sedan, leaving a dent in it the width of his thumb. Instead of pinning a note with his phone number to the sedan's windshield he had, to later twangs of guilt, simply driven away. What if the accident had in fact been witnessed by the car's owner, a gangster who filed away his hatred until, years later, he had time to spare for a slow and thorough vengeance . . . ? Eighteen months ago he had given witness's testimony to an auto collision. There had been no serious injuries, but what if gangsters had been involved who could measure their vindictiveness?

The bus stopped at a transfer point and another torrent of people compressed themselves inside in a din of buffeting and toe-stomping. Mr. Whilkie squeezed closer to the window as a large woman with two grocery sacks splashed down next to him.

But what *consequential* thing had he done, he pondered, staring out at the muggy landscape. What departure from his scarcely varying actions had made some one or more persons so very angry. . . . Last year, pausing to observe a Dacotah Indian rally outside the White House, he had stumbled, jostling a chief who in turn jostled a brave playing tom-toms. Mr. Whilkie dismissed the incident; when one had to contend with a government and a society that were indifferent when they were not actively genocidal, one was unlikely to take murderous umbrage at one clumsy onlooker. No, he must have done or learned something more serious, more fundamental, to require assassination.

Mr. Whilkie had come no closer to resolving his difficulties when he left the bus and walked the remaining two blocks to his rambledown brick home.

At the sound of their front door opening, Mrs. Whilkie, a well-kempt, black-haired woman of forty-six, called from upstairs, "The roast beef will be ready in half an hour, Mr. Whilkie. Help yourself to the tomato juice." So saying, she resumed her watering of the upper division of her army of plants.

Mrs. Whilkie—or Barbara, as he always called her when he addressed her by name (there were no nicknames between them, and Barbara, since five or six years into their marriage, had studiously spoken of and to him as "Mr. Whilkie")—Mrs. Whilkie was a woman of some ambition, born at a place and in a time where the closest she could come to fulfilling that ambition was to play the genial, ubiquitous helpmate to a successful husband.

Mr. Whilkie, when they married, had seemed to have all the ingredients she desired: he was intelligent and hardworking, with a good job and the likelihood of rising to real influence. Then one and two and ten years passed, and he did rise in position and salary, but he still remained in the same office. And he was still—there was no getting around it—a proofreader.

Having fed the last of her azaleas, Mrs. Whilkie gathered up the biography she was reading of the wife of Aaron Burr and commenced descending the stairs.

Once inside the house Mr. Whilkie had lost no time in beginning to examine the living room for signs of anything slightly out of place (A task, he reflected, rendered much easier than it might otherwise have been by the people living in this household. He and his wife could go for as much as a year without anything's falling out of place.). He was casting his eyes over the arrangement of coats on the coatrack when Mrs. Whilkie entered the room.

"Did you lose something, Mr. Whilkie?" she asked, possessing an eye as keen as his own for untidy actions. Her husband was not given to staring after things, whether coatracks or train accidents.

Mr. Whilkie turned—"jerked" was almost the word—to face her. "I'll get us some tomato juice."

"I hope you've remembered to invite everyone at the office to our party Friday," her voice followed him to the kitchen, not sternly but in the tone of one reciting out loud a grocery shopping list. "Be sure to remind Mr. Scully and that nice Mr. Burstein to come," she added during dinner. "I want everyone to hear his wonderful stories about the Riviera."

Her husband nodded compliance. Through dinner and afterward, as they played gin, he supplied the usual, requisite nods and "Oh, I see's" to their conversation, but Mrs. Whilkie could tell that, more than usual, his mind was elsewhere. More than that, he glanced at things, seeming surprised to find them where they always had been. As they were ascending the stairs for the evening she put a hand to his forehead but it seemed normal; if anything, a bit cool.

Feigning sleep, Mr. Whilkie thought about the occasion, seven months before, when the army colonel had entered the Printing Office irate about the printing of a document dealing with the manufacture of small bombs from parts lying about the home— a document that should still have been classified. Why hadn't they spotted it? Mr. Whilkie had heard no more about the complaint after Brubbage had kindly but clearly informed the colonel that such decisions were not made by the Printing Office, that the Printing Office simply processed the materials that came to them. Had—someone—checked further and learned that the proofing on that document had been done by Mr. Whilkie?

For the next two days Mr. Whilkie's behavior at the office was such as would be unlikely to make even the most suspicious coworker think that he found anything amiss. There were, it is true, the quick, darting glances above and behind him, coupled with the furtive siftings-through of his wastebasket, but so unostentatiously were these things done, so well did he maintain his quiet, vaguely mouselike demeanor, that, churn though his mind did those two days, he preserved the cloak of invisibility that had settled on him years before.

Lunch hours he spent in Union Station, peering over the top edge of a *Times* at the milling forms and faces embarking and disembarking. His three white-coated men were nowhere to be seen, either there or in the bookstore. That could mean nothing at all; then again, it could mean that they were onto him.

Friday evening, after eating a light dinner, Mr. Whilkie changed into his blue suit and read a *National Geographic* article about Lake Geneva until guests began arriving for his wife's party. Her parties drew a fair cross section of mid-level Washington society: people from their club and from the Rotary, both of which Mrs. Whilkie had sagely persuaded him to join in order to widen their circle of acquaintance. Mr. Whilkie had invited several people from his office, the ones he could depend on not to become drunk and back him into a corner and talk at him.

Mr. Whilkie sniffed at his brandy, allowing the aroma to work its subtle havoc with the metric orderliness of his thoughts. This party—friends, dyed-in-the-wool Washingtonians all, most of them arriving in the eager, adventure-loving bloom of youth, only to find as they grew middle-aged that if they were not as clever, or influential, or well-to-do, or happy, as they might once have hoped, still they were Washingtonians, and they couldn't leave (because they were Washingtonians). The older and closer to death they grew, the more they bragged of their insider's insight born of maturity. But did one grow wise living in such an environment, or merely wizened?

In R. W. Whilkie, as in all men, lay the seeds of his impending death. How long, if he took walks, and controlled his diet, and avoided thinking for more than an hour a day about the monomaniacal gold-starred clowns in Washington and Moscow who held Armageddon in their clenched fists, might a man of forty-seven hope to continue his existence? A quarter century, or thirty-five years? Forty? He thought about his Great-Grandmother Lydicke, who had become ninety-seven, spitting tobacco off her retired son's back porch. In two more quarters of a century how incomprehensibly different would this whirl-dervishing world be?

But enough of these misgivings; he would, as a matter of course, continue to live as long as he *could* live. The mind might think its secret thoughts, but the body struggled to preserve itself.

And here, very likely, at this party, were the person or persons who meant to kill him. Surely the plot must have been instigated by a friend or an acquaintance, someone who knew or worked with him. He might be important enough to stand in need of killing, but surely not so important that whatever threat he posed could be pinpointed from a distance.

He sipped the brandy, rolling it around on the tip of his tongue. Had he just poisoned himself? There were so many ways a really determined enemy could strike at one that it seemed almost quixotic to resist. Would they strike here, at a party ("'In the midst of life we are in death,'" as the spinster intoned in which Agatha Christie novel? *And Then There Were None?* Yes, that . . .) or wait for a more private moment, when an odd accident would be near impossible to trace? Unless— unless he were dealing with an organization so big and so callous that they would obliterate an entire floor of party-goers to get at their intended victims. For their sakes he should at least check the obvious places where one might plant a bomb.

Mr. Whilkie wended his way as unobtrusively as he could through the throng, some of whom paused in their conversations to nod at him. (He felt suddenly fortunate that he was not one whom most people felt an urge to seek out for conversation). Nothing behind the drapes or in the azalea pots appeared to be out of order; the books on the bookshelves—but how could he be sure?—seemed all undisturbed in their places. Heading back to the room's middle he scanned the tabletop for telltale disturbances in the hors d'oeuvres.

Waiting carefully until no one was looking in his direction, Mr. Whilkie poked his head, then his shoulders, through the tablecloth and peered under the table—only to find himself face to face with old Smathers from State. "Hello," said Mr. Whilkie.

"Hello, old tuff. You haven't seen any Communists poking about, have you?"

After the guests had safely departed, the Whilkies lay in their respective beds, she attempting to concentrate on a Barbara Cartland novel, he staring up at the ceiling, resolutely counting the holes in the tiles.

Eventually she looked in his direction. "Did you lose something underneath the table tonight?"

He continued to look upward. "I thought perhaps my handkerchief. It was in my pants pocket."

"Your pants pocket? I'm sure it wasn't when I pressed them
yesterday."

"It was in the rear pocket."

"I'm sure I don't know how it could—" Mrs. Whilkie shook
her head and switched off the light. Her husband, squinting into
the darkness, resumed his counting.

It was the following Monday, after an uneventful weekend,
that Mr. Whilkie got on the bus to his office at the usual time
only to step off eight blocks early. Even as a part of him watched
his actions in amazement, he knew that he would not be
reporting to work that day.

He could see, standing on this bustling street corner, that his
body had something in mind; but what, precisely . . . ? Why, to
throw a curve at his pursuers. It stood to reason that if you
were hunting an orderly and predictable man, your plans would
be considerably flummoxed if he began to be unpredictable
and disorderly. Yes, and more than that. If he began showing up
at unanticipated places at unforeseen times he might, serendi-
pitously, be able to ferret out his foes before they could get
him. He put his feet in motion.

Mr. Whilkie did not go to work that day, or the next, or the
day after. Nor, though it pained him terribly, did he alert the
enemy by phoning in. He roamed the streets, visited the monu-
ments, hung about in joints from plush to seedy, ever alert to
the potential clue about the motives and whereabouts of his
pursuers. Sometimes he would round a corner, half expecting
the boom to fall, in the form of blunt, plunging stone objects,
or bullets from a passing car.

And, searching, he came to realize how long it had been since
he had really *looked* at this city in which he had worked for so
many years. Outside the sheltering confines of his office he
soon found his head aching from the soup of aromas; the
Supreme Court building was covered with graffiti; the leaves on
all the cherry trees were brown. Once he sat above the banks
of the Potomac, studying its coating of fetid brown bubbles that
never burst. "It smells like milk from a dead cow," Mr. Whilkie

remarked to no one. To his left a pinkish gray pigeon, its feathers coming out, stood and picked at itself.

Thursday at half past three he sat at a small table in the rear of a bar, drinking milk-laced coffee and attempting to piece together his findings. Nothing that he had seen these past days pointed conclusively to his own situation—demonstrators, street missionaries, people whose hat brims covered their eyes. He had to keep in mind the fact that not everyone who did anything untoward had something to do with him. No, only one group of people. Somewhere in this city one person, or one group of people.

He gazed contemplatively at his table. It was sticky, covered with round spots left by beer glasses. Twenty years ago, when the Whilkies would drive in for nights on the town, bars had been gay, festive places full of sparkling lights. Now in daytime he could see that the sparkle came from tables stained with dust and alcohol, and spots on the bottles lining the counter. . . .

Not for the first time that week Mr. Whilkie pulled back from himself in wonder. Where, how, had he changed, to find himself so strongly and suddenly cynical? There was nothing new about these things he was noticing; why notice them now and not years before?

In his mind's eye he conjured up a face, a composite face of all the people at all the parties he had attended in Washington. It wore an artificial expression; it had to, because it had no real expression. People at those parties weren't actually enjoying themselves, but if what they were seeking from Washington was real, it must therefore follow that Washington entertainments were really entertaining, so they worked and worked at it.

And there it was: you were frozen in a pattern. The details that one noticed, the things that one thought about, were as automatic as leaving the house for one's bus every morning at seven twenty-two. The composite face faded and was replaced by stately marble buildings whose marble chipped to expose cheap cement underneath.

He stuck his chin determinedly on both fists. He had to go through all of the possibilities systematically, until he had covered all that he could possibly think of. There was the government, of course; foreign governments; the mob; ambitious office rivals . . . A new possibility entered his mind. His wife was still, certainly, a handsome woman; surely she hadn't lost her ability to turn heads. What if she had a fervent admirer, some one of their circle who knew her faithful nature and realized that he would have to get rid of Barbara's husband to get a chance at Barbara? Who? But there were so many people, and they would keep it well concealed, and Mr. Whilkie had never fancied himself a mind-reader.

He noticed that the hand that refilled his coffee cup was black. Looking up to nod a thank you he saw that the only black people in the establishment were attendants. *Nothing really changes.*

After a few swallows Mr. Whilkie stood up. There was time for another brief investigatory stroll before catching the bus that would bring him home at the usual time. If he could resolve these difficulties without Barbara's ever being the wiser, it would be much to the good.

At the street corner he was accosted by a ferretlike brown-cloaked man who pressed a pamphlet into his hand. After crossing the street Mr. Whilkie read the pamphlet, which proclaimed the existence of a benevolent Martian supercivilization that would bring its loving wisdom to the Earth upon such time as a billion of its peoples could be induced to simultaneously doff their clothes and chant "Ares in pacem" some hundreds of times. To the furtherance of that end, a rally would be held at five that afternoon on the grounds of the Washington Monument.

For some subtle reason that he could not altogether divine, the pamphlet stirred Mr. Whilkie's interest. Mars . . . In all his poring over those unusual happenings that might supply a clue to the identity of his hunters, he had overlooked one of the truly extraordinary moments of his life: the night he had seen three parallel lights, two green, one red, flying west in planelike fashion only to come to a full stop, hover, then shoot out of sight at a right angle.

Of course, many people had seen such things, and told of them, and lived on unscathed. But—he thought of a film he had seen with his wife years ago—suppose that some such witnesses were sought out, and replaced, by beings that looked and talked much like them? Mr. Whilkie was too level-headed to really believe in such things. Still—what would Samuel Spade—or Walter Mitty—do in his situation? What could throw Mr. Whilkie's foes, whoever they might be, more thoroughly off kilter than his attendance at a Martian unification rally?

Shortly after two that same afternoon Mrs. Whilkie had telephoned her husband's office to ask if he had any objections to Dr. and Mrs. MacKelroy's coming over the next evening for bridge, only to learn that Mr. Whilkie was not at work, had not in fact been to work all week. They had postponed calling home to inquire after him, assuming that a man of his exemplary record must have a good reason for being absent.

Mrs. Whilkie put down the phone in considerable trepidation. Pretending to go to work while really going somewhere else was *very* unusual for her husband. The obvious possibilities flitted across her mind, but she dismissed them. Mr. Whilkie was not that sort of man.

Then what *could* he be doing? He had spent many hours of their marriage quietly thinking goodness knew what thoughts, but beyond the fact that constancy is itself rare, he had never been unusual in his actions. From year to year the largest interruptions of his ordered habits were his bimonthly drives to Connecticut for two quarts of brandy.

Mrs. Whilkie's raveled brow smoothed at a surprising thought. Could he be a—spy? What better cover could a government agent ferreting out subversives have than her husband's job and his translucent personality?

Still, still, a wife would be able to tell such things. Whatever had come over Mr. Whilkie had come over him quite recently. She almost thought she could pinpoint it to the Wednesday before the party. Whatever was disturbing him, it could not be anything so horrendous that a wife's understanding could not help but make it better. (And if there actually *were* anything horrendous, there was always the additional understanding and help of Dr. MacKelroy.) She would simply have to broach it to him, gently, when he returned that evening from "work."

But Mr. Whilkie did not return that evening. She hesitated for

some time, assuming that, whatever was keeping him, he surely
knew what he was doing, but by nine-thirty she was sufficiently
alarmed to telephone the Washington police. The man who
took her call was in none too amiable a mood, the station
having been made particularly hectic that evening by the pro-
cessing of some two hundred religious cultists who had been
fished, nude, out of the Washington Monument's reflecting pool.
The man took down the description of her husband and called
her back within the half hour. Yes, they had information on an
R. W. Whilkie, had him, in fact, right there in the station . . .
behind bars???
    She drove to the station, paid her husband's bond, and drove
him home, listening to him mutter, between sneezes, about
"camouflage," and "escape." By 2:00 A.M., through gentle but
relentless coaxing, she had extracted from him in reasonably
connected form the tale of his doings, these past days, and the
reasoning behind those doings.

At 3:17 A.M., after Mrs. Whilkie has tucked him into bed and
herself fallen asleep, he lay fiercely thinking, although his eyes
were closed.
    He still had not told her everything. He had not told her of
the daft, good-hearted people splashing about in the reflecting
pool, of the young woman who giggled as she told him that he
reminded her of her uncle. He had not told her of the sadness
that enveloped him when the police arrived and compelled him
to re-don his identity, layer by layer and button by button. He
had not told Barbara that, for the first time in a dozen years, he
had had fun.
    His eyes blinked open. A fog that had been pressing down on
his shoulders, its tendrils blocking his eyes, was suddenly gone.
He saw that all of the clues led, indisputably, in one direction.
Although they hadn't met in too long a time, he knew the man
who wanted R. W. Whilkie dead.

Dr. MacKelroy sat on the Whilkies' living room couch, his right
arm about Mrs. MacKelroy and a scotch and soda dandling on
his left knee. "So you see, d'ya na, Roger, that ye have taken a

series of everyday moondane occurrences and blown them up into threats on your life. Ye follow me there?"

Mr. Whilkie laughed ruefully. "Yes. Yes. I've been very foolish, but I promise it won't happen again." He stood up, headed for the kitchen, paused to squeeze his wife's hand. "I'm going to have another glass of milk, dear." She nodded approval; when was the last time he had called her "dear"?

Quietly Dr. MacKelroy continued, "I canna' recommend a vacation for your husband too soon. He's been working turrible haird these twenty year an' a week or ten days in the mountains'd work wonders."

Mrs. Whilkie nodded dutifully as Dr. MacKelroy continued dispensing common sense. Her eyes wandered toward the kitchen doorway. Why was her husband taking so long? She called, "Mr. Whilkie?" adding, in a softer voice, "Roger?"

The small pipe bomb that knocked Mrs. Whilkie and her guests off their feet not only leveled the kitchen to smithereens. It also removed every trace of Roger W. Whilkie from the face of the earth. Only his wedding ring was found—its loop broken open by the blast.

The young man driving a Rabbit down an entrance to the Beltline Freeway slowed his car at the sight of the hitchhiker— a gray-spectacled, slightly built, fortyish man of medium height, with faded blue shirt, black corduroys, and a knapsack draped over his left shoulder. The driver opened the door and the hitchhiker, before he could dissuade him, had clambered over the seat divider into the back seat.

"Hi, the name's Bill," the driver said, extending a hand behind him. "What's yours?"

Grasping it firmly, the older man said, "Some people call me—Spike."

"Oh. Uhh . . . where are you heading?"

"Switzerland, by and by. There's no hurry, though. No hurry at all."

The perplexed driver swung his head forward and put the car back in motion. The compact man in the back seat closed his eyes, his entire face collaborating in a quiet smile.

REGINALD HILL
EXIT LINE

"Exit Line" belongs to a subgenre of escape-suspense fiction, which might include stories as different as "The Problem of Cell 13" and "The Most Dangerous Game." Like them, I believe it is destined to become an anthology favorite. I first read this story a few years ago in Hill's 1979 British collection, Pascoe's Ghost and Other Brief Chronicles of Crime *(Collins), a book that remains unaccountably unpublished in this country. Finally last year the story appeared in the U.S. edition of* John Creasey's Crime Collection 1987 *(St. Martin's), giving me an opportunity to reprint it at last.*

There is a chair.

There is a table.

There is an iron bedstead.

There is a bucket.

There is no window.

The walls, ceiling, and floor are of the same untreated concrete. Only gravity distinguishes them. Even the door does not help much. It is flush with the wall like the door of a squash court and it is set in the center of the wall about four feet from the ground and equidistant from the ceiling.

The only light in the room comes from a single bulb set above the door. It is protected by a metal muzzle. There is no switch. It goes out when I get into bed and comes on when I get up.

The door is made of some very hard wood. There is no handle or keyhole and it fits so snugly into the wall that no crack remains wide enough to admit even a sheet of paper.

I sleep wrapped in a square gray blanket on the metal mesh of the bedstead. The temperature of the room never varies. I would put it around sixty-five Fahrenheit.

Hunger, fatigue, and the movement of my bowels are my only clock.

There are a few inches of chemical solution in the bucket, but despite this the room must smell abominably. Fortunately I cannot tell.

My bucket is emptied and my rations supplied while I sleep. My rations consist of a soft plastic jug of water, a cob loaf, a lump of cheese, two apples, and a bone with a few scraps of meat on it.

I try to stay awake as long as possible after going to bed, but always sleep comes and I have neither seen nor heard any sign of those who clean out my bucket and bring my food.

I exercise each day, following a routine of press-ups, stretches, running on the spot, and deep breathing. I think I am still fairly fit despite everything they have done to me, but I have no mirror to check my appearance.

I cannot work out why the door is in the middle of the wall. Perhaps there was once a flight of steps leading up to it. I can find no trace of them, however.

There is always paper on the table and newly sharpened pencils. I have to write every day. If I do not write, I get no food, only water.

The door is made of very hard wood and has no handle or keyhole. If I am to get out of here I must find some means of opening it.

I have to write the story of my life. Each morning I look to see if what I wrote the previous day has gone. If it is still there, then I know I must rewrite it. Sometimes I have done the same episode a dozen times before it is accepted. Sometimes the alteration of a single word is enough.

These notes are the framework of my sanity.

My clothes consist of a pair of blue denim trousers with zipped flies and no belt, a loose shirt, or rather smock, of gray cotton, a pair of open sandals without buckles or laces. I also have a wristwatch on a canvas strap. The face is cracked and it does not work. Hunger, fatigue, and the movement of my bowels are my only clock.

Sometimes I think that the walls of the room are getting closer together. I have measured the breadth and width of the room with my feet, placing one in front of the other from corner to corner. It is fifteen foot-lengths square. I do this measurement at least once every day. I know it will not change, but I cannot sit writing for any length of time without doing the measurement.

I have tried banging on the door with my chair but no one comes and the door shows no sign of damage. It sounds so solid that perhaps no noise is audible outside. Not that that matters. I do not doubt I am watched all the time.

I have developed a habit of doodling and scribbling on sheets of paper. Then sometimes I tear and fold these sheets to make aeroplanes, dancing men, flowers, or cockleshell boats. But always I contrive to secrete that one of the torn scraps which has my note on it. I dare not write more but I need what I write. These notes are the framework of my sanity.

Any hope I have lies in that door. I laid a trap, putting my toilet bucket directly beneath it. It wasn't much of a trap and absolutely worthless if I am being watched. I tried to lie awake but eventually fell asleep. The bucket was emptied and back in its usual place when I woke.

I suspect I am being injected with drugs as I sleep. I have noticed tiny punctures appearing in my skin and I can think of no other explanation. Perhaps they are trying to make me dependent on some drug so that withdrawal will force me to talk. About what?

I must make contact. Only through contact can there be a future for me.

I need these notes to keep some check on the present. Without them I would not know if things change. I keep them concealed beneath my smock. My broken watch has a luminescent dial. By this tiny light I read my notes under the blanket before I fall to sleep. Without them I think I should be mad. Even with them, I have no certainty of survival. Above all I fear those punctures in my skin. I must force them to show themselves.

Yesterday I stood on my chair and poured cold water through the protective muzzle on to the light bulb. It cracked and went out. I then stood by the door holding the chair ready to attack anyone who entered. But no one came. The room was in pitch darkness. I waited for what seemed several hours, then I grew so fatigued that I sat on the floor. Eventually I fell asleep. When I awoke the light was on again.

I need these notes to keep some check on the present. I have scarcely any memory of the recent past. My broken watch is stopped at a quarter to four. I cannot recall how it got broken. Perhaps I do not want to. But the more autobiography I write, the more my childhood comes back to me. I write in such detail that I shall be old before I reach my youth. Yet whenever I omit anything the writing is not accepted.

My fears that the room is contracting are with me always. I must make contact. I shall refuse to write until they contact me or I starve.

I have written nothing for three days. On the third day I woke up very weak from lack of food and found I was lying on the ceiling of the room. Up above, or down below, I could see the chair, the table, the bucket, and the bed. I tried to crawl down the walls to them but I stuck to the ceiling like a fly. Finally I either fainted or fell asleep. When I awoke I was in my bed again and there was food on the table. I ate and started writing immediately.

The door is set in the center of the wall. There is no crack big enough to admit even a razor blade. It is so solid that it cannot be broken down. Perhaps it will burn. I have an idea for starting a fire. But I have had ideas for so many things.

I have been trying to write of the death of my mother for the past three? four days? Each time what I write is rejected. Why? What do they want of me? I shall write no more.

I have to write again. More and more I think of death but it must be quick. I have no will to die of starvation. My attempt to start a fire was a fiasco. I cleared everything from my table, picked a few small splinters of wood from the surface with my fingernails, then held a pencil between both my palms and rubbed violently, trying to generate heat where the pencil point touched the woodwork. It got warm but nothing more.

I have writen that I was not wholly sorry at my mother's death. This is a lie but they have accepted it. They have accepted a lie. How many other lies have they made me tell? I must make an end to this while I still can.

I have decided to hang myself. There is no other way. I thought of slashing my wrists as I lay under my blanket one night, but I have nothing to use. I tried to break my water jug but it just bounces. If I had the courage I could bite through the veins but even in my despair that thought revolts me. But I shall use my teeth to cut through the bound edge of my blanket so that I can tear off a strip to make a noose.

The only light in the room comes from a single bulb set above the door. It is protected by a metal muzzle fitted into the wall. This must be my gallows. The thought frightens me more than I can say, but I see no alternative. I write lies all the time now, descriptions of childhood hatreds and deceptions and odious lusts and imaginings, all lies, all lies. Yet they are accepted, every one of them.

I have my noose. I wish it had not to be this way. How much better to slash my wrists as I lie on my bed and feel the life pour softly from me.

I keep my noose around my waist. All is ready. I climbed on my chair today and examined the light. Let them think what they will.

I had to make sure I had the right length of "rope." No point in ending up on tiptoe slowly strangling. Oh, God! But I will strangle. The drop cannot be deep enough to break my neck.

Perhaps they will come if they see me strangling. Perhaps my piece of blanket will break or stretch and leave me flat-footed on the ground. If only I could be certain. Sometimes in the past I have had in my rations a flat brittle shoulder bone. If I had one of these now I could break a splinter off and stab myself with it or slash my wrists. I must have certainty. I cannot face being hauled back from the brink.

More lies today. And another knuckle bone. I cannot go on much longer.

Oh, God! Today a shoulder! They will wonder at my appetite to see me gnawing and cracking at it. I have a long thin splinter, surprisingly strong but with a point like a needle. I feel as joyous as if someone had given me freedom.

Was it yesterday I was so joyful? Yet I am still here. A noose round my waist, a dagger of bone at my side, yet I am still here. Is it illusion that I think I remember a time when I had will and courage and conviction? If there was a button on the table before me that I merely had to press to obliterate all this place and me with it, could I reach out my finger and press it? Perhaps I have arrived where they want me to arrive. Perhaps now all I have to do is wait.

My dear friends, for what else should I call those who have watched over me with such unstinting care all these weeks? months? years?—My dear friends, these are the last words I shall write in this stinking cell. Yesterday you saw me sitting like a zombie staring blindly into space. Today you will be interested to observe this sudden last outburst of creative energy. And when it is finished you shall at last see me make my suicide attempt. All will be as you have doubtless forecast. Why should it not be, for you must be clever men? But you must not retain to yourself sole claim on the power of prognostication. We on our side have been trained also. And whose school is the better?

I laid my plans within a couple of days—so far as I can gauge—of arriving here. I knew I had to. It's all a question of taking the initiative. Sit and wait, and very soon you are totally under control. This business of autobiography is very seductive. By the time I came to the politically significant period in my life I've no doubt I would have been providing you with dense detail just to convince you of my accuracy! So against your routine I had to set a counter-routine. But *I* am not so stupid as to imagine *you* are so stupid as not to look for this. So I worked out a double routine, the top layer of which you could penetrate easily enough. All those little notes of mine with their hints of breakdown, their wild hopes, their repetitions, did you imagine I would not guess that you would read them? More! I have lain there and felt your hands remove them from under my smock, then replace them after they'd been copied. That surprises you? There is much to surprise you!

I let all my hopes for escaping from here seem to center on the door. But within a very short while I'd worked out that the door was a dummy. A little piece of hair stuck across the wood and the wall confirmed that it never opened or shut. I then set about discovering the real door. My exercises enabled me to examine most of the floor area without being too obvious and my "shrinking cell" fears allowed me to pace slowly right into the corners and stand there, as if making sure that the walls weren't moving. Really, of course, what I wanted to discover was that the walls did move! But your interior decorator is pretty good and it took another hair in the corner to convince me that the section of wall behind my bed must slide or swing open.

The next thing was to confirm this. I'd worked out that I was certainly being drugged to put me to sleep so soundly that your visits did not disturb me. This meant the food or the water had been tampered with, probably both. Not to eat would draw too much attention, I thought, but you cooperated to the extent of withdrawing my food if I did not write. So I deliberately did not write one day and this just left me with the problem of the water. I had noticed the calibrations on the inside of the jug and I knew it was not merely enough to pretend to drink—this was not just a one-off thing. I would need to repeat it at least once, probably twice, till all my theories were checked. So I decided to kill two birds with one stone and see if I could put the light out of action.

It worked beautifully. When the cold water cracked the hot bulb I crouched in the darkness as though waiting to attack the first man through that dummy door. Gradually, as you would expect having seen me apparently drink quite a lot of water before my experiment, I pretended to grow drowsy. Finally I flopped over as if asleep. I could have embraced the man who came through the wall and picked me up, even when he stuck a pin in me to check the depth of my sleep! Fortunately I had already worked out what this rash of punctures meant and I was ready for it. I hope my fears of being turned into a junkie entertained you. Fear and the human imagination are all the drugs the expert interrogator needs.

Now I needed to do this once more to establish the routine. I hope I kept you amused with my attempts to break down the door and set fire to it! How natural that at last full of despair I should turn to thoughts of suicide. And how equally natural, I hope, that in my search for a weapon I should attempt to shatter my jug and thus spill all the water again—on a day, of course, when I was foodless for being naughty.

Again I had to go through the motions of drowsiness and finally sleep. I hope I got the timing right, but as this must be uncertain in any case as it's related to the amount of water I drink, perhaps it didn't matter. But it mattered thereafter.

Counting seconds, I reached eighty minutes before the wall slid open. I have had to take what happened then as the routine sequence for I do not dare risk another trial run.

The light went on as the wall slid open (I'm writing this for my benefit, dear friends, not yours!), a single figure entered, stuck a pin into me as before. Ready though I was I twitched slightly and he tried again. This time I showed no reaction and this satisfied him. That must be some drug you're using!

His job seemed to be pretty menial so far as I could make it out. He simply removed the jug and the toilet bucket. As he left, another two men arrived. They removed my notes from their hiding place and photographed the latest one before returning them. Then they photographed what I had written during the day. (The original I found on the table still when I got up, so clearly rejection has nothing to do with content. It is merely aimed at setting up doubts and anxieties in the writer so that the search for detail is pursued with great vigor each time. *What* clever men you must be!)

I knew that these two were not you, my dear friends, for they talked like underlings. Not indiscreetly, of course, for they too would be on your video screen, but of ordinary things like the foulness of the weather and the approach of Christmas.

As they finished, the first man (I assume) returned with my bucket and my next day's rations. I had written that day, so my food was restored.

Now I had all the information I needed or at least was likely to get to enable me to escape. So now the plan could really get under way.

I wrote more and more of suicide. I made a noose. I was interested to observe that although you knew I had a noose, you didn't take it off me. So I wondered if you could be provoked into giving me a weapon, that is the bone dagger.

I bet this caused some debate between the two of you. Yes, I've come to the conclusion that there are probably two of you sitting up there like gods watching my behavior on a flickering gray screen. One of you will be a military man, concerned with security, duty, following orders, protecting the state. He wouldn't be very happy at the thought of my having anything that could be called a weapon.

The other must be a scientist, fascinated by the opportunity to acquire new knowledge and to test old. This is no weapon, but a token, he would say. The prisoner has no real intention of committing suicide. To give the possibility of death is to give the hope of life and it is from this that true confessions will spring. Besides, what if I did die? Even failed experiments are useful. The unexpected becomes expected once it has happened.

So I got my weapon. A bonus of bone! See, I can still make jokes, scientist. What does that prove of the human spirit? But it really was a bonus. The main function of my suicide pretensions has been to permit me to play around with the light again. You've seen me examine it, ostensibly as a hook to hang myself on. Shortly you shall see me get back up there once again, and I doubt if you'll be surprised. I must look as if I'm building up to some climax of action, which indeed I am. Yesterday I sat as if in a coma, staring into space. Today I have been scribbling in an agitated fashion. I bet you can hardly wait to see what I've been writing, scientist!

Very shortly I shall jump up and begin to pace around the room looking as if I'm breaking up. Then suddenly I will push the chair under the light. Next I shall unwind my noose of blanket from my waist and examine it as though both fascinated and horrified. I shall put my hand to my throat, have a bout of coughing as though the very *thought* of hanging restricts my breathing. (I bet you make a note of that!) Picking up my jug, I shall take a draught of water to stop the coughing. And finally I shall climb on the chair and loop the noose over the light fitment.

This is the big moment. The soldier may want to interfere (they can be very humane, soldiers; they like to kill to time-tables). The scientist will say *wait*. The struggle will show itself in every angle of my body.

And life will win. I will relax, sob convulsively, almost be sick. The scientist will preen himself.

And I shall be squirting the water held in my mouth into the little cockleshell of paper I have tied into the noose. The keel of this paper boat, of a kind you've grown very used to seeing over the past few weeks, has a tiny hole in it. As I clamber off the chair, the water will already begin to seep through. I shall look exhausted. Who wouldn't be in my circumstances, drained of emotion and topped up with drugged water?

I shall stagger across the room and fall on the bed. The light will go out. (Is it economy or convention that makes you switch off when I go to bed?) And a moment or so later, if all goes well and the fates who have so maligned me these past months decide to wink, while the bulb is still red hot the water will drip through and crack the glass and you up aloft in your godlike observation post will not be aware of it.

So in one hour and twenty minutes (if he is as punctilious as my military friend must surely require) the man with the pin will open the door. Only this time no light will go on and I shall be waiting with my pin also.

After that, who knows? If once I get outside, I'm sure that I shall find myself in remote enough terrain to make escape possible. The way my photographer friends talked about the rough winds and snow on the hills gives me a picture of a countryside with plenty of undulations to hide in, lots of flowing water to shake off dogs, lots of trees (pine forests, perhaps?) to ward off helicopters.

We shall see. You, my friends, I should have liked to meet. But I shall not be able to arrange it, I fear. If I escape, distance—and if I don't, death—will separate us beyond hope of encounter. Either way, you my soldier with all your schemes of security, and you my scientist with all your charts of the human mind, you both will have been defeated. You deserve death also, but perhaps defeat will serve as well for your puffed-up egos. Let the curtain rise!

"The thing about the human mind," said the scientist with great satisfaction, "is that even its deceits are forecastable. A lie is as good as the truth to the discerning eye."

"If you were so sure 128 was going, I wouldn't have a man in hospital with a punctured lung," growled the soldier.

"I'm sorry about that," said the scientist. "but I had to let things run their course. All those notes! What ingenuity. I look forward to observing the reaction to recapture."

"If there is a recapture," said the soldier.

"What on earth do you mean? You assured me security was complete!" said the scientist.

"It is," said the soldier. "Look at the map on the screen. That bleep and flashing light comes from the bugs. Every item of 128's clothing has got one attached. Lose a sandal, it makes no difference. My men can track every movement. Only . . ."

"Only what?"

"Only there's nothing but your fancy theories to say that it won't be a corpse they bring back!"

"I've told you," said the scientist. "128's not suicidal. All this talk of death or escape is self-deceit. That light seems to be following the line of the stream, doesn't it?"

"Yes. The usual pattern. We could have worked it out even without the bugs. The letter told us, though we hardly needed that either. A valley for concealment, running water to throw the dogs off the scent. Dogs! They must think we live in the dark ages."

"The light's moving pretty fast."

"It's a fast-moving stream."

"You don't mean 128's actually in the water?" said the scientist, suddenly alarmed.

"Why not? Swimming, floating, it's the fastest way down to the sea."

"Let's have a look at the file," said the scientist. "Nothing here about being a strong swimmer."

"You don't have to be," said the soldier with grim satisfaction. "Dead or alive, that water'll move you fast. Don't look so worried! There's a net across the mouth of the stream and my men are waiting there."

"I hope so. I hope so," said the scientist. "But nets are more holes than string."

"There's no way through. And even if there were, no one's going to stay alive for long in the Irish Sea on a winter's day. Poor sod. The things I do for England. Look, there you are! Like I said, in the net."

The light had halted where the line of the stream intersected the line of the shore.

A telephone rang.

"Back in the fold," said the soldier, picking it up.

He listened for a few moments and then said, "Good God!"

"What's up?" demanded the scientist. "Not dead?"

"No," said the soldier. "All they found was a bundle of clothes tied to a log."

"Maximum security screen!" he barked into the mouthpiece. "Then start searching. I'm coming down."

He replaced the receiver.

"Maximum security?" sneered the scientist.

The soldier paused at the door.

"Has it struck you yet that the letter was probably just as big a smoke screen as the notes?" he asked coldly. "So much for psychology."

"Rubbish," said the scientist, peering into the thick file before him. "No one's that controlled. Show 'em freedom or vengeance, every time they'll run."

The soldier said nothing but gave a little gasp and stepped back a pace from the open doorway.

The scientist looked up from the file.

"You okay?" he asked.

The soldier turned. His hands clutched his belly. About his tight-laced fingers was coiled a thread of blood.

"Psychology!" he whispered scornfully.

Then he fell.

Behind him in the doorway stood a naked woman. She stepped into the room.

In her hand was a dagger of bone.

EDWARD D. HOCH

LEOPOLD AND THE BROKEN BRIDE

I seem to have a compulsion to use at least one "impossible crime" story in this collection each year. This time it's one of my own.

Captain Leopold's wife, Molly, had known Susan Richter since her days in criminal law, when the two of them often met for lunch at the restaurant across from the courthouse. Susan was a bright, attractively tall woman a few years younger than Molly, who worked as a paralegal in the prestigious law firm of Buckley & Oates. Though she rarely talked about her personal life, she'd dropped enough hints so that Molly wasn't completely surprised to hear the news of Matt Buckley's divorce and subsequent engagement to Susan.

"I'm so happy for you," Molly told her over lunch the day the news became official. It was the first time in months they'd lunched together. Molly had shifted her practice to corporate law to avoid conflict with her husband's position in the police department and she rarely had occasion to visit the courthouse as she did in the old days.

"You must have suspected, Molly," Susan told her. "I used to mention him often enough."

"Oh, I knew you liked him," Molly agreed, picking at her salad, "I just didn't realize it had grown so serious. I met his wife once and she seemed like a strong-willed woman. I'm surprised she let him go."

"Believe me, it wasn't easy. Poor Matt had a very messy divorce. I'll have to make it up to him the best I can. I'm leaving my job now that we're engaged, but I intend to find something else after the honeymoon. I don't believe in relaxing at home on his money."

"What does his father think of it?" Justin Buckley was Buckley & Oates's senior partner, a man in his sixties who was painfully aware of the image his family presented to the community.

"Well, naturally he wasn't too happy. He's planning to retire from the firm next year and he wanted Matt to carry on the family name."

"He still can, can't he?"

"Of course. But Justin is taking a while to come around, that's all. And good old Janet is doing her best to poison his mind against me, claiming that I broke up her marriage.—That marriage was badly cracked before I ever met Matt."

"When's the wedding?"

"Next month. I'm planning a big one with all the trimmings. It may be Matt's second marriage but it's my first and I'm having a wedding gown, attendants, a choir and organist, flower girls. You're invited, of course, and we want you and Jules over for dinner one night before the wedding."

"You'll be awfully busy."

"You're one of my dearest friends, Molly. I wanted to have you in the wedding party, but there's family pressure for me to have my cousin Pearl from Cleveland—"

"Think nothing of it," Molly assured her, secretly thankful she hadn't been asked. "Don't worry, we'll be there. And if you have time to invite us over before the wedding we'd love to come."

Leopold had never been a particularly social person, and when the wedding invitation arrived two weeks later he looked on it as a minor annoyance. "Wedding at St. Mark's Episcopal Church with a reception at the Pines Party House. I didn't think Matt Buckley would go for such a fancy affair the second time around."

"Susan told me she wants the works," Molly said. "And who can blame her?"

"What about Janet?"

"I gather she's making life difficult, but divorces are never pleasant."

"You don't have to tell me that."

They went to dinner at Susan's apartment on a September evening the week before the wedding. Leopold knew Matt

Buckley casually from his trial work and he was surprised to find him casually dressed in a turtleneck sweater, helping Susan prepare dinner as if they'd already been married for years.

"Wedding gifts are arriving every day now," Susan said, leaning across the dinner table to light the candles.

"Gifts from all the judges I've appeared before," Matt joked from the kitchen.

Susan showed them the spare bedroom, which was piled high with silver trays, cocktail shakers, a toaster oven, bedding, glassware, clocks, and even a portable television set.

"Oh, these are delightful," Molly exclaimed over a framed pair of paintings. "Will you have room for all these things here?"

"Matt wants to buy a house when we get back from the honeymoon, and I suppose we will. Janet's still living in their old house. She got that as part of the settlement. Speaking of Janet, I have to show you this." Susan lowered her voice a bit, presumably so Matt wouldn't hear her from the kitchen. She opened a small box and removed the styrofoam packing to extract a delicate glass figure of a bride. "It's crystal," she said. "Matt thinks it's probably worth several hundred dollars."

"It's lovely," Molly said. "Who sent it?"

"Janet. Without a note—just one of her calling cards."

"You mean Matt's invited her to the wedding?"

"Of course not—she just sent it on her own. I suppose I should be happy it wasn't a bomb."

"It seems awfully civilized of her," Molly said dubiously.

Susan held the crystal bride to the light, turning it slowly in her hand. "It was a gift from Matt's parents when he married Janet. Even with the hard feelings about the divorce, she must have decided it belonged with him. Still, there's something a bit eerie about it. You can see right through this bride, as if she isn't really there. Do you think Janet's trying to tell me something?" she laughed.

The wedding was at noon the following Saturday and as Leopold helped Molly from the car he said, "We only seem to go to church for weddings and funerals. I suppose some Sunday we should go for no special reason."

Molly looked at him. "I never thought I'd hear you say that.

You're usually content to spend Sunday morning lounging around the house."

"I'm getting old," he replied only half seriously. "A few aches and pains can do wonders for bringing back the old-time religion."

They crossed the street to the splendid Gothic building. The first familiar face they encountered belonged to Whitney Oates, the silver-haired partner in Matt's firm. "Captain Leopold—and Molly! It's a pleasure to see you! Come over and say hello to Grace."

Oates and his wife were pleasant, down-to-earth people Leopold had known for years. Whitney specialized in civil law and had given Molly some helpful pointers when she decided to abandon criminal practice. They stood at the back of the church amidst lavender-clad bridesmaids and a bustling florist, a tall woman with gray hair, while Leopold shook hands and exchanged wedding-day pleasantries. "The sun's breaking through just in time," he observed. "It's going to be a nice day after all."

Whitney Oates stepped out of the path of two young women in flowing red choral robes hurrying through the door to the choir loft. "I don't think Susan has overlooked anything. Matt is really going to know he's been married." Then, as a man about his own age entered the church wearing the formal dress of the wedding party, he asked, "Have you met Susan's father?" and he proceeded to introduce Leopold and Molly.

Bill Richter looked decidedly uncomfortable in his dark tuxedo, running a finger inside his collar as he spoke to them. "I never thought Susan would get me into this outfit," he grumbled. "The things you put up with for a daughter. But she's the only one I've got, and her mother's been dead four years. I guess it's the least I can do for her." Molly frowned and seemed about to say something but to think better of it. Other wedding guests were arriving and the ushers were anxious to escort them to their seats.

When they were seated, near the back on the bride's side, Leopold whispered, "What was bothering you?"

"Did it show? It was just that I don't remember Susan's mother dying four years ago. I knew Susan then and I would have gone to the funeral or sent flowers."

"There's Susan now," Leopold said, glancing toward the rear of the church, where the bride had just arrived, a veiled vision in white as she leaned over to kiss her father.

One of the ushers started down the aisle with Matt's parents, then after a few moments the organ started up. Leopold glanced toward the choir loft. The choir was in position, but apparently they were saving their song for later. The first pair of ushers began the procession and off to the side Leopold saw Matt Buckley appear in the transept with the best man at his side. A photographer hurried to position himself halfway down the center aisle.

The organist began the familiar "Here Comes the Bride," and all eyes turned toward the rear of the church. After the ushers came the bridesmaids, followed by a pair of tiny flower girls, holding small bouquets provided by the florist who gave them a nudge to start them on their way. The maid of honor followed, and then Susan's father glanced around for the bride. He seemed momentarily puzzled, and Leopold saw him say, "Susan, where are you?"

The rest of the procession had reached the altar before the wedding guests realized something was wrong. A growing murmur filled the church and Bill Richter groped like a blind man in the vestibule, the florist trying to calm him. "I'd better see what the trouble is," Leopold whispered to Molly. He slipped out of their pew and walked quickly to the rear.

"Where is she?" Richter was demanding. "She couldn't just disappear as she was about to go down the aisle."

"She's not outside," the florist assured him.

"There must be a rest room someplace," Leopold suggested.

The woman stepped quickly to a door near the side entrance and opened it. "Susan, dear—are you in there?" But Leopold could see the tiny room was empty.

"Why would she run away?" Richter asked. "She wanted this marriage."

The rest of the wedding party was waiting with the minister at the altar. The best man detached himself from the others and hurried back up the side aisle to investigate the delay. "What is it?" he said. "Where's Susan?"

"We're looking for her," Leopold assured him. But even as he spoke, he had an uneasy feeling of disaster. He could hear the organist improvising to fill the empty time as the minister peered up the aisle with growing concern. And he could smell—what?

His sensitive nose took him to a wastebasket the florist had been using as she made last-minute adjustments to the bouquets. He dug around in it and came up with a small gauze pad in with the litter.

"What is it?" Richter asked.

Leopold took a careful sniff. "Chloroform."

"What are you saying?" Susan's father was alarmed.

"That a crime may have been committed. I'm going to ask that everyone remain here while I call in some officers to search the church."

"What sort of a crime? What's happened to my daughter?"

"I wish I knew," Leopold told him. "I've never seen anything like it."

"If you're implying someone attacked Susan while we stood right here, that's out of the question," the florist insisted.

"Could you tell me your name, please?"

"Michelle Power, from Flower Power. My shop handled all the floral arrangements."

"Would you know anything about this chloroform pad?"

"Certainly not. But Mr. Richter and I were right here with Susan all the time, Captain. Nothing could have happened to her."

"But something did."

"Right before our eyes?"

"That's the way it seems."

An hour later they were no closer to a solution. In fact, the police search of the church had yielded nothing at all. The missing bride was nowhere to be found and nothing else was amiss.

"What could have happened to her?" Molly asked Leopold when she finally managed to reach him outside the church.

"I wish I knew, Molly. It's as if she just faded away. We found a gauze pad soaked with chloroform, but it seems impossible that she could have been kidnapped before our eyes."

"Her father is frantic."

"I know. So is Matt Buckley. I'm going to drive him over to Susan's apartment to see what we can find. Maybe she just changed her mind and slipped out of the church and went home."

"Do you believe that?"

Leopold shook his head. "There were three neighborhood women standing out in front of the church for a look at the bride. They saw her go in and swear she didn't come out."

"You're telling me what happened is impossible?"

"No, I'm only telling you we haven't explored all the possibilities. That's why Matt and I are going to the apartment."

Matt Buckley was trying hard to keep the analytical mind of a lawyer. He sat next to Leopold in the front seat of the car, staring straight ahead and talking all the time. "I remember the first day she started work as a paralegal. They talk about love at first sight and that's what it was with me. For a moment I even forgot I was married. I was a high-school kid again, in love with the new girl in class. That's how I'll always remember her."

"You talk as if she's dead. There might be a simple explanation for what's happened."

Matt just shook his head.

He had a key to Susan's apartment. Inside, everything seemed the same as it had when Leopold and Molly came to dinner. Through the open door to the spare bedroom he could see that the number of wedding gifts had grown. But there was something on the floor just inside the door.

"What's this?" Leopold asked, stopping to pick it up. Then he recognized it. "Isn't this the gift your former wife sent?"

"Yes. How did it get on—?" Matt stopped. The crystal statuette of the bride had been broken in half.

"I think we'd better pay a call on your ex-wife," Leopold suggested.

They drove across town to a white colonial house in a fashionable neighborhood. "I'm proud of this house," Matt said. "I'm kind of sorry Susan's never been here."

Janet Buckley opened the front door with a frown, staring at her former husband in his tuxedo. "What in heaven's name are you doing here? And Captain Leopold, isn't it?"

Leopold nodded. "We'd like a few words with you."

"But isn't the wedding—?"

"The wedding's been delayed," Matt told her. "Susan's disappeared."

"I don't understand." Janet Buckley was a small woman whose soft features had hardened over the years. Leopold had never seen her smile.

"Just that—she disappeared from the church as the ceremony was about to begin. We think—Captain Leopold thinks she's been kidnaped."

"Who would do a thing like that?" she asked doubtfully, leading them into the living room.

"That's what we're trying to find out," Leopold said. "I believe you sent Matt and Susan a wedding gift."

"The crystal bride? It was given to me by Matt's parents when we were married. I didn't want it under the circumstances."

Leopold interrupted before Matt could respond. "When was the last time you saw Susan, Mrs. Buckley?"

"Saw her? I suppose when I came to the office during the alimony hearing."

"Did you ever visit her apartment?"

"Certainly not."

"You weren't there today?"

"Of course not."

"We found your wedding gift broken on the floor. Do you know anything about that?"

"No."

"You didn't feel any special anger that Susan had destroyed your marriage and was taking your husband?"

His words were deliberately harsh and both of them reacted with emotion. "That's enough, Captain Leopold," Matt said.

"I didn't touch her," Janet insisted. "I wouldn't dirty my hands."

Leopold got to his feet. "I may be back," he told Janet. "If you know anything at all you'd better tell us now."

"I have no idea where she is or what happened to her. Maybe

being inside a church was such a blow to her conscience she just ran away."

Outside in the car, Leopold said, "Where do you want me to drop you?"

Matt thought a moment and then said, "Back at Susan's. If she's alive and free, she'll come there."

Leopold had assigned Lieutenant Fletcher to the case immediately, and when he returned to his office Fletcher came in with his report, pausing to get two cups of coffee from the new self-service percolator that had recently replaced the old coin-operated monster. "The coffee's better and it's free," he said, forgetting for the moment that is was paid for by a monthly collection.

Leopold grunted and barely tasted his. "What have you got on Susan Richter?"

"Not much, Captain. Her maid of honor, a cousin from Cleveland named Pearl Wayne, helped her dress this morning. They were driven to the church in a limousine her father hired for the day. Miss Wayne says Susan acted normal and just a little nervous."

"Did she notice the broken figurine?"

"Negative. She'd seen all the presents last night after the rehearsal. She can't say if it was broken before they left for the church today."

"Did you check on the flower woman, Michelle Power?"

"Yes. Nothing suspicious. She has no record of any sort."

"And yet it seems that she or Susan's father had to play a part in whatever happened."

"Did anything happen, Captain? Could it just be some sort of publicity stunt?"

"For what purpose? Matt Buckley and his firm hardly need this kind of publicity." Leopold drummed his fingers nervously on the desktop. "Weddings, Fletcher. I'm remembering the one I went to fifteen years ago when my ex-wife was killed at the reception. This thing is just as impossible."

"Former spouses have a way of being bad news. Want me to get a search warrant for the Buckley home?"

"Not yet. You said there was a rehearsal last night?"

"Sure. There's always a rehearsal."

"Let's go back to the church."

The minister was not around, but they could hear the organ playing as they entered. Leopold glanced about the rear of the church, noting it was much as he'd left it a few hours earlier. He opened the door to the choir loft and climbed the circular stairway. The man playing the organ had an angelic appearance, his bald head ringed with a tuft of white hair.

He stopped playing when he saw Leopold. "Oh, the police again. I stayed to practice. I'd given up my afternoon for the wedding—I hope it's all right."

"Of course it's all right," Leopold assured him. "You're Mr. Fitzgibbon?"

"That's correct. Have you found the missing bride?"

"Not yet. I wanted to ask you a few questions. Were you here last evening for the rehearsal?"

"No—they seldom have the organist at rehearsals."

"Do you always use the choir?"

"No, that was the bride's choice. I sat down with her last month and ran through the entire program. She made it clear she wanted the best, the full thirty-voice choir."

"Did you see Miss Richter at all this morning?"

"No, I was already up here when one of the girls came up and said she'd just arrived."

"Do you have any idea what could have happened?"

"She got cold feet, I suppose."

"No one saw her leave the church."

"But she must have left it, whether she was seen or not."

"I suppose so," Leopold said. He thanked the organist and went down the stairway. Fletcher was still in the back of the church searching through the shelves where the hymn books were stored.

"Nothing here, Captain, except an empty florist box over there."

The large flat box had Flower Power written on it in red magic marker, though it was hard to imagine what sort of flower arrangement could have fit inside. It seemed more suitable for a sweater or a pair of slacks. "Go by Michelle Power's shop and find out what was in this box. I'm going to call on the father of the bride."

Bill Richter was at the Buckley home with Matt's parents and the rest of the wedding party. He sat alone on a screened-in back porch, nursing a scotch and soda. Leopold said a few words to the others, dashing their hopes that he'd come with good news, before he retreated to the porch with Susan's father.

Leopold sat down in the chair next to him, but he had to address Richter before the white-haired man realized he was there. Then he turned all the way around and stared hard at him before he spoke. "Captain Leopold—I didn't hear you come out! Is there any news yet?"

"No. I wanted to ask you some questions."

"About Susan?"

"Yes. Did she have any enemies?"

"Everyone liked Susan. She was popular all through school. She was a girl who always got what she wanted."

"There's no need to speak of her in the past tense, Mr. Richter."

"That chloroform—"

"It may mean nothing. When you say Susan always got what she wanted, does that include Matt Buckley?"

"Oh, she wanted him, all right. Even when Matt's wife started making her life hell, she hung in there."

"How did Janet make her life hell?"

"For one thing, she called up Whitney Oates and demanded Susan be fired from the firm. Told everyone Susan had stolen her husband."

"Then your daughter has at least one enemy," Leopold observed.

"I suppose so. But with a divorce settlement and alimony as large as she was getting, I don't see what Janet Buckley had to complain about."

"Maybe she still loved her husband."

"I suppose so."

A garden spider had lowered itself from the porch ceiling and settled on the rim of Richter's glass. Leopold waited for him to brush it away and then finally did it himself. "Can I ask you something of a personal nature, Mr. Richter?"

"What's that?"

"How long has your eyesight been failing?"

"My eyes are perfectly all right," he answered defensively.

"I noticed you groping around the back of church today after Susan disappeared and you didn't see me just now until I spoke to you."

Richter sighed. "I've got glaucoma and most of my peripheral vision is gone. I can see straight ahead well enough."

Leopold nodded. "Tunnel vision. How many people know you have it?"

"No one except Susan, unless she told them. I wanted it kept secret. I use eyedrops to control it."

"When did it come on?"

"I was under a great deal of tension at the time my wife died four years ago. That was the start of it."

"Molly says Susan never mentioned her mother dying."

"Susan's always been an odd girl in many ways. The death notice was in the newspaper. If Molly missed it, I suppose Susan didn't want to embarrass her by bringing it up. They didn't see each other that often. Susan was never close to other women. That's why I was so pleased when she told me she was getting married. Even with all the trouble over the divorce I was sure it would work out."

"Maybe it still will," Leopold said. He patted Richter's arm and left him seated on the porch.

Back at the squad room, Fletcher's news was negative. "Michelle Power never saw this box before, Captain. It's not one of hers."

Leopold nodded. "Dust it for prints."

"I already have. Just yours and mine, plus a few smudges."

"Interesting. If it was wiped off, that implies the kidnaper used it. But for what?"

"You really think it was a kidnaping? There's been no ransom demand."

"Maybe money wasn't the motive."

"I spoke to the maid of honor, Pearl Wayne, but she couldn't add anything. She was busy watching the flower girls to make sure they started down the aisle on cue."

"Michelle Power would have been watching them too, bending down to hand them their bouquets. And Susan's father has poor eyesight, with no side vision at all. Almost anything might have happened if it happened fast enough. But what?"

He was still pondering that question when he called Molly at dinnertime to say he'd be late.

"Any news yet?" she asked.

"Not a thing. She seems to have vanished off the face of the earth."

Matt Buckley arrived after seven, looking haggard. He'd exchanged his wedding tuxedo for a sport shirt and jacket and beige cuffed slacks. "I have to find her, Captain. I've agreed to go on the eleven o'clock news with an appeal to her kidnapers. I'll pay anything they ask."

"It may not be as simple as that. Ordinary kidnapers probably would have contacted the family by now."

"These aren't ordinary kidnapers, Captain. We've already established that they had to be invisible to grab her in the back of that church without being seen."

"Not necessarily," Leopold told him.

"What do you mean?"

"The florist and the maid of honor were busy with the flower girls. Richter's eyesight is failing. For a crucial moment or two no one was looking at the bride."

"But someone would have seen the kidnaper approach."

"Perhaps not. We've heard testimony that no one was back there but the bridal party, yet I know of at least thirty people who passed through other than the wedding guests—thirty people who must have been seen but not noticed."

"Thirty—"

"The women's chorus of the Church of St. Mark."

Lieutenant Fletcher interrupted them. "Captain, the 911 operator just took a call that could be important. A woman, either drunk or hysterical, said she couldn't go through with it. She gave an address where she said we could find Susan Richter."

Leopold was on his feet, snatching the address from Fletcher.

He recognized it at once and his eyes went to Matt Buckley's face. "You'd better come with us, Matt. It's your old house. Janet must be involved."

They went in Leopold's car with the siren wailing all the way. A radio-dispatched patrol car was already on the scene and an officer stood in the open doorway. "It was unlocked, Captain," he reported. "We've got a dead woman inside."

Leopold turned quickly to Buckley. "Wait out here, Matt," he ordered. Then he and Fletcher followed the officer into the house.

Janet Buckley was sprawled on the living-room carpet near the telephone, a small-caliber automatic pistol near her right hand. "Fletcher, search the rest of the house," Leopold said. "Upstairs and the basement."

He knelt and carefully retrieved the pistol, then examined the ugly powder-burned hole in Janet's right temple, just at the hairline. A sniff of the barrel told him the weapon had been fired. He searched the floor and the loose folds of Janet's dress, but found nothing else. He checked the tables and chairs in the room, lifting and feeling in the cushions, and again found nothing. There was no note.

Fletcher appeared at the door to the basement stairs. "I found her, Captain. Chloroformed and handcuffed to a cot in the basement, but she's alive."

He led the way downstairs to a small inside room that had been finished off with wood paneling and wall-to-wall carpeting. Leopold noted a bottle of chloroform and a cloth pad on a table.

Susan Richter wore the remnants of her wedding gown. Part of the long, layered skirt had been ripped away. Her white shoes were on the floor and her wrists were handcuffed to the metal rim of the cot on which she lay. As Leopold waited with her for medical help, she opened her eyes, blinked, and turned from the light. "What happened? Where am I?"

"Don't try to move. We'll have these handcuffs off you in a minute."

"What happened to me?" she asked again, closing her eyes.

"You were kidnaped from the church just before your wedding. Do you remember anything about it?"

She opened her eyes again and as Fletcher returned with a key he'd found in Janet's purse and freed her hands, she managed to sit up on the cot. Leopold massaged her wrists and encouraged her to tell them what she remembered.

"I came to the church with my maid of honor, Pearl. My father was there, telling me it was late. The procession started almost at once. I remember watching them walk down the aisle. I remember the little flower girls. Then someone was there, next to me. Someone in a red robe. That's all I remember."

"You didn't recognize the woman who assaulted you?" Fletcher asked.

"I just remember the red robe. It was someone who looked familiar but—" She glanced around at the paneled walls. "I want Matt. Is he upstairs?"

"We'll get him."

Matt came downstairs and took her in his arms. "It's all right now. You're safe," he told her.

"Where am I?"

"At Janet's. She tried to prevent the wedding."

"Janet's? Of course! It was Janet in the robe!"

Matt helped her up the stairs to the first floor, carefully steering her away from the living room where the police photographer was at work. They sat at the table in the breakfast nook off the kitchen and Leopold continued his questioning. "You're sure you don't remember anything from the time you passed out in the back of the church until you woke up just now?"

"Not a thing. This is all such a horrible dream." She turned to Matt for comfort. "What are those men doing in the other room?" she asked him. "Where's Janet?"

"She's dead, Susan."

Leopold glanced up as one of the officers came to the kitchen door. "It's not here, Captain. We went over every inch of the room."

"Thanks, Mike."

"What's not there?" Matt Buckley asked.

Leopold turned to him. "The cartridge case. Automatic pistols eject the cartridge case when they're fired. I noticed when I examined the body there wasn't one on the floor or in any of the chairs."

"What does that mean?"

"It means that Janet couldn't have shot herself. Either she was shot somewhere else or the killer took the cartridge case away. Either way, it has to be murder."

Susan Richter shook her head as if to clear it. "I don't understand what you're saying."

"I'm saying I'm going to have to arrest you on suspicion of murder. You have the right to remain silent . . ."

The color had drained from Susan's face as Leopold recited her rights under the law. "I didn't kill her," she managed to whisper as he finished. "I'm not going to prison for this."

"Susan," Leopold said. "No one kidnaped you from St. Mark's. You staged your own disappearance, and no one but you could have done it. Last night during the rehearsal you left a box in the back of the church with the florist's name written on it. Inside was one of the red choir robes, and probably a wig as well. While Michelle Power was busy with the flower girls' bouquets, as you knew she would be, and your father was looking away, you merely removed the robe and the wig from the box and stepped through the door to the choir loft. It wouldn't have taken more than five seconds.

"In the stairwell you quickly removed your veil and ripped away the bulky bottom of your wedding gown, which you'd probably cut and stitched earlier in preparation. You slipped on the robe and wig and stuffed the pieces of your gown under the robe. Then you joined the other young women in the choir loft. You knew you wouldn't have to sing because there'd be no wedding, and no one would question an unfamiliar face in such a large group. They'd assume you were a last-minute substitution. When the wedding was cancelled, you simply filed out unnoticed with the others."

"Why can't you believe the story she told you?" Matt wanted to know. "Why couldn't Janet have kidnaped her?"

"A small woman like Janet couldn't have carried a woman as tall as Susan out of the church unconscious, even if no one was watching. And that wouldn't explain the box with the florist's name on it. Then, too, the success of the plan depended in large part on Bill Richter's poor eyesight, a condition known only to Susan. Remember, it was Susan who arranged for the choir, Susan who knew the name of the florist so she could write it on the box."

"What if there had been late-arriving wedding guests in the back of the church admiring the bride?" Fletcher asked.

"She was purposely late so everyone would be seated. If there had been other people, she simply would have postponed the vanishing act until later—perhaps disappeared less dramatically at the reception."

"But why would she do it?" Matt asked angrily. "She already had me. It wasn't any lovers' triangle. Janet and I were divorced."

"Exactly. She had you, but Janet had a large divorce settlement with generous alimony payments for years to come. The alimony would stop when she died, of course. It just had to be done in such a way that no suspicion fell on you or Susan."

"Me or—"

"The plot was far-fetched in the extreme, but with some neat little touches along the way. When Janet sent that crystal bride as a wedding gift, Susan broke it before leaving for the church— as if Janet were threatening to break her. She tossed the chloroformed pad in the wastebasket, knowing we'd find it, and she left more chloroform in the basement room. She took a small whiff of it and handcuffed herself to the cot, of course."

"How do you know that?" Matt challenged again.

"When she pretended to regain consciousness, she asked if you were upstairs. She told us she remembered nothing since the church, and you told me earlier she never saw this house. How did she know that carpeted, paneled room without windows was in the basement?"

Matt sighed, avoiding Susan's eyes.

"You're saying she made the phone call to headquarters?" Fletcher asked.

"I'm sure of it. We keep a tape of all 911 calls. A voiceprint should confirm it was Susan and not Janet. After she made the

call, she went downstairs to handcuff herself to the cot and
await rescue."

Susan was trembling now. "Matt, tell them I didn't shoot her."

"Susan, try to control yourself—"

"Control myself!" She was suddenly on her feet. "You told
me it was safe! You told me we were in it together! You said we
needed that alimony money, that you weren't going to slave
away at the law firm the rest of your life to keep Janet in crystal
and champagne!" She turned wildly to Leopold. "I did the rest
of it, but he shot her. Do you think she'd have let me into the
house alone? He used some of the chloroform to knock her out
and then he wrapped her fingers around the gun and shot her!"

Matt shook his head. "Susan, no one's going to believe that.
You're carrying on like a madwoman."

Captain Leopold addressed Susan. "He shot her there in the
living room?"

"Yes—she was passed out on the floor."

"What happened to the missing cartridge case?"

"I don't know! I waited until he had time to reach your office,
to establish an alibi, and then I phoned 911, pretending to be
hysterical."

Leopold turned to Matt Buckley. "I can't believe either of you
would have removed that ejected cartridge case deliberately,
but one of you might have accidentally, if it lodged in your
clothing. If you're innocent, you'll agree to be searched."

Matt hesitated only a second. "Of course. I have nothing to
hide."

Fletcher found it in the cuff of his trousers.

Molly was waiting up when Leopold arrived home after midnight. "They had it on the late news," she said. "I still can't
believe it. Susan and Matt planning a terrible thing like that."

"I suppose it was love," he told her, "and greed. They wanted
each other but they wanted the money too. Now they have
neither. She'll probably end up testifying against him."

Molly shook her head sadly. "Let's go to bed, darling."

JOHN D. MACDONALD
BIMINI KILL

*Considering the late John D. MacDonald's obvious love
for boating and the sea, it's surprising that so few of his
short stories had nautical backgrounds. This one, published in a yachting magazine just a few months after his
death, makes fine use of that background while reaffirm-
ing MacDonald's position as one of the leading American
mystery writers.*

I don't like it, Vince," Nan was saying. "I don't like any part of
it. It scares me, sort of. But he actually begged me, for old times'
sake, and the lawyer said I ought to give him a last chance
before I start the divorce thing."

It was a Sunday afternoon in Lauderdale in the off-season, a
hot and lazy day, and I had been aboard my joy and my
mortgaged burden, my three-year-old Bertram 54 sport fisher-
man, the *Faraway Gal*, when Nan Brogan had come out onto
the big dock and stepped aboard.

I was just back from a long charter, and I had been putting
the lines and the gear back in first class shape. I was reassem-
bling one of the big marlin reels when Nan appeared. Now she
sat on the transom in the sunlight and touched the opened can
of cold beer to her cheek and looked at me in a wry way and
said, "So I guess I'm asking you for old times' sake too, Vince."

It is a sour thing to endure when your girl marries someone
else, particularly when you know in your heart she is making a
mistake. The cruel ones said she married Yates Brogan for his
money, but I knew that wasn't true. She thought she loved him,
I know. And it was partly my fault for having taken her too
much for granted before Yates came along, and then, out of
injured pride, putting up no fight at all when I saw her being
attracted to him. But the worst part of it was watching how the
two years of marriage had slowly changed her, had taken the

sweet high edge off her spirits, had saddened her dark blue eyes.

"I'll do it," I said. "I won't like it any better than you will, Nan. But I'll do it. And I can use the five hundred bucks I'll charge him for the transportation."

It was exactly the sort of twisted, tension-laden situation you would expect a man like Yates Brogan to cook up. He knew Nan was my girl before he came into her life. The only good thing I can find to say about him is that he is a superb sailor. His custom motorsailer, the *Reefcomber,* is a jewel to take your breath away, and he has taken her to most of the fine waters of the world. He has inherited money and has never done one day's work in his life. He has always had a bottle problem and a woman problem, and marriage to my Nan had not lessened either of them. After they were married, Brogan based the *Reefcomber* in Lauderdale so Nan could be near her folks. They lived aboard and took extended cruises out of Lauderdale, usually with some of Brogan's hard-living friends aboard. I had seen her after those cruises, looking more dispirited each time they returned.

The final ugliness had taken place in Nassau a month ago, and she had left him there and flown home to begin divorce proceedings. Apparently he hadn't believed her serious until the first legal documents had caught up with him at Bimini. Then last week he had left the *Reefcomber* there and flown back to talk her out of it.

"It's just his darn pride," Nan said. "I'm not after a penny of his money. We don't love each other any more. I'm just sort of a possession, somebody a little bit decorative who can handle the lines and chart a course and take a wheel shift. Nothing is going to change my mind, Vince. But, in all decency, I guess I have to give him a chance to speak his piece."

Yates Brogan had found out I was running over to Bimini on Monday to pick up a charter there, and he wanted me to run him and Nan over so he could bring Nan back on the *Reefcomber.*

"Why doesn't he just ask you to fly over with him?" I asked her.

She sighed and shrugged. "I don't know. Yates likes everything as complicated as possible. I guess he thinks it gives him an advantage or something. He thrives on confusion. But he's acting very strange. Maybe it's a silly thing to say, but I have the feeling he might do some strange, violent thing. Anyway, I know I'll feel safer with you nearby."

"I won't be nearby aboard the *Reefcomber,* Nan."

"By then I'll either be over this scary feeling about him or I won't. He wants to bring her back across the stream on Wednesday. Your charter starts Tuesday morning, doesn't it?"

"Yes."

"And because of Chet being in the hospital, you're going to pick up a Bahamian to crew for you after you get into Bimini, aren't you?"

I was puzzled, wondering what she was driving at. "That's right."

Her blush darkened her deep-water tan. "So . . . to sort of add injury to insult, Vince, could . . . Johnny Welch crew for you on the way across? Then he'd be there in Bimini if I decided not to come back with Yates, and Yates tried to force me to come with him."

Maybe it could be a good thing to watch your girl's marriage going sour if you had the comfortable knowledge you were going to be there to pick up the pieces. And I would have been glad to. I've never loved anybody else, and I never will. But I had been off on a long charter at the wrong time, and Johnny Welch had been there to field the rebound.

"*Crew* for me!" I said with disgust.

She knew what I meant. Johnny is a big hearty young man, a local realtor with various land development interests. A few times in the past I had taken him and some of his hot prospects out to fish the stream. Few men have ever been as inept aboard a small boat. That was one world he could not share—a world that Yates Brogan, Nan, and I belonged in, a world of boats and the sea, the textures of wind and weather.

"Not for pay," Nan said, "but Yates wouldn't have to know that. Actually, it was Johnny's idea. He's terribly nervous about this whole idea. He wants to be near me. And I guess I would . . . like to have him near me. I know Johnny is an idiot about boats; he can't pick up a line without getting it all wound around his ankles. But . . . I'm not as intolerant of the lubbers as I used to be, Vince. Yates has given me a new kind of . . . sickness of the sea. Maybe it won't ever be the same for me again."

Just as I thought the tears might start, she moved neatly and swiftly to collect my empty beer can and climb up onto the dock to drop it and hers into the white trash bin. She dropped lightly back onto the broad transom, a smallish girl in blue shorts and a white blouse, with frayed old topsiders, a sea tan, cropped black hair that I knew would smell fresh as ocean winds if I could but hold her in my arms as I had done long ago and could never do again. This was a sea girl, a small-boat girl, moving with the sureness that could but accentuate the lurching clumsiness of powerful Johnny Welch.

"You don't really mean that," I told her.

"I guess not. But it will take a while. I won't give you a play by play. I'll spare you that. But it's been . . . grim. I tried to make it work, Vince. I keep telling myself that. I really tried. What about Johnny?"

I shrugged. "He can come along. Makes a cozy little group, huh?"

She knew what I meant and had the grace to blush. The old boyfriend—dating from way back when she had been a scrawny sun-blackened twelve-year-old who'd helped me sail my first boat—and the man she shouldn't have married and the new boyfriend, the one who had been there for her to lean on at just the right time.

"Things work out in such stupid ways," she said. "I'm very sorry about the way things have worked out, Vince. You're the most . . ."

"Don't tell me now. How will Johnny react to your coming back on the *Reefcomber* with Brogan?"

"Maybe I'm hoping he just won't let me. And maybe I'm making things just a little more complicated than Yates figured on. And I don't catch him off balance very often. So I'm taking a nasty feline pleasure in that. What time tomorrow, Vince?"

"Miami Marine says the wind will pick up in the afternoon, so let's roll it by seven."

When she left I watched her walk shoreward along the dock

and saw her wave a couple of times to friends who called to her. I finished putting the reel back together, cursing Yates Brogan and Johnny Welch and that stupid restraint of mine that had at last landed me in the hopeless category of treasured friend to the woman I love.

I visited Chet in the hospital at eight o'clock that evening. The crisp white pillow made his chunky face look as red as old bricks. They were going to take out his appendix in the morning. We'd hoped to be able to wait until we were between charters, but this last time it had acted up just enough to alarm both of us a little.

"By Thursday," he said, "I fly over and go to work."

"So a marlin is a little green when it comes to gaff, and you pop open."

"So I run the *Gal* and you handle the fish."

"It would confuse the charter, boy. I'm the skill and you're the muscle."

"Skill? Who was it busted the piling at Frazier's Hog Key?"

I got off that painful subject by telling him about the passengers I'd have the next day. Chet whistled through his broken tooth. "Don't get too far from a marlin spike, Cap. Keep your mind on where the shark rifle is stowed. Brogan is a nut, and he's mean. Why'd you let yourself in for a deal like that?"

"For laughs," I said.

He looked at me, and I knew he knew why I'd agreed. He knew there was nothing Nan couldn't ask of me. "Sure," he said. "For laughs." He grinned. "Lash Johnny to a cleat so as he don't fall overboard before you clear the sea buoy."

After I'd wished him luck he let me get as far as the door before he asked sternly, "You take that number three reel down?"

"Yes."

"The drag is smooth now?"

"Seems to be."

"Find some fish, Vince."

"I'll be looking."

"And . . . don't let her bother you too much, hear?"

"I'm just running the boat."

Yates Brogan was first aboard Monday morning. I had the

coffee on, and I'd just finished making up my bunk. He tossed his duffle bag in onto the bunk. He's tall and hard, but the liquor has started to blur the hawk-lines of his face. I could smell the drink on him, and his eyes weren't quite in focus, but he was steady on his feet.

"*Good* morning, Vincent," he said in his mocking way. "You should be very happy to help such a deserving couple find their way back to bliss."

"I'm going to Bimini. You're paying for the ride."

"Surly in the early? I've paid for it, lad," he said, tucking ten fifties into my shirt pocket. "I thought you had a sentimental interest in the lady."

"Knock it off, Brogan."

"Nan just gets a little too impulsive sometimes. And then it doesn't do a bit of good to knock her around. You have to reason with her and talk soft and sweet."

As I was wondering if I could knock him all the way up onto the dock or if he'd drop between the boat and the pilings of the finger slip, he looked beyond me and the grin slid off his face.

"What the hell," he said softly.

I turned and saw Nan and Johnny coming toward us. Johnny looked flushed, indignant and uncomfortable. Nan said good morning with icy formality. I took her gear. Johnny tried to come aboard with his after Nan was aboard and managed to hook a toe in my spring line and narrowly avoided landing flat on his face in the cockpit. As he recovered his balance, Brogan said, "Upsy daisy, pal. Back on the dock. The passenger list is complete."

"Welch isn't a passenger," I said. "He's crewing for me."

Brogan turned and looked at me, and then he looked at Nan. He made a short ugly laughing sound and said, "Nice! Very cute, dear wife. Very conspiratorial. But what good will it do you?"

"Listen to me, Brogan!" Johnny said bravely.

"Please, dear boy. Not on an empty stomach."

As Brogan turned away from him, Welch started to follow him, his big freckled fists clenched. "Get the lines, Welch," I told him, and swung up to the flying bridge and kicked the two big GM 1271 TIs into rumbling life. I peered down and saw Welch making ineffectual motions while Nan was deftly taking in the lines. Brogan was pouring himself some coffee and looking amused. Welch's next error was to try to shove us off, a type of assistance I do not need when I'm at the dual throttles of the *Faraway Gal.* I slid the stern away from the pilings just as he started to push, and if he hadn't caught the base of an outrigger, he'd have gone over the side then and there. Brogan laughed at him, too long and too loud.

We left the big marina, went down the waterway and under the bridge and out through the pass into the Atlantic. As soon as I'd cleared the tide chop just outside the pass, Nan came up with coffee for me.

"Lovely morning," she said with no conviction.

"Lovely people." Brogan had moved forward along the boat deck as soon as we had begun to run dry beyond the chop, and he sat on the bow hatch looking forward, sipping his coffee. Johnny Welch sat slumped, gloomy, inert in the port fighting chair staring back toward the mainland. Neither of them could hear what we were saying.

"Yates is furious," Nan said. "Maybe he thought he could really talk me into changing my mind. But as soon as he saw Johnny, he knew it wouldn't work."

"Take it a minute," I said. I left my coffee there and went down and estimated how much to allow for the movement of the stream and the southeast wind in relation to cruising speed, and kicked it into automatic pilot. It held just where I wanted it the first time. I moved the starboard engine up a few revolutions to put it in better sync, and the course still held true. Then I went back up to my coffee and my ex-girl and the dazzle of the morning sun and the incredible indigo of the Gulf Stream, the skitter of flying fish, the long swells, the limber flex of the outriggers—all the components of my world, which on this day gave me no pleasure.

I ran at the most economical cruising speed, which would give us Bimini in four hours. Nan went down to the galley and fixed breakfast. I ate only because she had fixed it. Johnny Welch ate hugely. Nan nibbled. Yates Brogan refused food. He took more coffee, spiking it with black rum from a bottle out of his duffle bag, giving me a white meaningless smile as he did so. After Nan had cleaned up, Yates took her up on the bow. I sat on the transom splicing a new loop into one of my dock lines to replace one that had become frayed. I could hear little wisps of the angry discussion, fragmented words blown past me by the wind, muffled by the engine drone. I knew Johnny could hear it too. We avoided each other's eyes.

Yates came back to the cockpit, unsmiling. As he went to pour more coffee and rum I stood up and looked forward. She sat up there, her back to me, and I could tell from her posture that she was crying. I sat down and continued working on the splice.

"Stop bullying her, Yates," Johnny Welch said.

Yates came to stand near me and stare at Welch. "You touch my heart, boy. That woman is my wife."

"Not for long."

"And you're standing by? You're next in line? Johnny boy, are you sure she's worth what I could do to you?"

Welch stared at him with a kind of dull wonder. Johnny is almost an all-American boy, except perhaps a shade too meaty, and with promise of becoming bald too soon. "What kind of an idea is that?"

"I might get cross with you, Johnny. I've looked you up. I could buy up some paper from people who'd be glad to sell. I could squeeze you, and it wouldn't take much of a squeeze, would it?"

"You can't scare me, Brogan."

"I can't? I've made you look highly nervous." He turned to me. "Skipper, can I ride in your tuna tower?"

"Please don't slip and fall, Brogan."

He went up nimbly, a man accustomed to masts, rigging, and the swing and dip of the sea. He sat up there and we could hear him singing.

"I don't care what he tries to do to me," Johnny said. "I don't want him to hurt Nan. I think he's crazy. I think he could do anything. I don't think he knows what he's going to do next. Nobody ever walked out on him before."

"Whatever happens, you be good to her, Johnny."

He stared at me, a decent, somewhat bovine young man. "Sure, Vince. You know I will. Sure."

At a little after eleven we went in over the bar and into Bimini harbor. The upcoming tuna tournament had packed the place with sport fishermen. I moved the length of the harbor at dead slow and tucked it into my dock reservation, made my mooring and went to the office to check on my charter. There was a message for me saying my people wouldn't arrive until noon of the next day. When I went back to the *Faraway Gal,* my three passengers were gone. I was hosing the salt off her when Brogan appeared.

"Where'd they go?" he demanded.

"Nan and Johnny? I haven't the faintest idea."

He gave me a long ugly look, then turned on his heel and walked away. I watched him walk to the next dock, and I recognized the *Reefcomber* in the second slip. He hopped aboard and disappeared.

Friends of mine started coming over to say hello and exchange gossip and trade news, but I was alone and eating a cheese sandwich when Yates Brogan came back, a little bit unsteady on his feet this time.

"You seen 'em yet?"

"No."

"Their gear still aboard?"

"Yes."

"Hand me up her stuff. I'll take it aboard the *Reefcomber.*"

"That would be up to her."

"Hand it up here, or I'm coming aboard and get it."

"You've got no permission to come aboard, Brogan. You hired a ride and the ride's over. Come aboard, and I'll heave you over the side."

He looked so indecisive, I half turned away from him. I saw the movement out of the corner of my eye as he launched himself into the air, and I turned back in time to get such a monstrous thump in the mouth it spun the sky, blinded my eyes, and dropped me belly-down across the starboard rail. By the time I had rejoined reality, he was clambering up onto the dock with Nan's kit. I lurched and caught him by the ankle. He pulled free but fell sprawling. It gave me time to get up onto the dock as he came to his feet, and I settled into the business of knocking him loose from that white grin.

We attracted a large noisy audience, appreciative of this

special entertainment. He hit me well a few times, enough to loosen my knees, but I shook the mists out of my head and kept my arms going and soon felt the sweet solidity of impact from knuckles to elbow. He went down with the grin and came up with the grin, and went down without it and came up without it, and then went sprawling back wildly and off the dock, missing the stern of the *Faraway Gal* as he went into that harbor water, so clear that you can read every word on the labels of the more recently jettisoned cans, nine feet deep. I saw him start to swim slowly toward a dock ladder. I sat on the edge of the dock and leaned forward to drip the random blood into the water, exploring damage with the tip of my tongue, gasping for air.

Nan was kneeling beside me, her hand sweet on my shoulder, her voice tender in my ear, "Oh, Vince. Vince, dear, he hurt you!"

"Wanted your gear," I said thickly. "Tried to take it. Bring me the hose."

She brought the nozzle and turned it on. I ran the water over my head. She brought me a towel from my boat, and I left some pink smears on it when I swabbed my face, but the bleeding was about over. I looked over and saw Brogan, sopping wet, boarding the *Reefcomber*. He didn't hop aboard. He went aboard like an old old man, and I took a certain satisfaction in that.

Our audience dispersed. I stood up. Nan stood as tall as she could, and her eyes were that brighter blue that happens when she is angry. "This was the dumbest thing I ever did! I'm going to tell him right now, right this minute, that I wouldn't go back to him if he . . . if he only had one more hour to live. And the only thing I want from him is to be left alone."

She started marching toward the *Reefcomber*. Johnny started after her. I caught him by the arm.

"But he might hurt her!"

"Let her do it her way."

"Don't you give a damn, Vince?"

"Stay out of it, Johnny."

"But this isn't the way to do it. She should make him understand. People can . . . separate in a reasonable way."

"Brogan isn't a very reasonable guy."

I think she was in the cabin of the *Reefcomber* for fifteen minutes, and I don't think Johnny or I took our eyes off that boat for more than ten seconds at a time. I heard Johnny's sigh when she reappeared and came walking back to us at a much slower pace.

She did not speak or focus on either of us as I helped her aboard. She sat and looked at nothing and said in a small voice, "This time he believed me."

"About time," I said.

"He took it very badly. He said I would be very very sorry, and Johnny would be very very sorry for doing this to him. His face is all banged up."

I looked at my puffed fists. I was not surprised.

She looked up at me. "I will *not* run from him. We won't take a plane back until tomorrow, Johnny. He's started drinking already. He'll either pass out or do something foolish. Johnny, you find a place ashore. I'll stay aboard if I may, Vince."

"Now wait a minute!" Johnny said.

"It's okay with me, Nan. You can lock the cabin. I can use the forward hatch to the crew quarters. If that makes you nervous, Welch, you can bunk in with me."

He looked uneasy. "No. No, that's okay."

Brogan didn't appear again. Johnny found a place ashore and came back. The three of us had drinks aboard, and then in the blue Bimini dusk we walked down the narrow main street and had dinner at the Big Game Fishing Club. We were all trying to make the effort to be festive, but it didn't quite come off. Johnny laughed too loudly at nothing. Nan seemed distracted. I kept wondering if it was worse to lose a girl the second time than the first time. I knew that after the tensions and cruelties of the relationship with Brogan, she felt she needed the quiet devotion of a Johnny Welch.

Johnny walked back to the dock with us. All the boats were in, and most of them were lighted. We heard the laughter of women, heard some amateur guitar, some slightly drunken harmony, and music from several radios. We had a nightcap beer under the stars and pointedly avoided mentioning Brogan. His motorsailer was dark. Nan said good night to us and closed herself into the cabin. Shortly after her lights went out, Johnny said good night and left. I sat with my dreary thoughts and outworn dreams for a little while, then went forward and lowered myself into the crew compartment. After I was in the bunk I was all too aware of her presence on the other side of the bulkhead, with her head perhaps ten inches from mine and her heart ten thousand miles from mine. As I was moving closer to sleep I heard the wind freshen and felt the increased motion of the boat and heard the creak of lines and chafing gear. It was out of the east and would grow stronger.

I could not guess how many people were awakened by her first scream. But by the third she must have had one hundred percent attention. I got to her a moment after the third spine-chilling scream. I was convinced Brogan had gotten to her and was killing her. I yanked on a pair of shorts, grabbed my sheath knife, and tried the intercabin door. It was locked on her side. I went up through the hatch so fast I gouged a piece of meat out of my shoulder. I erupted into a cool gray world that paled the dock lights. The sky was pink in the east. The screams had started roosters crowing, dogs barking.

She was in the cockpit, staring toward the *Reefcomber,* her fists against her throat, her eyes bulging with shock and hysteria. She wore slacks and a cotton coolie jacket. I looked where she was looking, and I did not take the time to cuff the hysteria out of her. I went up onto the dock and toward the *Reefcomber* at a dead run, and the closer I got to him, the more unpleasant he looked. The *Reefcomber* moved in the east wind, and he swayed with each movement, swayed at the end of the short length of nylon line. I went up on the trunk cabin, clasped one arm around his thighs, severed the line with one slash, caught his full weight, and brought him down to the deck. As I was doing it, I kept wondering why I could not force myself to move more slowly, more clumsily.

The half-inch nylon had bitten deeply into the flesh of his throat. I worked the slipknot loose and pulled the loop off over his head. I rolled him onto his back and began artificial respiration, but I knew from the feel of the body of Yates Brogan that he was irrevocably dead. Hoarse questions were shouted. People gathered around. A fat man in pink pajamas identified himself as a doctor and immediately confirmed the fact of death.

I went back to my boat. It was getting lighter every minute. I heard Nan sobbing. I looked in on her. She was face down on the bunk. I went below and sat next to her. She turned and looked up at me. "He's dead." It was more statement than question.

"Yes."

"I . . . I woke up and I couldn't go back to sleep. I couldn't stop thinking about . . . everything. So I came out to watch . . . the sun come up. The first time I glanced over there, I didn't see him. I just got the feeling something was wrong. I looked again and then I saw . . . what it was."

"There's a doctor there. He says it happened maybe a couple of hours ago."

"What a mess! What a dreadful mess!"

I shrugged. "It simplifies a lot of things, doesn't it?"

"Don't be so callous, Vince."

"I'm being honest. He wasn't one of my favorite people. I won't miss him a bit."

She sat on the edge of the bunk, frowning. "I thought he'd do some crazy thing. But I didn't think it would be that."

"So instead of a divorcée, you're a widow. And pretty well off."

"I won't *touch* it! Not a dime of it!" She looked speculatively at me. "I suppose he left some vile note of farewell."

"I don't know. I didn't look."

"I'm sorry I went to pieces. But . . ."

"You don't have to explain or apologize, Nan. You know that."

Johnny appeared at eight o'clock. When he heard what had happened he turned pale and sweaty and sat down abruptly, his mouth sagging.

The Bahamian officials appeared a little after nine. Three men, two of them young, two of them in uniform. They questioned us together and separately. Brogan had left no suicide note. They seemed most curious about the fact of the public brawl I'd had with Brogan. The spelling out of the relationship between Brogan, Nan, and Johnny seemed to pain them. And they acted very weary, as though they could see an endless wilderness of forms, red tape, and complex documents ahead of them. Suicide is incorrect and troublesome.

We were told more investigators would fly in from Nassau, and we could expect a visitation of reporters from Nassau as well as the States. Nan and Johnny were politely requested to remain in Bimini until officially released. By then perhaps Mrs. Brogan could arrange to have the *Reefcomber* taken back to Lauderdale, its port of registry.

Suicide is troublesome, but in Bimini tuna is king. I would be permitted to fulfill my charter.

After the questioning I lined up a good boy to crew for me and set him to work acquiring the bait fish we would need. Nan and Johnny had gone off into town. I felt restless. I looked over at the *Reefcomber.* For once there was no one standing on the dock staring at where a man had died. I sauntered over and stood and figured out how he had done it. He had stood atop the trunk cabin and put the noose around his neck, and reached as high as he could to tie the other end of the line to a stay and then had stepped off.

The line still hung where I had slashed it apart, and the breeze had unraveled the end of it into an Irish pennant.

I stared at that clean white line.

Suddenly the world had a entirely different look. In the midmorning silence I heard Nan's voice. I turned and saw her with Johnny. He went into the dockmaster's office. She came walking toward me.

She came up to me. "Vince . . . you have such a strange look." I could not speak. I pointed at the end of the line. "What do you mean, Vince. What am I supposed to . . . Oh!"

It took her as long to see it as it had me. Her fingers closed convulsively around my wrist. The color went out of her face so that her tan looked yellowish and sickly. She moistened her lips. "Even . . . even when Yates was so drunk you couldn't understand a word he said, he would never never . . ."

"I know. It would be the same with you or with me."

Then she said in a very small voice, "Johnny has been telling me it would be childish not to accept the money."

"What's going on?" Johnny Welch asked, cheerfully enough. We both turned and stared at him. He was alien, a creature of the land, whereas we were of both the land and the sea, with skills he would never know. Johnny's face changed. "What's the matter with you two?"

In a voice that did not seem like my own, I said, "Was he so drunk he wasn't any problem, or did you have to hit him? You could safely hit him. I left enough marks on him so one more wouldn't be noticed."

"What the hell are you talking about, Vince?"

"About murder. For love and money. Maybe mostly money. You aren't in very good shape, are you?"

"Are you accusing me of killing him?"

"You came back in the night, after everybody had settled down for the night. You hoisted him up onto that trunk cabin. Then I think you made the line fast, made a loop in the other end, lifted him up, worked the noose around his neck, and let him fall free."

"Nan, he's talking nonsense! Why are you looking at me like that!"

I took a small gamble. "Somebody saw you do it, Johnny. Those Bimini cops are on their way back here, looking for you."

For a moment he smiled. Then his face went blank. He turned away and began to run, with a frantic, ludicrous, hopeless haste, like an overweight kid being chased across a schoolyard. We watched him run over the grass, past the swimming pool, and out through the open gate into the road and disappear. There was no need to follow him. Bimini is a small island.

Nan sagged heavily against me for a girl so small. I put my arm around her. I took her slowly back to the *Faraway Gal.*

I had them call the officials back. I took them to the *Reefcomber* and showed them the frayed line. I told them how Johnny had run when I had tricked him. They nodded. They accepted the evidence of the line because they were men who lived close to the sea and knew boats and lines, and they came to the same conclusion as Nan and I had. The line was the evidence, and his flight was the confession.

When a child is learning to tie a square knot and makes the second loop the wrong way, the result is an awkward, untrustworthy knot, one that is a symbol of scorn among seafaring people. And a seaman like Yates Brogan, no matter how fumbling drunk he might have been, how depressed or how suicidal, would never have made the hangman rope fast with a granny knot.

Every ending is, of course, a beginning. They caught him, and he confessed and was convicted and sentenced. I had good charters and killed big fish and kept up the payments on the *Faraway Gal.* Each time we came back to our home dock, I called on Nan. It took a time of mending and forgetting, but one time, at last, she was waiting for me, and I knew from her eyes the big wheel had turned all the way around, all the way back to our beginning, so that now the only regret we have is for the time we lost, and that is only a faint regret nowadays because life is as rich as the sea itself, and she has come back to the sea with a sound heart, love in her eyes, and a sweetness of lips.

BILL PRONZINI

STACKED DECK

Bill Pronzini's popular Nameless detective, one of the most impressive private eyes of the past two decades, has always been more interested in fair-play solutions to classic mystery puzzles than in the sort of tough action that many eyes thrive on. For this story Pronzini created a new character, Deighan, who's a bit tougher than Nameless, a bit faster with a gun. He reminds us of the best of the pulp heroes, the sort of characters a writer like Paul Cain knew so well, but with the depth and shading that mark him as a Pronzini original.

1

From where he stood in the shadow of a split-bole Douglas fir, Deighan had a clear view of the cabin down below. Big harvest moon tonight, and only a few streaky clouds scudding past now and then to dim its hard yellow shine. The hard yellow glistened off the surface of Lake Tahoe beyond, softened into a long silverish stripe out toward the middle. The rest of the water shone like polished black metal. All of it was empty as far as he could see, except for the red-and-green running lights of a boat well away to the north, pointed toward the neon shimmer that marked the North Shore gambling casinos.

The cabin was big, made of cut pine logs and redwood shakes. It had a railed redwood deck that overlooked the lake, mostly invisible from where Deighan was. A flat concrete pier jutted out into the moonstruck water, a pair of short wooden floats making a T at its outer end. The boat tied up there was a thirty-foot Chris-Craft with sleeping accommodations for four. Nothing but the finer things for the Shooter.

Deighan watched the cabin. He's been watching it for three hours now, from this same vantage point. His legs bothered him

183

a little, standing around like this, and his eyes hurt from squinting. Time was, he'd had the night vision of an owl. Not anymore. What he had now, that he hadn't had when he was younger, was patience. He'd learned that in the last three years, along with a lot of other things—patience most of all.

On all sides the cabin was dark, but that was because they'd put the blackout curtains up. The six of them had been inside for better than two hours now, the same five-man nucleus as on every Thursday night except during the winter months, plus the one newcomer. The Shooter went to Hawaii when it started to snow. Or Florida or the Bahamas—someplace warm. Mannlicher and Brandt stayed home in the winter. Deighan didn't know what the others did, and he didn't care.

A match flared in the darkness between the carport, where the Shooter's Caddy Eldorado was slotted, and the parking area back among the trees. That was the lookout—Mannlicher's boy. Some lookout: he smoked a cigarette every five minutes, like clockwork, so you always knew where he was. Deighan watched him smoke this one. When he was done, he threw the butt away in a shower of sparks, and then seemed to remember that he was surrounded by dry timber and went after it and stamped it out with his shoe. *Some* lookout.

Deighan held his watch up close to his eyes, pushed the little button that lighted its dial. Ten-nineteen. Just about time. The lookout was moving again, down toward the lake. Pretty soon he would walk out on the pier and smoke another cigarette and admire the view for a few minutes. He apparently did that at least twice every Thursday night—that had been his pattern on each of the last two—and he hadn't gone through the ritual yet tonight. He was bored, that was the thing. He'd been at his job a long time and it was always the same; there wasn't anything for him to do except walk around and smoke cigarettes and look at three hundred square miles of lake. Nothing ever happened. In three years nothing had ever happened.

Tonight something was going to happen.

Deighan took the gun out of the clamshell holster at his belt. It was a Smith & Wesson .38 wadcutter, lightweight, compact— a good piece, one of the best he'd ever owned. He held it in his hand, watching as the lookout performed as if on cue—walked to the pier, stopped, then moved out along its flat surface. When the guy had gone halfway, Deighan came out of the shadows and went down the slope at an angle across the driveway, to the rear of the cabin. His shoes made little sliding sounds on the needled ground, but they weren't sounds that carried.

He'd been over this ground three times before, dry runs the last two Thursday nights and once during the day when nobody was around; he knew just where and how to go. The lookout was lighting up again, his back to the cabin, when Deighan reached the rear wall. He eased along it to the spare-bedroom window. The sash went up easily, noiselessly. He could hear them then, in the rec room—voices, ice against glass, the click and rattle of the chips. He got the ski mask from his jacket pocket, slipped it over his head, snugged it down. Then he climbed through the window, put his penlight on just long enough to orient himself, went straight across to the door that led into the rec room.

It didn't make a sound, either, when he opened it. He went in with the revolver extended, elbow locked. Sturgess saw him first. He said, "Jesus Christ!" and his body went as stiff as if he were suffering a stroke. The others turned in their chairs, gawking. The Shooter started up out of his.

Deighan said, fast and hard, "Sit still if you don't want to die. Hands on the table where I can see them—all of you. Do it!"

They weren't stupid; they did what they were told. Deighan watched them through a thin haze of tobacco smoke. Six men around the hexagonal poker table, hands flat on its green baize, heads lifted or twisted to stare at him. He knew five of them. Mannlicher, the fat owner of the Nevornia Club at Crystal Bay; he had Family ties, even though he was a Prussian, because he'd once done some favors for an East Coast *capo*. Brandt, Mannlicher's cousin and private enforcer, who doubled as the Nevornia's floor boss. Bellah, the quasi-legitimate real-estate developer and high roller. Sturgess, the bankroll behind the Jackpot Lounge down at South Shore. And the Shooter—hired muscle, hired gun, part-time coke runner, whose real name was Dennis D'Allesandro. The sixth man was the pigeon they'd lured in for this particular game, a lean guy in his fifties with Texas oil money written all over him and his fancy clothes—Donley or Donavan, something like that.

Mannlicher was the bank tonight; the table behind his chair was covered with stacks of dead presidents—fifties and hundreds, mostly. Deighan took out the folded-up flour sack, tossed it on top of the poker chips that littered the baize in front of Mannlicher. "All right. Fill it."

The fat man didn't move. He was no pushover; he was hard, tough, mean. And he didn't like being ripped off. Veins bulged in his neck, throbbed in his temples. The violence in him was close to the surface now, held thinly in check.

"You know who we are?" he said. "Who I am?"

"Fill it."

"You dumb bastard. You'll never live to spend it."

"Fill the sack. *Now.*"

Deighan's eyes, more than his gun, made up Mannlicher's mind for him. He picked up the sack, pushed around in his chair, began to savagely feed in the stacks of bills.

"The rest of you," Deighan said, "put your wallets, watches, jewelry on the table. Everything of value. Hurry it up."

The Texan said, "Listen heah—" and Deighan pointed the .38 at his head and said, "One more word, you're a dead man." The Texan made an effort to stare him down, but it was just to save face; after two or three seconds he lowered his gaze and began stripping the rings off his fingers.

The rest of them didn't make any fuss. Bellah was sweating; he kept swiping it out of his eyes, his hands moving in little jerks and twitches. Brandt's eyes were like dull knives, cutting away at Deighan's masked face. D'Allesandro showed no emotion of any kind. That was his trademark; he was your original iceman. They might have called him that, maybe, if he'd been like one of those old-timers who used an ice pick or a blade. As it was, with his preferences, the Shooter was the right name for him.

Mannlicher had the sack full now. The platinum ring on his left hand, with its circle of fat diamonds, made little gleams and glints in the shine from the low-hanging droplight. The idea of losing that bothered him even more than losing his money; he kept running the fingers of his other hand over the stones.

"The ring," Deighan said to him. "Take it off."

"Go to hell."

"Take it off or I'll put a third eye in the middle of your forehead. Your choice."

Mannlicher hesitated, tried to stare him down, didn't have any better luck at it than the Texan. There was a tense moment; then, because he didn't want to die over a piece of jewelry, he yanked the ring off, slammed it down hard in the middle of the table.

Deighan said, "Put it in the sack. The wallets and the rest of the stuff too."

This time Mannlicher didn't hesitate. He did as he'd been told.

"All right," Deighan said. "Now get up and go over by the bar. Lie down on the floor on your belly."

Mannlicher got up slowly, his jaw set and his teeth clenched as if to keep the violence from spewing out like vomit. He lay down on the floor. Deighan gestured at Brandt, said, "You next. Then the rest of you, one at a time."

When they were all on the floor he moved to the table, caught up the sack. "Stay where you are for ten minutes," he told them. "You move before that, or call to the guy outside, I'll blow the place up. I got a grenade in my pocket, the fragmentation kind. Anybody doubt it?"

None of them said anything.

Deighan backed up into the spare bedroom, leaving the door open so he could watch them all the way to the window. He put his head out, saw no sign of the lookout. Still down by the lake somewhere. The whole thing had taken just a few minutes.

He swung out through the window, hurried away in the shadows—but in the opposite direction from the driveway and the road above. On the far side of the cabin there was a path that angled through the pine forest to the north; he found it, followed it at a trot. Enough moonlight penetrated through the branches overhead to let him see where he was going.

He was almost to the lakefront when the commotion started back there: voices, angry and pulsing in the night, Mannlicher's the loudest of them. They hadn't waited the full ten minutes, but then he hadn't expected them to. It didn't matter. The

Shooter's cabin was invisible from here, cut off by a wooded finger of land a hundred yards wide. And they wouldn't be looking for him along the water, anyway. They'd be up on the road, combing that area; they'd figure automatically that his transportation was a car.

The hard yellow-and-black gleam of the lake was just ahead, the rushes and ferns where he'd tied up the rented Beachcraft inboard. He moved across the sandy strip of beach, waded out to his calves, dropped the loaded flour sack into the boat, and then eased the craft free of the rushes before he lifted himself over the gunwale. The engine caught with a quiet rumble the first time he turned the key.

They were still making noise back at the cabin, blundering around like fools, as he eased away into the night.

2

The motel was called the Whispering Pines. It was back off Highway 28 below Crystal Bay, a good half mile from the lake, tucked up in a grove of pines and Douglas fir. Deighan's cabin was the farthest from the office, detached from its nearest neighbor by thirty feet of open ground.

Inside he sat in darkness except for flickering light from the television. The set was an old one; the picture was riddled with snow and kept jumping every few seconds. But he didn't care; he wasn't watching it. Or listening to it: he had the sound turned off. It was on only because he didn't like waiting in the dark.

It had been after midnight when he came in—too late to make the ritual call to Fran, even though he'd felt a compulsion to do so. She went to bed at eleven-thirty; she didn't like the phone to ring after that. How could he blame her? When he was home and she was away at Sheila's or her sister's, he never wanted it to ring that late either.

It was one-ten now. He was tired, but not too tired. The evening was still in his blood, warming him, like liquor or drugs that hadn't quite worn off yet. Mannlicher's face . . . that was an image he'd never forget. The Shooter's too, and Brandt's, but especially Mannlicher's.

Outside, a car's headlamps made a sweep of light across the curtained window as it swung in through the motel courtyard. When it stopped nearby and the lights went out, Deighan thought: It's about time.

Footsteps made faint crunching sounds on gravel. Soft knock on the door. Soft voice following: "Prince? You in there?"

"Door's open."

A wedge of moonlight widened across the floor, not quite reaching to where Deighan sat in the lone chair with the .38 wadcutter in his hand. The man who stood silhouetted in the opening made a perfect target—just a damned airhead, any way you looked at him.

"Prince?"

"I'm over here. Come on in, shut the dor."

"Why don't you turn on a light?"

"There's a switch by the door."

The man entered, shut the door. There was a click and the ceiling globe came on. Deighan stayed where he was, but reached over with his left hand to turn off the TV.

Bellah stood blinking at him, running his palms along the sides of his expensive cashmere jacket. He said nervously, "For God's sake, put the gun away. What's the idea?"

"I'm the cautious type."

"Well, put it away. I don't like it."

Deighan got to his feet, slid the revolver into his belt holster. "How'd it go?"

"Hairy, damned hairy. Mannlicher was like a madman." Bellah took a handkerchief out of his pocket, wiped his forehead. His angular face was pale, shiny-damp. "I didn't think he'd take it this hard. Christ."

That's the trouble with people like you, Deighan thought. You never think. He pinched a cigarette out of his shirt pocket, lit it with the Zippo Fran had given him fifteen years ago. Fifteen years, and it still worked. Like their marriage, even with all the trouble. How long was it now? Twenty-two years in May? Twenty-three?

Bellah said, "He started screaming at D'Allesandro. I thought he was going to choke him."

"Who? Mannlicher?"

"Yeah. About the window in the spare bedroom."

"What'd D'Allesandro say?"

"He said he always keeps it locked, you must have jimmied it some way that didn't leave any traces. Mannlicher didn't believe him. He thinks D'Allesandro forgot to lock it."

"Nobody got the idea it was an inside job?"

"No."

"Okay then. Relax, Mr. Bellah. You're in the clear."

Bellah wiped his face again. "Where's the money?"

"Other side of the bed. On the floor."

"You count it?"

"No. I figured you'd want to do that."

Bellah went over there, picked up the flour sack, emptied it on the bed. His eyes were bright and hot as he looked at all the loose green. Then he frowned, gnawed at his lower lip, and poked at Mannlicher's diamond ring. "What'd you take this for? Mannlicher is more pissed about the ring than anything else. He said his mother gave it to him. It's worth ten thousand."

"That's why I took it," Deighan said. "Fifteen percent of the cash isn't a hell of a lot."

Bellah stiffened. "I set it all up, didn't I? Why shouldn't I get the lion's share?"

"I'm not arguing, Mr. Bellah. We agreed on a price; okay, that's the way it is. I'm only saying I got a right to a little something extra."

"All right, all right." Bellah was looking at the money again. "Must be at least two hundred thousand," he said. "That Texan, Donley, brought fifty grand alone."

"Plenty in his wallet too, then."

"Yeah."

Deighan smoked and watched Bellah count the loose bills and what was in the wallets and billfolds. There was an expression on the developer's face like a man has when he's fondling a naked woman. Greed, pure and simple. Greed was what drove Lawrence Bellah; money was his best friend, his lover, his god. He didn't have enough ready cash to buy the lakefront property down near Emerald Bay—property he stood to make three or four million on, with a string of condos—and he couldn't raise it fast enough any legitimate way; so he'd arranged to get it by knocking over his own weekly poker game, even if it meant crossing some hard people. He had balls, you had to give him that. He was stupid as hell, and one of these days he was liable to end up in pieces at the bottom of the lake, but he did have balls.

He was also lucky, at least for the time being, because the man he'd picked to do his strong-arm work was Bob Prince. He had no idea the name was a phony, no idea the whole package on Bob Prince was the result of three years of careful manipulation. All he knew was that Prince had a reputation as dependable, easy to work with, not too smart or money-hungry, and that he was willing to do any kind of muscle work. Bellah didn't have an inkling of what he'd really done by hiring Bob Prince. If he kept on being lucky, he never would.

Bellah was sweating by the time he finished adding up the take. "Two hundred and thirty-three thousand and change," he said. "More than we figured on."

"My cut's thirty-five thousand," Deighan said.

"You divide fast." Bellah counted out two stacks, hundreds and fifties, to one side of the flowered bedspread. Then he said, "Count it? Or do you trust me?"

Deighan grinned. He rubbed out his cigarette, went to the bed, and took his time shuffling through the stacks. "On the nose," he said when he was done.

Bellah stuffed the rest of the cash back into the flour sack, leaving the watches and jewelry where they lay. He was still nervous, still sweating; he wasn't going to sleep much tonight, Deighan thought.

"That's it, then," Bellah said. "You going back to Chicago tomorrow?"

"Not right away. Thought I'd do a little gambling first."

"Around here? Christ, Prince. . . ."

"No. Reno, maybe. I might even go down to Vegas."

"Just get away from Tahoe."

"Sure," Deighan said. "First thing in the morning."

Bellah went to the door. He paused there to tuck the flour sack under his jacket; it made him look as if he had a tumor on his left side. "Don't do anything with that jewelry in Nevada. Wait until you get back to Chicago."

"Whatever you say, Mr. Bellah."

"Maybe I'll need you again sometime," Bellah said. "You'll hear from me if I do."

"Any time. Any old time."

When Bellah was gone, Deighan put five thousand dollars into his suitcase and the other thirty thousand into a knapsack he'd bought two days before at a South Shore sporting goods store. Mannlicher's diamond ring went into the knapsack too, along with the better pieces among the rest of the jewelry. The watches and the other stuff were no good to him; he bundled those up in a hand towel from the bathroom, stuffed the bundle into the pocket of his down jacket. Then he had one more cigarette, set his portable alarm clock for 6:00 A.M., double-locked the door, and went to bed on the left side, with the revolver under the pillow near his right hand.

3

In the dawn light the lake was like smoky blue glass, empty except for a few optimistic fishermen anchored close to the eastern shoreline. The morning was cold, autumn-crisp, but there was no wind. The sun was just beginning to rise, painting the sky and its scattered cloudstreaks in pinks and golds. There was old snow on the upper reaches of Mount Tallac, on some of the other Sierra peaks that ringed the lake.

Deighan took the Beachcraft out half a mile before he dropped the bundle of watches and worthless jewelry overboard. Then he cut off at a long diagonal to the north that brought him to within a few hundred yards of the Shooter's cabin. He had his fishing gear out by then, fiddling with the glass rod and tackle—just another angler looking for rainbow, Mackinaw, and cutthroat trout.

There wasn't anybody out and around at the Shooter's place. Deighan glided past at two knots, angled into shore a couple of hundred yards beyond, where there were rushes and some heavy brush and trees overhanging the water. From there he had a pretty good view of the cabin, its front entrance, the Shooter's Caddy parked inside the carport.

It was eight o'clock, and the sun was all the way up, when he switched off the engine and tied up at the bole of a collapsed pine. It was a few minutes past nine-thirty when D'Allesandro came out and walked around to the Caddy. He was alone. No chippies from the casinos this morning, not after what had gone down last night. He might be going to the store for cigarettes, groceries, or to a café somewhere for breakfast. He might be going to see somebody, do some business. The important thing was, how long would he be gone?

Deighan watched him back his Caddy out of the carport, drive it away and out of sight on the road above. He stayed where he was, fishing, waiting. At the end of an hour, when the Shooter still hadn't come back, he started the boat's engine and took his time maneuvering around the wooded finger of land to the north and then into the cove where he'd anchored last night. He nosed the boat into the reeds and ferns, swung overboard, and pushed it farther in, out of sight. Then he caught up the knapsack and set off through the woods to the Shooter's cabin.

He made a slow half circle of the place, keeping to the trees. The carport was still empty. Nothing moved anywhere within the range of his vision. Finally he made his way down to the rear wall, around it and along the side until he reached the front door. He didn't like standing out here for even a little while because there was no cover; but this door was the only one into the house, except for sliding doors to the terrace and a porch on the other side, and you couldn't jimmy sliding doors easily and without leaving marks. The same was true of windows. The Shooter would have made sure they were all secure anyway.

Deighan had one pocket of the knapsack open, the pick gun in his hand, when he reached the door. He'd got the pick gun from a housebreaker named Caldwell, an old-timer who was retired now; he'd also got some other tools and lessons in how to use them on the various kinds of locks. The lock on the Shooter's door was a flush-mounted, five-pin cylinder lock, with a steel lip on the door frame to protect the bolt and strike plate. That meant it was a lock you couldn't loid with a piece of plastic or a shim. It also meant that with a pick gun you could probably have it open in a couple of minutes.

Bending, squinting, he slid the gun into the lock. Set it, working the little knob on top to adjust the spring tension. Then he pulled the trigger—and all the pins bounced free at once and the door opened under his hand.

He slipped inside, nudged the door shut behind him, put the pick gun away inside the knapsack, and drew on a pair of thin plastic gloves. The place smelled of stale tobacco smoke and stale liquor. They hadn't been doing all that much drinking last night; maybe the Shooter had nibbled a few too many after the rest of them finally left. He didn't like losing money and valuables any more than Mannlicher did.

Deighan went through the front room. Somebody'd decorated the place for D'Allesandro: leather furniture, deer and antelope heads on the walls, Indian rugs on the floors, tasteful paintings. Cocaine deals had paid for part of it; contract work, including two hits on greedy Oakland and San Francisco drug dealers, had paid for the rest. But the Shooter was still small-time. He wasn't bright enough to be anything else. Cards and dice and whores-in-training were all he really cared about.

The front room was no good; Deighan prowled quickly through the other rooms. D'Allesandro wasn't the kind to have an office or a den, but there was a big old-fashioned rolltop desk in a room with a TV set and one of those big movie-type screens. None of the desk drawers was locked. Deighan pulled out the biggest one, saw that it was loaded with Danish porn magazines, took the magazines out, and set them on the floor. He opened the knapsack and transferred the thirty thousand dollars into the back of the drawer. He put Mannlicher's ring in there too, along with the other rings and a couple of gold chains the Texan had been wearing. Then he stuffed the porn magazines in at the front and pushed the drawer shut.

On his way back to the front room he rolled the knapsack tight around the pick gun and stuffed them into his jacket pocket. He opened the door, stepped out. He'd just finished resetting the lock when he heard the car approaching on the road above.

He froze for a second, looking up there. He couldn't see the car because of a screen of trees; but then he heard its automatic transmission gear down as it slowed for the turn into the

Shooter's driveway. He pulled the door shut and ran toward the lake, the only direction he could go. Fifty feet away the log-railed terrace began, raised up off the sloping ground on redwood pillars. Deighan caught one of the railings, hauled himself up and half rolled through the gap between them. The sound of the oncoming car was loud in his ears as he landed, off balance, on the deck.

He went to one knee, came up again. The only way to tell if he'd been seen was to stop and look, but that was a fool's move. Instead he ran across the deck, climbed through the railing on the other side, dropped down, and tried to keep from making noise as he plunged into the woods. He stopped moving after thirty yards, where ferns and a deadfall formed a thick conceal-ing wall. From behind it, with the .38 wadcutter in his hand, he watched the house and the deck, catching his breath, waiting.

Nobody came up or out of the deck. Nobody showed himself anywhere. The car's engine had been shut off sometime during his flight; it was quiet now, except for birds and the faint hum of a powerboat out on the lake.

Deighan waited ten minutes. When there was still nothing to see or hear, he transcribed a slow curl through the trees to where he could see the front of the cabin. The Shooter's Caddy was back inside the carport, no sign of haste in the way it had been neatly slotted. The cabin door was shut. The whole area seemed deserted.

But he waited another ten minutes before he was satisfied. Even then, he didn't holster his weapon until he'd made his way around to the cove where the Beachcraft was hidden. And he didn't relax until he was well out on the lake, headed back toward North Shore.

4

The Nevornia was one of North Shore's older clubs, but it had undergone some recent modernizing. Outside, it had been given a glass and gaudy-neon face-lift. Inside, they'd used more glass, some cut crystal, and a wine-red decor that included carpeting, upholstery, and gaming tables.

When Deighan walked in a few minutes before two, the banks

of slots and the blackjack tables were getting moderately heavy play. That was because it was Friday; some of the small-time gamblers liked to get a jump on the weekend crowds. The craps and roulette layouts were quiet. The high rollers were like vampires: they couldn't stand the daylight, so they only came out after dark.

Deighan bought a roll of quarters at one of the change booths. There were a couple of dozen rows of slots in the main casino—flashy new ones, mostly, with a few of the old scrolled nickel-plated jobs mixed in for the sake of nostalgia. He stopped at one of the old quarter machines, fed in three dollars' worth. Lemons and oranges. He couldn't even line up two cherries for a three-coin drop. He smiled crookedly to himself, went away from the slots and into the long concourse that connected the main casino with the new, smaller addition at the rear.

There were telephone booths along one side of the concourse. Deighan shut himself inside one of them, put a quarter in the slot, pushed 0 and then the digits of his home number in San Francisco. When the operator came on he said it was a collect call; that was to save himself the trouble of having to feed in a handful of quarters. He let the circuit make exactly five burrs in his ear before he hung up. If Fran was home, she'd know now that he was all right. If she wasn't home, then she'd know it later when he made another five-ring call. He always tried to call at least twice a day, at different times, because sometimes she went out shopping or to a movie or to visit with Sheila and the kids.

It'd be easier if she just answered the phone, talked to him, but she never did when he was away. Never. Sheila or anybody else wanted to get hold of her, they had to call one of the neighbors or come over in person. She didn't want anything to do with him when he was away, didn't want to know what he was doing or even when he'd be back. "Suppose I picked up the phone and it wasn't you?" she'd said. "Suppose it was somebody telling me you were dead? I couldn't stand that." That part of it didn't make sense to him. If he were dead, somebody'd come by and tell it to her face; dead was dead, and what difference did it make how she got the news? But he didn't argue with her. He didn't like to argue with her, and it didn't cost him anything to do it her way.

He slotted the quarter again and called the Shooter's number. Four rings, five, and D'Allesandro's voice said, "Yeah?"

"Mr. Carson?"

"Who?"

"Isn't this Paul Carson?"

"No. You got the wrong number."

"Oh, sorry," Deighan said, and rang off.

Another quarter in the slot. This time the number he punched out was the Nevornia's business line. A woman's voice answered, crisp and professional. He said, "Mr. Mannlicher. Tell him it's urgent."

"Whom shall I say is calling?"

"Never mind that. Just tell him it's about what happened last night."

"Sir, I'm afraid I can't—"

"Tell him last night's poker game, damn it. He'll talk to me."

There was a click and some canned music began to play in his ear. He lit a cigarette. He was on his fourth drag when the canned music quit and the fat man's voice said, "Frank Mannlicher. Who's this?"

"No games. Is it all right to talk on this line?"

"Go ahead, talk."

"I'm the guy who hit your game last night."

Silence for four or five seconds. Then Mannlicher said, "Is that so?" in a flat, wary voice.

"Ski mask, Smith & Wesson .38, grenade in my jacket pocket. The take was better than two hundred thousand. I got your ring—platinum with a circle of diamonds."

Another pause, shorter this time. "So why call me today?"

"How'd you like to get it all back—the money and the ring?"

"How?"

"Go pick it up. I'll tell you where."

"Yeah? Why should you do me a favor?"

"I didn't know who you were last night. I wasn't told. If I had been, I wouldn't have gone through with it. I don't mess with people like you, people with your connections."

"Somebody hired you, that it?"

"That's it."

"Who?"

"D'Allesandro."

"What?"

"The Shooter. D'Allesandro."

". . . Bullshit."

"You don't have to believe me. But I'm telling you—he's the one. He didn't tell me who'd be at the game, and now he's trying to screw me on the money. He says there was less than a hundred and fifty thousand in the sack; I know better."

"So now you want to screw him."

"That's right. Besides, I don't like the idea of you pushing to find out who I am, maybe sending somebody to pay me a visit someday. I figure if I give you the Shooter, you'll lose interest in me."

More silence. "Why'd he do it?" Mannlicher said in a different voice—harder, with that edge of violence it had held last night. "Hit the game like that?"

"He needs big money, fast. He's into some kind of scam back east; he wouldn't say what it is."

"Where's the money and the rest of the stuff?"

"At his cabin. We had a drop arranged in the woods; I put the sack there last night, he picked it up this morning when nobody was around. The money's in his desk—the big rolltop. Your ring too. That's where it was an hour ago, anyhow, when I walked out."

Mannlicher said, "In his desk," as if he were biting the words off something bitter.

"Go out there, see for yourself."

"If you're telling this straight, you got nothing to worry about from me. Maybe I'll fix you up with a reward or something. Where can I get in touch?"

"You can't," Deighan said. "I'm long gone as soon as I hang up the phone."

"I'll make it five thousand. Just tell me where you—"

Deighan broke the connection.

His cigarette had burned down to the filter; he dropped it on the floor, put his shoe on it before he left the booth. On his way out of the casino he paused long enough to push another quarter into the same slot machine he'd played before. More lemons and oranges. This time he didn't smile as he moved away.

5

Narrow and twisty, hemmed in by trees, old Lake Road branched off Highway 28 and took two miles to get all the way to the lake. But it wasn't a dead-end; another road picked it up at the lakefront and looped back out to the highway. There were several nice homes hidden away in the area—it was called Pine Acres—with plenty of space between them. The Shooter's cabin was a mile and a half from the highway, off an even narrower lane called Little Cove Road. The only other cabin within five hundred yards was a summer place that the owners had already closed up for the year.

Deighan drove past the intersection with Little Cove, went two-tenths of a mile, parked on the turnout at that point. There wasn't anybody else around when he got out, nothing to see except trees and little winks of blue that marked the nearness of the lake. If anybody came along they wouldn't pay any attention to the car. For one thing, it was a '75 Ford Galaxy with nothing distinctive about it except the antenna for the GTE mobile phone. It was his—he'd driven it up from San Francisco—but the papers on it said it belonged to Bob Prince. For another thing, Old Lake Road was only a hundred yards or so from the water here, and there was a path through the trees to a strip of rocky beach. Local kids used it in the summer; he'd found that out from Bellah. Kids might have decided to stop here on a sunny autumn day as well. No reason for anybody to think otherwise.

He found the path, went along it a short way to where it crossed a little creek, dry now and so narrow it was nothing more than a natural drainage ditch. He followed the creek to the north, on a course he'd taken three days ago. It led him to a shelflike overhang topped by two chunks of granite outcrop that leaned against each other like a pair of old drunks. Below the shelf, the land fell away sharply to the Shooter's driveway some sixty yards distant. Off to the right, where the incline wasn't so steep and the trees grew in a pack, was the split-bole Douglas fir where he'd stood waiting last night. The trees were fewer and more widely spaced apart between here and the cabin, so that from behind the two outcrops you had a good look at the Shooter's property, Little Cove Road, the concrete pier, and the lake shimmering under the late-afternoon sun.

The Caddy Eldorado was still slotted inside the carport. It was the only car in sight. Deighan knelt behind where the outcrops came together to form a notch, rubbed tension out of his neck and shoulders while he waited.

He didn't have to wait long. Less than ten minutes had passed when the car appeared on Little Cove Road, slowed, turned down the Shooter's driveway. It wasn't Mannlicher's fancy limo; it was a two-year-old Chrysler—Brandt's, maybe. Brandt was driving it: Deighan had a clear view of him through the side window as the Chrysler pulled up and stopped near the cabin's front door. He could also see that the lone passenger was Mannlicher.

Brandt got out, opened the passenger door for the fat man, and the two of them went to the cabin. It took D'Allesandro ten seconds to answer Brandt's knock. There was some talk, not much; then Mannlicher and Brandt went in, and the door shut behind them.

All right, Deighan thought. He'd stacked the deck as well as he could; pretty soon he'd know how the hand—and the game—played out.

Nothing happened for maybe five minutes. Then he thought he heard some muffled sounds down there, loud voices that went on for a while, something that might have been a bang, but the distance was too great for him to be sure that he wasn't imagining them. Another four or five minutes went by. And then the door opened and Brandt came out alone, looked around, called something back inside that Deighan didn't understand. If there was an answer, it wasn't audible. Brandt shut the door, hurried down to the lake, went out onto the pier. The Chris-Craft was still tied up there. Brandt climbed on board, disappeared for thirty seconds or so, reappeared carrying a square of something gray and heavy. Tarpaulin, Deighan saw when Brandt came back up the driveway. Big piece of it—big enough for a shroud.

The Shooter's hand had been folded. That left three of them still in the game.

When Brandt had gone back inside with the tarp, Deighan stood and half ran along the creek and through the trees to where he'd left the Ford. Old Lake Road was deserted. He yanked open the passenger door, leaned in, caught up the mobile phone, and punched out the emergency number for the county sheriff's office. An efficient-sounding male voice answered.

"Something's going on on Little Cove road," Deighan said, making himself sound excited. "That's in Pine Acres, you know? It's the cabin at the end, down on the lake. I heard shots—people shooting at each other down there. It sounds like war."

"What's the address?"

"I don't know the address, it's the cabin right on the lake. People *shooting* at each other. You better get right out there."

"Your name, sir?"

"I don't want to get involved. Just hurry, will you?"

Deighan put the receiver down, shut the car door, ran back along the path and along the creek to the shelf. Mannlicher and Brandt were still inside the cabin. He went to one knee again behind the outcrops, drew the .38 wadcutter, held it on his thigh.

It was another two minutes before the door opened down there. Brandt came out, looked around as he had before, went back inside—and then he and Mannlicher both appeared, one at each end of a big, tarp-wrapped bundle. They started to carry it down the driveway toward the lake. Going to put it on the boat, Deighan thought, take it out now or later on, when it's dark. Lake Tahoe was sixteen hundred feet deep in the middle. The bundle wouldn't have been the first somebody'd dumped out there.

He let them get clear of the Chrysler, partway down the drive, before he poked the gun into the notch, sighted, and fired twice. The shots went where he'd intended them to, wide by ten feet and into the roadbed so they kicked up gravel. Mannlicher and Brandt froze for an instant, confused. Deighan fired a third round, putting the slug closer this time, and that one panicked them: they let go of the bundle and began scrambling.

There was no cover anywhere close by; they both ran for the Chrysler. Brandt had a gun in his hand when he reached it, and he dropped down behind the rear deck, trying to locate Deighan's position. Mannlicher kept on scrambling around to the passenger door, pulled it open, pushed himself across the seat inside.

Deighan blew out the Chrysler's near front tire. Sighted, and blew out the rear tire. Brandt threw an answering shot his way, but it wasn't even close. The Chrysler was tilting in Deighan's direction as the tires flattened. Mannlicher pushed himself out of the car, tried to make a run for the cabin door with his arms flailing, his fat jiggling. Deighan put a bullet into the wall beside the door. Mannlicher reversed himself, fell in his frantic haste, crawled back behind the Chrysler.

Reloading the wadcutter, Deighan could hear the sound of cars coming fast up on Little Cove Road. No sirens, but revolving lights made faint bloodred flashes through the trees.

From behind the Chrysler Brandt fired again, wildly. Beyond him, on the driveway, one corner of the tarp-wrapped bundle had come loose and was flapping in the wind off the lake.

A county sheriff's cruiser, its roof light slashing the air, made the turn off Little Cove onto the driveway. Another one was right behind it. In his panic, Brandt straightened up when he saw them and fired once, blindly, at the first in line.

Deighan was on his feet by then, hurrying away from the outcrops, holstering his weapon. Behind him he heard brakes squeal, another shot, voices yelling, two more shots. All the sounds faded as he neared the turnout and the Ford. By the time he pulled out onto the deserted road, there was nothing to hear but the sound of his engine, the screeching of a jay somewhere nearby.

Brandt had thrown in his hand by now; so had Mannlicher.

This pot belonged to him.

6

Fran was in the backyard, weeding her garden, when he got home late the following afternoon. He called to her from the doorway, and she glanced around and then got up, unsmiling, and came over to him. She was wearing jeans and one of his old shirts and a pair of gardening gloves, and her hair was tied in a long ponytail. Used to be a light, silky brown, her hair; now it was mostly gray. His fault. She was only forty-six. A woman of forty-six shouldn't be so gray.

She said, "So you're back." She didn't sound glad to see him, didn't kiss him or touch him at all. But her eyes were gentle on his face.

"I'm back."

"You all right? You look tired."

"Long drive. I'm fine; it was a good trip."

She didn't say anything. She didn't want to hear about it, not any of it. She just didn't want to know.

"How about you?" he asked. "Everything been okay?"

"Sheila's pregnant again."

"Christ. What's the matter with her? Why don't she get herself fixed? Or get Hank fixed?"

"She likes kids."

"I like kids too, but four's too many at her age. She's only twenty-seven."

"She wants eight."

"She's crazy," Deighan said. "What's she want to bring all those kids into a world like this for?"

There was an awkward moment. It was always awkward at first when he came back. Then Fran said, "You hungry?"

"You know me. I can always eat." Fact was, he was starved. He hadn't eaten much up in Nevada, never did when he was away. And he hadn't had anything today except an English muffin and some coffee for breakfast in Truckee.

"Come into the kitchen," Fran said. "I'll fix you something."

They went inside. He got a beer out of the refrigerator; she waited and then took out some covered dishes, some vegetables. He wanted to say something to her, talk a little, but he couldn't think of anything. His mind was blank at times like this. He carried his beer into the living room.

The goddamn trophy case was the first thing he saw. He hated that trophy case; but Fran wouldn't get rid of it, no matter what he said. For her it was like some kind of shrine to the dead past. All the mementoes of his years on the force—twenty-two years, from beat patrolman in North Beach all the way up to inspector on the narcotics squad. The certificate he'd won in marksmanship competition at the police academy, the two citations from the mayor for bravery, other crap like that. Bones, that's all they were to him. Pieces of a rotting skeleton. What was the sense in keeping them around, reminding both of them of what he'd been, what he'd lost?

His fault he'd lost it, sure. But it was their fault too, goddamn them. The laws, the lawyers, the judges, the *system*. No convictions on half of all the arrests he'd ever made—half! Turning the ones like Mannlicher and Brandt and D'Allesandro loose, putting them right back on the street, letting them make their deals and their hits, letting them screw up innocent lives. Sheila's kids, his grandkids—lives like that. How could they blame him for being bitter. How could they blame him for taking too many drinks now and then?

He sat down on the couch, drank some of his beer, lit a cigarette. Ah, Christ, he thought, it's not them. You know it wasn't them. It was *you*, you dumb bastard. They warned you twice about drinking on duty. And you kept on doing it, you were hog-drunk the night you plowed the departmental sedan into that vanload of teenagers. What if one of *those* kids had died? You were lucky, by God. You got off easy.

Sure, he thought. Sure. But he'd been a good cop, damn it, a cop inside and out; it was all he knew how to be. What was he supposed to do after they threw him off the force? Live on his half-pension? Get a job as a part-time security guard? Forty-four years old, no skills, no friends outside the department—what the hell was he supposed to do?

He'd invented Bob Prince, that was what he'd done. He'd gone into business for himself.

Fran didn't understand. "You'll get killed one of these days," she'd said in the beginning. "It's vigilante justice," she'd said. "You think you're Rambo, is that it?" she'd said. She just didn't understand. To him it was the same job he'd always done, the only one he was any good at, only now *he* made up some of the rules. He was no Rambo, one man up against thousands, a mindless killing machine; he hated that kind of phony flag-waving crap. It wasn't real. What he was doing, that was real. It meant something. But a hero? No. Hell, no. He was a sniper, that was all, picking off a weak or a vulnerable enemy here and there, now and then. Snipers weren't heroes, for Christ's sake. Snipers were snipers, just like cops were cops.

He finished his beer and his cigarette, got up, went into Fran's sewing room. The five thousand he'd held out of the poker-game take was in his pocket—money he felt he was entitled to because his expenses ran high sometimes, and they had to eat, they had to live. He put the roll into her sewing cabinet, where he always put whatever money he made as Bob Prince. She'd spend it when she had to, parcel it out, but she'd never mention it to him or anyone else. She'd told Sheila once that he had a sales job, he got paid in cash a lot, that was why he was away from home for such long periods of time.

When he walked back into the kitchen she was at the sink, peeling potatoes. He went over and touched her shoulder, kissed the top of her head. She didn't look at him, stood there stiffly until he moved away from her. But she'd be all right in a day or two. She'd be fine until the next time Bob Prince made the right kind of connection.

He wished it didn't have to be this way. He wished he could roll back the clock three years, do things differently, take the gray out of her hair and the pain out of her eyes. But he couldn't. It was just too late.

You had to play the cards you were dealt, no matter how lousy they were. The only thing that made it tolerable was that sometimes, on certain hands, you could find ways to stack the damn deck.

JULIAN SYMONS

HAS ANYBODY HERE SEEN ME?

With all his other activities—mystery novelist, critic, biographer, essayist—it's not surprising that new short stories from Julian Symons are a rarity these days. But when they arrive, they're always something special.

Out of the Underground train, along the platform, up the stairs, onto the escalator. Advertisements moving past—best pizza in London, it's mouthwateringly M-m-m-moreish, Michael Frayn play at Savoy, see-thru nightie that turns him on, Smirnoff the vodka, Morland's Can Find That Job You're Looking For, Dance All Night at the Fandango, Alligator Jeans Go Snap.

To the top, present ticket, up more stairs, out. Where?

Why, he thought, looking at the bookshop on one corner, Great Newport Street beside it, newsstand nearby, the theater showing *He Did What She Wanted,* a new comedy, I know this place, of course I do. Then, seeing the Undergound entrance saying Leicester Square, he shook with laughter. All I had to do was look at the station name as I came out, silly me. Leicester Square station, just round the corner the Hippodrome, then the Square itself. *Used* to be the Hippodrome, now Talk of the Town, something like that. I know where I am, of course I do. Couldn't recognize Leicester Square, did you ever? No I never, no I never did.

So here I am, but the question remains—most unfortunately, the question remains. Not where, but who? Face up to it, the name's gone. Who knows it, who's seen me, am I the invisible man? Familiar lines came into his head, he had to restrain himself from singing them:

"Has anybody here seen me?
M-e-double-e, me,

207

Where can me be?
I left home at half past ten,
Haven't seen myself since then,
Has anybody here seen m-e-double-e, me, double-e, me?"

A clever little song, but its entrance into memory was disturbing. Something wrong with it, something he didn't want to remember, something that made movement imperative. He said aloud, "No use standing here," bought an evening paper, crossed the road, walking in a businesslike manner as if he knew where he was going. He passed a shop that showed in the window brass doorknobs, door knockers, bathroom fittings, gilded mirrors. Stopped to consider his reflection in a mirror.

A tallish man, thin dark-blue jacket and trousers, mouse-colored hair receding a little, smooth, almost delicate features, good figure, elegant really. Lines about the eyes, though, and, oh dear, as he looked more closely, some wrinkles in the delicate features. Age? Oh, say thirty-five—well, perhaps forty, no more than forty. Why should thought of age make alarm bells ring in his head?

And now that I've seen him: who is this stranger?

But *of course,* he mentally told the figure in the glass, there's really no problem in this case of lost identity. Just—it's so simple—just look at his wallet, credit cards, any stray envelopes bearing name and address that may be about his person. The figure in the glass felt its inner breast pocket. Nothing there. He watched with detachment as the figure, now a little agitated, felt in jacket, trouser, hip pockets, dredging up some five pounds in coins, and a shopping list made on a piece of paper evidently torn from a memo pad. Fillet steak, new potatoes, courgettes. Is that my writing? The figure in the glass put the paper against the shop window to write on it, then checked himself. No pen.

Never mind, he told himself, no cause for alarm, I'm not lost, I know just where I am, could find my way without trouble around Central London, no trouble at all, I assure you. All that's happened is a temporary blackout, happens to almost everybody at some time or another. A blockage, like that caused by wax in the ear. In ten minutes or perhaps less, something in my head will go *click* as the ear goes *pop* and I shall remember.

A drink might help.

Within a hundred yards, a pub revealed itself. The sign outside showed two men staring at each other, one a respectable whiskered top-hatted Victorian, the other a jaunty crouching creature, half man and half ape, arms stretching well below his knees. The pub was called The Jekyll and Hyde. He pushed open the saloon-bar door and went in.

"What'll it be?"

"A pint of best bitter."

Did he know this pub, did he often drink bitter? The place was crowded, but he saw a vacant seat at one table, sat down, drank some bitter, gave an involuntary shudder.

The other man at the table was thickset, sandy, with a sharp inquiring nose. "Great weather we're having. Can't have enough of it as far as I'm concerned." The words were said challengingly, in apparent fear of contradiction.

He realized that he was hot, uncomfortably so, shirt clinging to him. He nodded.

"The wife now, she don't like it. Get out in the garden, I say, enjoy the sun while you can, don't get much of it, this ain't California. Know what she says? Too much sun gives you skin cancer. I ask you, how many days do we get like this in a year— ten? Twenty? Say thirty, the most I'll give you is thirty." The glare seemed to call for a response, but he did not make it. "All right, thirty. And that gives you skin cancer, I say to her, thirty days in the sun, is that what you're telling me? No good, though—she covers herself up like she was wearing one of those Arab things."

"Yashmaks."

"Right you are." The man looked at him with respect. "You a regular? Seen you in here before, have I?"

"If you'll excuse me, there's something I want to read in the paper." It was true, he had an overwhelming feeling that the evening paper contained vital information about his identity.

"Suit yourself." The man picked up his empty glass, ordered a refill at the bar, took it to another table.

He opened the paper, an early edition. He could not have said what he expected to find, perhaps a name he would recognize, perhaps a picture of the man in the shop mirror. He turned the pages quickly, not reading, but looking for a name, a picture, something he felt must be there.

Nothing. Now he went through the pages more slowly, lingering over the news stories. On the front page discussions about an atomic pact, and in a separate panel "This Time the Wolf Kills." The Wolf, it seemed, was a burglar and rapist who had terrorized an area in South London. He was uncannily skillful in entering houses through skylights, windows closed but not locked, basement areas. He cased houses carefully, making sure that only one person was there, and that a woman. Mostly they were married, and the Wolf struck in the late morning or early afternoon. He threatened the woman with a knife, raped her, then took any jewelry he could find. In this case, the woman had resisted, there had been a struggle, and the Wolf had stabbed her to death. Significant clues, the story said, were being followed up by police.

What else? Scandal in a Home for Young Delinquents, Big Drugs Haul at Heathrow, Pop Star Tells All, Arson Suspected in City Fire, Man in Spy Inquiry Vanishes. "Civil Servant James Hetherington, recently interrogated in relation to the missing Ministry of Defense papers, left his home in Clapham yesterday morning and has apparently disappeared. His wife Jennifer said he left just as usual after breakfast, taking his briefcase and saying he might be a little late that evening . . ."

"Is this seat taken?"

A woman stood beside his table, glass in hand, half smiling. He said it was free, and she sat down. A young woman, thirty-five perhaps, unobtrusively dressed, gold ring on wedding finger. Was there something about her he recognized? Now she did laugh, raised her glass. "Seen enough?"

"I beg your pardon. It's just that I thought—"

"Yes?"

"Do we know each other?"

She looked at him over the rim of the glass, a short drink, probably gin and something. "Well. What do you think?"

"I think perhaps we've met before."

"Tell me the old old story. I mean, I wouldn't call that a new approach, would you?" Her voice was artificially refined.

"It isn't an approach. It's simply that I can't remember—"

"Where it was we met? That one's as old as the hills too. Never mind, I'm Rosemary. What's your name?"

"John."

She had noticed the pause before he said it. "That's not very original, either. Are you going to buy me one, John? Gin and french."

As he went up to the bar and ordered the drink he wondered: Do we really know each other or not? Can I tell her the truth? The barman seemed to look at him oddly. Perhaps they knew each other too, he was expecting to be greeted.

"Do we know each other?"

The barman had a toothbrush moustache, hair cut very short. "How's that?"

"I've been in this pub before, thought I recognized you."

"You looking for trouble?"

"Of course not. Why should you think so?"

"You stay on your side of the counter, I'll stay on mine, right?" The barman stuck his face forward, pores were visible in his broad cheeks. "Or put it this way, I don't know you, you don't know me, let's keep it that way, right?"

Rosemary was reading his paper. "I hope you don't mind."

"Of course not."

"You've spilt something, John—stepped in it too, from the look of it. Cheers." He looked down and saw two dark patches on his left trouser leg, one near the bottom, the other above the knee. Another patch, or stain, marked his left shoe.

"This Wolf, I don't know what things are coming to, you're not safe in your own home. What you been up to then, John?"

Confession seemed inevitable. "I don't know."

"How do you mean, don't know?"

"This is important." He leaned across the table, grasped for her hand, but she withdrew it. "Do we know each other or not?"

She looked away. "That's a funny question. It was you said we knew each other."

"Please listen. I said my name was John, but I don't know if it is or not, I don't know what it is, I've lost my memory. I think I only lost it a little while ago." He was conscious that the words must sound absurd, as he saw her looking from side to side as if in fear of attack. The overlay of refinement had gone from her voice when she spoke again.

"I'll tell you what I think, John, you're a bloody nutter. I'm a working girl, I thought you meant business, it wasn't me who started this what's-your-name lark. I don't know what you're after, but whatever the game is I'm not playing. I'm going out of that door now and if you come after me I swear I'll turn you in. Now you remember that, *John.*"

She left the pub, hips swaying. As the door closed after her, the barman stopped polishing a glass and stared at him as it seemed accusingly. He shook his head as if the action might help to shake those lost bits of memory back into place. Instead, it brought to the surface another line or two of that song:

"I'm an actress on the stage
And I should be all the rage
But I'm always losing *some*thing."

How did it go on? Da da *da,* da da *da,* then the last line of the verse, "And now I've lost meself." Very careless, John or whatever your name is, you'd better find yourself again.

He looked at the pub clock. Two-fifteen. As good a time as any other for discovering your identity. He folded the paper carefully, put it on the table, got up, left the pub.

A fine afternoon in London. Two-fifteen, by now two-sixteen. *I left home at half past ten, Haven't seen myself since then.* Did I buy the fillet steak, if so, where is it? Let's hope I didn't leave it out so the cat could get at it. Do you own a cat then, John? Don't know.

Take the first right, second left, leads down to the river. Is that so, how do I know it? But I do. Down to the river, onto the bridge, vault the parapet—no problem, it's quite low—then down, down, an endless descent that lasts only seconds. The water cold, dirty. Make no resistance. Finish.

That's what you may *think,* John, but things aren't that simple. Always a dozen busybodies around just waiting for people to jump off bridges, raise the alarm, strip off, jump in, lifesavers to a man or woman. Man or woman created he them. But did he, is that so?

For that matter, they say the moment you hit the water you struggle, don't want it, never meant things to end like this, swim with a nice easy crawl to safety. Never meant to enter that cold river, officer, just leaning over the parapet to look at my reflection, Narcissus complex you might say, leaned that tiny bit too far.

Stop it, stop it, he said to himself—or had the words been spoken aloud? He took the first right. A narrow street this, small shops, shabby, seems familiar. Newsagent's, antique shop Victoria Regina, "We sell all the rubbish Grandma threw out," barber's pole, heads bent over basins, attendant waves and smiles. At me? Go in, ask, Excuse me, who am I? Have you seen me? Has anybody here seen me? Drawn a blank, oh, dear, thank you kindly, sorry you've been troubled. But where can me be?

A couple of lines of patter: *I'm so forgetful, you know, last night I got home, took me clothes off and tucked 'em in bed, then hung meself up in the wardrobe.* But let's be frank about it, this is no joke. *Has* anybody here seen me? Waiting, waiting for the click of recognition.

It did not come. He took the second left, and at once felt uneasy: I know this. On the left there will be an Italian restaurant named Ruggiere, a cut-price men's clothing shop, a block of flats named Atlas Court. And on the right? The right was boarded up. There were cracks in the posters and he crossed the road, looked through. A half-demolished building stood there, a sign in front of it: *For All Demolition Work Come To D. E. Stroyer.* On the damaged facade of the building the word *Theater* remained, and on the walls below two or three torn placards. One showed the picture of a top-hatted, monocled Victorian toff and said, *Burlington Bertie Is One of the Boys,* another was of a woman wearing an enormous picture hat, with *Outrageous Olivia, Outré with Oomph* beneath.

"Good afternoon to you."

He turned. A tramp, perhaps, but if so a burly and upright one. Clothes old and shabby, trousers with old-fashioned turn-ups and slightly frayed at the bottom, but gray hair neatly brushed, and a waxed gray moustache giving an air somewhat military yet hardly genuine. The voice too had something assumed about it, rather as though it issued from a ventriloquist.

"Lookin' at the old place, then? Victim of the property developers, a damned shame. And what do they do with it? Two years now, and it still isn't even properly knocked down. Just sittin' on it, every month it's worth another few thou. A damned shame, I say."

"Perhaps you can remind me, what was it called?"

The man stared. "Remind you? Ay should say so. Remind you of the Old Tyme Theater, that's extremely droll."

He gestured at what lay behind the boarding. "I've forgotten exactly your connection, I'm afraid."

The man pulled at his moustache, faintly clicked his heels. His voice took on momentarily the stentorian tones of a circus barker. "Percy Cudmore at your service, formerly sarn't major in Her Majesty's Indian Army, now employed to keep this rabble in order. Remember now, old man? Kind of combined commissionaire and chucker-out line, though some of the lads got a bit above themselves at times. *You* remember that, or should do." His left eye closed in an unmistakable wink.

"I'm afraid not."

"If you say so. No offense meant—none taken, I hope." He stood a little closer, garlic and beer discernible. "Times are diff for an ex-sarn't major, old man. Can't even get a job as a pub bouncer, say I'm too old and not up to it, can you believe it? The same not true of your good self, I hope—you're lookin' remarkably well an' flourishin'. Wish I could say similar. If you happen to have a bit of foldin' money superfluous to present needs it'd be much appreciated."

Here was somebody who knew him. What could be simpler than to say: I remember we were both associated with this theater, but exactly what did I do there, who was I? But the words were literally unspeakable. He had a feeling of dread, his limbs trembled, his throat seemed choked so that he could hardly breathe. He opened his jacket, felt for the wallet that was not there, then buttoned it again hurriedly, aghast at what the opened jacket had shown. But Percy Cudmore seemed to have noticed nothing.

He felt in his pocket, found two of the golden coins, put them in the hand that almost surreptitiously received them, then took a step backward to remove himself from the body so close to his own. Hand closed on coins, transferred them swiftly to pocket, encounter over. Hand sketched a near-salute, jeering rather than respectful, and the words too seemed jeering, though they were harmless enough.

"Left the foldin' money at home, worried about gettin' mugged I daresay, very wise. Many thanks, old man. Do the same for you one day, I hope." Now Percy Cudmore, done with him, walked up the road, fifty yards away turned into a pub.

Hand shaking, he unbuttoned the jacket again. The right side of his shirt was spotted and smeared with red and there were stains on the jacket lining. He buttoned it once more.

Now his actions became decisive. He walked down to the end of the road, crossed it. The river was there, as he had known it would be. He walked along beside it until he came to the bridge, but hardly glanced at the water. Left at the bridge, over the Thames. Now on the south side, he went through a minor maze of narrow streets without troubling to look at their names, steps unerring.

All this was a kind of sleepwalking. He had no idea of who he was or what would be at the end of this apparently purposeful left-right, left-right. He no longer sought to find a name for himself. I am me, he thought, no need to look further. Has anybody here seen me? Never mind whether they have or not, whether I left home at half past ten or not. If I did hang myself up in a wardrobe and put my clothes to bed, it's nobody's business but mine. The only person concerned is m-e double-e, me, double-e, me.

Steady now, only a song. Don't take it seriously. Petrol station on corner. Turn right.

But honestly, admit it. I'm always losing something, and now I've lost meself.

Do I wish to find me, him, or it?

He turned another corner, stopped still. This was a mews, the street cobbled, garages on either side, little houses above them. The houses had been tarted up, newly painted blue, pink, white. Pot plants outside the front doors. At the far end a knot of people, two or three police cars. He made his way toward them over the cobbles, treading delicately as a cat. Faces turned toward him expectantly. He smiled, nodded. Yes, I know you. It is me, not you, that has disappeared.

A copper in uniform at the door looked inquiring, but feet

clattered on the stairs, a man appeared. "Chief Inspector Hawkins, just the man we're looking for, come on up." He followed the chief inspector up the stairs into the living room, then put hand to mouth in dismay.

It was, or had been, a pretty room. The Italian china ornaments on walls and tables in the shapes of gloves, shoes, opened books, were a little chichi, the *trompe l'oeil* window opening on a country scene with real curtains over it was rather preposterous, the tubular chairs and tables were out of key with the ornaments and the window, but still it had been a pretty room. Now most of the ornaments were smashed, the curtain had been pulled down, lighting fittings were broken. Glass and china littered the floor.

"Somebody went a bit berserk, wouldn't you say?" Hawkins was rosy-faced, smiling, his manner jolly. "But you ain't seen nothing yet." He led the way along past a tidy kitchen to a bedroom. There was blood everywhere here. It had spurted over the walls, marked the white carpet, there were splotches of it on the pink sheets. He shook his head, he could not have said why.

"Looking for the body? Went half an hour ago, no need to worry. Now then, sir. Your name is Oliver Raynes and you share this delightful residence with one Archibald Burton, now the late Archibald Burton, agreed? And the said Archie had recently been showing an undue interest in a young actor by the name of Leon Padici, agreed? And according to your next-door neighbor, Archie had been communicating to you the idea that he'd prefer your room to your company, as the old saying goes—he'd like you to move out and Leon to move in.

"And this same neighbor heard a most tremendous barney going on early this morning—couldn't help hearing, he says, the shouts and shrieks woke him up—as a conclusion to which Archie succumbed to attacks with a meat chopper from the kitchen, the assailant being apparently under the impression that Archie was a side of beef that needed carving. He then did the demolition job you've seen in the next room and exited into the street, where the ever-watchful neighbor saw him. Or you."

The words made no impact on him. He was staring at a poster

on the wall that had escaped the general carnage, except for a spot or two of blood. It was one he had seen outside the theater, showing the woman in the picture hat. It was signed *Dearest Archie, with all my love, Olivia.* The chief inspector was still talking.

"Now here you are, come back to save us the trouble of looking for you, which I must say is very helpful. And with marks that show just what a naughty boy you've been." He wagged his round, rosy head in reproof. "I couldn't be sorrier, I'm one of your admirers."

"Not me," he said. "It wasn't me. I could never have done such a thing. This isn't me." He took off his jacket, threw it on the ground, unzipped his trousers. "Please. These are not mine. The clothes I wear are not me, nothing of all this is me. I am not me. Has anybody here seen me?"

He looked wildly round, but the chief inspector was his only audience. His trousers dropped to the floor. Beneath them he wore frilly pants, lettered *Naughty But Nice.*

Hawkins laughed heartily. "Your famous song, of course. *I left home at half past ten, Haven't seen meself since then.* And very well you always delivered it. Pity the Old Tyme packed up. I used to enjoy those shows, took my old lady, we sang the choruses. Quite fancied you myself, as a matter of fact."

He laughed again, to show that this was a joke. "And 'I am not me'—that sounds a promising line. It wasn't me hacked my friend to death, it was somebody else, please judge I wasn't there. Yes, very comical, I like it." He restrained his amusement, as it seemed, with difficulty. "But now, Oliver Raynes, I must ask you to put these clothes on again. I am arresting you on the charge of murdering Archibald Burton and must warn you that anything you say may be used in evidence. So come along, Oliver. Or should I say Olivia?"

THE YEARBOOK OF THE MYSTERY and SUSPENSE STORY

THE YEAR'S BEST
MYSTERY and SUSPENSE NOVELS

Linda Barnes, *A Trouble of Fools* (St. Martin's)
William Bayer, *Pattern Crimes* (Villard)
Simon Brett, *A Nice Class of Corpse* (Scribner's)
Mary Higgins Clark, *Weep No More, My Lady* (Simon and
    Schuster)
Michael Collins, *Minnesota Strip* (Donald I. Fine)
Bill Crider, *Shotgun Saturday Night* (Walker)
Dorothy Salisbury Davis, *The Habit of Fear* (Scribner's)
James Ellroy, *The Black Dahlia* (Mysterious Press)
Jonathan Gash, *Moonspender* (St. Martin's)
Sue Grafton, *"D" Is For Deadbeat* (Henry Holt)
Joyce Harrington, *Dreemz of the Night* (St. Martin's)
Tony Hillerman, *Skinwalkers* (Harper & Row)
Michael J. Katz, *Murder Off the Glass* (Walker)
Stephen King, *Misery* (Viking)
Elmore Leonard, *Bandits* (Arbor House)
Ed McBain, *Tricks* (Arbor House)
Brian Moore, *The Color of Blood* (Dutton)
Shizuko Natsuki, *The Third Lady* (Ballantine)
Francis M. Nevins Jr., *The Ninety Million Dollar Mouse*
    (Walker)
Steve Sohmer, *Favorite Son* (Bantam)
Ross Thomas, *Out on the Rim* (Mysterious Press)
Scott Turow, *Presumed Innocent* (Farrar, Straus & Giroux)
Barbara Vine, *A Fatal Inversion* (Bantam)
Charles Willeford, *Sideswipe* (St. Martin's)

BIBLIOGRAPHY

I. Collections

1. Bellem, Robert Leslie. *Spicy Detective Encores #1.* Framingham, MA 01701 (P.O. Box 921): Winds of the World Press. Three Dan Turner stories from a 1930s pulp magazine. (1986)

2. ———. *Spicy Detective Encores #5.* Framingham, MA 01701 (P.O. Box 921): Winds of the World Press. Three more Dan Turner stories from a 1930s pulp magazine. See also item 6 below.

3. Bloch, Robert. *Midnight Pleasures.* Garden City, NY: Doubleday. Fourteen stories of crime, fantasy, and horror, mainly from the past decade.

4. Brown, Fredric. *Brother Monster.* Miami Beach, FL: Dennis McMillan Publications. Part of an unfinished science fiction novel plus five mysteries from the pulps. Introduction by Brown's former agent, Harry Altshuler.

5. ———. *Sex Life on the Planet Mars.* Miami Beach, FL 33141 (1995 Calais Dr. #3): Dennis McMillan Publications. Five mysteries from the pulps plus a previously unpublished fantasy and two chapters from an unfinished nonfiction book about science fiction. Introduction by Charles Willeford.

6. Case, Justin. *Spicy Detective Encores #2.* Framingham, MA 01701 (P.O. Box 921): Winds of the World Press. Three "Eel" stories from a 1930s pulp magazine. "Justin Case" was a pseudonym of Robert Leslie Bellem.

7. Chesterton, G. K. *The Annotated Innocence of Father Brown.* New York: Oxford University Press. A new edition of the first Father Brown collection (1911), with introduction, extensive annotations, and bibliography by Martin Gardner.

8. ———. *The Best of Father Brown.* London: Dent. Sixteen stories chosen and introduced by H. R. F. Keating.

9. ———*Thirteen Detectives.* New York: Dodd Mead. Nine stories from prior Chesterton collections plus two stories collected for the first time—one about Father Brown.

10. Davis, Norbert. *The Adventures of Max Latin.* New York: Mysterious Press. Five novelettes from *Dime Detective,* 1941–1943. Introduction by John D. MacDonald.

11. de la Torre, Lillian. *The Exploits of Dr. Sam: Johnson, Detector.* New York: International Polygonics. Seven stories and novelettes from *EQMM,* in the fourth collection of Dr. Sam: Johnson's cases.

12. Dent, Lester. *The Sinister Ray.* Brooklyn, NY 11228 (P.O. Box 209): Gryphon Books. Three pulp stories about Lynn Lash, scientific sleuth.

13. Doyle, Sir Arthur Conan. *The Baker Street Dozen.* New York: Congdon & Weed. Thirteen Sherlock Holmes stories, including the author's personal favorites, each with an essay by a prominent Sherlockian. Edited by P. J. Doyle and E. W. McDiarmid.

14. Fraser, Antonia. *Jemima Shore's First Case and Other Stories.* New York: Norton. Five stories about investigative reporter Jemima Shore plus eight other crime and fantasy tales, some published for the first time in America.

15. Garron, Robert A. *Spicy Detective Encores #3.* Framingham, MA 01701 (P.O. Box 921): Winds of the World Press. Three stories from a 1930s pulp magazine.

16. Hensley, Joe L. *Robak's Firm.* Garden City, NY: Doubleday. Fifteen stories, eight new, including four about Hensley's series sleuth, lawyer Dan Robak.

17. Hill, Reginald. *There Are No Ghosts in the Soviet Union and Other Stories.* London: Collins. Six stories and novelettes including one about detectives Dalziel and Pascoe.

18. MacLeod, Charlotte. *Grab Bag.* New York: Avon. Seventeen stories, five new, 1963–1987.

19. Moran, Cary. *Spicy Detective Encores #6.* Framingham, MA 01701 (P.O. Box 921): Winds of the World Press. Three Jarnegan stories from a 1930s pulp magazine.

20. Mortimer, John. *Rumpole's Last Case.* Harmondsworth, England: Penguin Books. Seven stories and novelettes about

the British barrister. Also included in *The Second Rumpole Omnibus* (Viking).

21. Pirkis, Catherine Louisa. *The Experiences of Loveday Brooke, Lady Detective.* New York: Dover Publications. First U.S. edition of an 1894 collection of seven stories, with a new introduction by Michele Slung. (1986)

22. Price, E. Hoffman. *Spicy Detective Encores #4.* Framingham, MA 01701 (P.O. Box 921): Winds of the World Press. Three Cliff Cragin stories from a 1930s pulp magazine.

23. Ritchie, Jack. *The Adventures of Henry Turnbuckle.* Carbondale, IL: Southern Illinois University Press. Twenty-nine humorous detective stories, 1971–1984. Edited by Francis M. Nevins Jr. & Martin H. Greenberg, with an introduction by Nevins.

24. Sanders, Lawrence. *The Timothy Files.* New York: Putnam. Three novelettes about Wall Street sleuth Timothy Cone.

25. Shannon, Dell. *Murder by the Tale.* New York: Morrow. Eight new stories about Lt. Luis Mendoza plus seven non-series stories, some fantasy.

26. Skvorecky, Josef. *The Mournful Demeanour of Lieutenant Boruvka.* New York: Norton. Twelve stories set in Czechoslovakia and Italy, one from *EQMM.* First published in Britain in 1973.

27. van de Wetering, Janwillem. *The Sergeant's Cat and Other Stories.* New York: Pantheon. Fourteen stories, eight about Amsterdam sleuths Grijpstra and de Gier.

II. Anthologies

1. Adler, Bill, concept by. *Murder in Los Angeles.* New York: Morrow. Eight new stories by California mystery writers. Introduction by Thomas Chastain.

2. Apostolou, John L. & Martin H. Greenberg, eds. *Murder in Japan: Japanese Stories of Crime and Detection.* New York: Dembner. Fourteen stories by Japanese writers, four from *EQMM.*

3. Asimov, Isaac, Martin H. Greenberg & Carol-Lynn Rössel

Waugh, eds. *Hound Dunnit.* New York: Carroll & Graf. Seventeen mysteries concerning dogs.

4. Breen, Jon L. & John Ball, eds. *Murder California Style.* New York: St. Martin's. Twenty-one stories, seven new, by members of the Southern California chapter of Mystery Writers of America.

5. Bruccoli, Matthew J. & Richard Layman, eds. *A Matter of Crime, Vol. 1.* San Diego: Harcourt Brace Jovanovich. First of a new anthology series, containing twelve original stories, a novel excerpt, and an interview with James Ellroy.

6. ———. *A Matter of Crime, Vol. 2.* San Diego: Harcourt Brace Jovanovich. Thirteen new stories, a novel excerpt, and interviews with Joe Gores and Linda Barnes.

7. ———. *The New Black Mask, No. 8.* San Diego: Harcourt Brace Jovanovich. Final volume in an anthology series, containing thirteen new stories and a brief interview with John D. MacDonald.

8. Carr, John Dickson, et al. *Crime on the Coast & No Flowers By Request.* New York: Berkley. First U.S. edition of two round-robin novelettes by eleven mystery writers, serialized in England in 1953–54 and collected in a British edition in 1984.

9. Clark, Mary Higgins, ed. *Murder on the Aisle.* New York: Simon & Schuster. Fifteen stories involving theatrical or sporting events, in the annual anthology from MWA.

10. Gorman, Edward, ed. *The Black Lizard Anthology of Crime Fiction.* Berkeley, CA: Black Lizard/Creative Arts. Twenty hardboiled stories, seven new, in the first of an annual series. Includes Clark Howard's 1980 Edgar winner.

11. ———. *Mystery Scene Reader.* Cedar Rapids, IA: Fedora. Five stories, three new, plus 27 brief tributes to the late John D. MacDonald, seven interviews with authors, and a memoir by a former pulp writer.

12. Greenberg, Martin H. & Edward D. Hoch, eds. *Great British Detectives.* Chicago: Academy Chicago. Four novelettes by Charteris, Chesterton, Sayers, and Michael Gilbert, in the fourth volume of the Academy Mystery Novellas series.

13. ———. *Women Write Murder.* Chicago: Academy Chicago. Four novelettes by McCloy, Rendell, Eberhart, and Craig

Rice, in the fifth volume of the Academy Mystery Novellas series.

14. Greenberg, Martin H. & Carol-Lynn Rössel Waugh, eds. *The New Adventures of Sherlock Holmes.* New York: Carroll & Graf. Fourteen new stories plus reprints of a brief drama and essay.

15. Greene, Douglas G. & Robert C. S. Adey, eds. *Death Locked In.* New York: International Polygonics. Twenty-three stories of locked rooms and impossible crimes, from pre-Poe to the present.

16. Haining, Peter, ed. *Supernatural Sleuths.* London: William Kimber. Twelve stories of occult investigators, 1866–1963, mainly fantasy. (1986)

17. Hale, Hilary, ed. *Winter's Crimes 19.* London: Macmillan. Ten new stories in an annual anthology series.

18. Harris, Herbert, ed. *John Creasey's Crime Collection 1987.* London: Gollancz. Sixteen stories, four new, in the annual anthology from the Crime Writers Association. (U.S. edition: St. Martin's.)

19. Hoch, Edward D., ed. *The Year's Best Mystery and Suspense Stories 1987.* New York: Walker. Thirteen of the best stories published during 1986.

20. Jones, Richard Glen, ed. *Unsolved! Classic True Murder Cases.* New York: Peter Bedrick. Nine accounts of true crimes written by well-known authors.

21. Jordan, Cathleen, ed. *Alfred Hitchcock's A Brief Darkness.* New York: Davis. Twenty-eight stories from *AHMM,* 1962–1979.

22. ———. *Alfred Hitchcock's The Shadow of Silence.* New York: Davis. Twenty-eight stories from *AHMM,* 1965–1968.

23. Kahn, Joan, ed. *Ready or Not.* New York: Greenwillow/Morrow. Fourteen stories for young adults, some fantasy.

24. Layman, Richard & Matthew J. Bruccoli, eds. *Crime Wave.* London: Robinson. Fourteen stories and two interviews, published in the U.S. as issues #5 and #6 of *The New Black Mask.*

25. Manguel, Alberto, ed. *Dark Arrows.* New York: Clarkson N. Potter. Eighteen stories of revenge, including Frederick Forsyth's 1982 Edgar winner.

26. McSherry, Frank D., Jr., Charles G. Waugh & Martin H. Greenberg, eds. *Sunshine Crime.* Nashville: Rutledge Hill Press. Thirteen stories set in the thirteen southern and border states.

27. Pronzini, Bill, Carol-Lynn Rössel Waugh & Martin H. Greenberg, eds. *Manhattan Mysteries.* New York: Avenel. Twenty-four stories plus Donald E. Westlake's Edgar-winning novel *God Save the Mark.*

28. Pronzini, Bill & Martin H. Greenberg, eds. *Prime Suspects.* New York: Ivy/Ballantine. Thirteen stories, one new, in the first volume of an anthology series. See also #29 below.

29. ———. *Suspicious Characters.* New York: Ivy/Ballantine. Thirteen stories in the second volume of an anthology series.

30. ———. *Uncollected Crimes.* New York: Walker. Fourteen stories not previously anthologized.

31. Queen, Ellery, ed. *Ellery Queen's Six of the Best.* London: Hale. Six novelettes from *EQMM,* chosen by the London publisher.

32. ———. *Masters of Mystery.* New York: Galahad. Fifty-six stories from prior Queen anthologies.

33. Roberts, Garyn G., ed. *A Cent a Story! The Best From Ten Detective Aces.* Bowling Green, OH: Bowling Green State U. Popular Press. Ten stories and novelettes from an early pulp magazine, 1933–1936. (1986)

34. Sellers, Peter, ed. *Cold Blood: Murder in Canada.* Oakville, Ontario: Mosaic Press. Thirteen stories, six new, by Canadian writers or with Canadian settings. Introduction by Edward D. Hoch.

35. Sullivan, Eleanor, ed. *Ellery Queen's Bad Scenes.* New York: Davis. Twenty-five stories, mainly from *EQMM.*

36. ———. *Prime Crimes 5.* New York: Davis. Twenty-eight stories, all but one new, in the final volume of an anthology series.

37. (Taylor, Imogen, ed.) *Ladykillers: Crime Stories by Women.* London: Dent. Thirteen stories, two previously unpublished. (No editor credited but British library catalogue data indicates editor is Imogen Taylor.)

38. Waugh, Carol-Lynn Rössel, Martin H. Greenberg & Frank D.

McSherry, eds. *Murder and Mystery in Boston.* New York: Dembner. Thirteen stories from various sources.

III. Nonfiction

1. Bargainnier, Earl F. & George N. Dove, eds. *Cops and Constables: American and British Fictional Policemen.* Bowling Green, OH: Bowling Green State U. Popular Press. Thirteen essays about U.S. and British mystery writers and their series detectives. (1986)
2. Browne, Ray B. *Heroes and Humanities: Detective Fiction and Culture.* Bowling Green, OH: Bowling Green State U. Popular Press. Fifteen essays on U.S., British, Australian, and Canadian mystery writers. (1986)
3. Ffinch, Michael. *G. K. Chesterton.* New York: Harper & Row. A biography of Father Brown's creator, with more emphasis on his life than on his writings.
4. Granovetter, Pamela & Karen Thomas McCallum. *The Copperfield Checklist of Mystery Authors.* New York: Copperfield Press. A checklist of the complete works of one hundred crime and mystery writers.
5. Haining, Peter. *James Bond: A Celebration.* London: W. B. Allen. Thirty-five years of James Bond, in books and on screen.
6. Hamilton, Cynthia S. *Western and Hard-Boiled Detective Fiction In America.* London: Macmillan. A study of the two forms and the links between them.
7. Keating, H. R. F. *Crime & Mystery: The 100 Best Books.* New York: Carroll & Graf. Brief essays on the author's choices, from Poe to P. D. James.
8. Lellenberg, Jon L., ed. *The Quest for Sir Arthur Conan Doyle.* Carbondale, IL: Southern Illinois U. Press. Essays by thirteen Conan Doyle scholars.
9. Masters, Anthony. *Literary Agents: The Novelist as Spy.* Oxford & New York: Basil Blackwell. Essays on twelve spy novelists, mainly British, who began their careers in intelligence work. Introduction by Len Deighton.
10. Milward-Oliver, Edward. *The Len Deighton Companion.*

London: Grafton Books. An alphabetical list of characters and themes from all of Deighton's fiction and nonfiction, with an interview and a complete bibliography through 1987.

11. Monaghan, David. *Smiley's Circus.* London: Orbis. A guide to John le Carré's seven novels about George Smiley, including a Who's Who of characters and places mentioned in the books. (1986)

12. Nieminski, John. *John Nieminski: Somewhere a Roscoe.* Madison, IN: Brownstone Books. A chapbook of thirteen essays by the late Chicago writer, well known in mystery fan circles. Selected and edited by Ely Liebow and Art Scott.

13. Panek, LeRoy Lad. *An Introduction to the Detective Story.* Bowling Green, OH: Bowling Green State U. Popular Press. A history of the genre, from pre-Poe days to the present, with emphasis on the nineteenth century.

14. Pike, B. A. *Campion's Career: A Study of the Novels of Margery Allingham.* Bowling Green, OH: Bowling Green State U. Popular Press. First serialized in *the Armchair Detective.*

15. Pronzini, Bill. *Son of Gun in Cheek.* New York: Mysterious Press. A companion volume to *Gun in Cheek,* continuing the author's study of neglected classics of substandard mystery writing.

16. Sampson, Robert. *Yesterday's Faces, Volume 3: From the Dark Side.* Bowling Green, OH: Bowling Green State U. Popular Press. A study of series villains in early pulp magazines.

17. Skinner, Robert E. *The New Hard-Boiled Dicks: A Personal Checklist.* Madison, IN: Brownstone Books. A sixty-page chapbook briefly examining the work of twelve modern hard-boiled writers.

18. Stewart, J. I. M. *Myself and Michael Innes.* London: Gollancz. An autobiography, with comments on his detective fiction.

19. Symons, Julian. *Conan Doyle.* New York: Mysterious Press. First U.S. edition of a brief illustrated biography published in Britain in 1979.

20. Ward, Elizabeth & Alain Silver. *Raymond Chandler's Los Angeles.* Woodstock, NY: Overlook Press. Photos of Los Angeles accompanied by pertinent quotes from Chandler's novels and stories.
21. Wolfe, Peter. *Corridors of Deceit: The World of John le Carré.* Bowling Green, OH: Bowling Green State U. Popular Press. A study of le Carré's novels up to 1985.

AWARDS

Mystery Writers of America

Best novel: Aaron Elkins, *Old Bones* (Mysterious Press)

Best first novel: Deidre S. Laiken, *Death Among Strangers* (Macmillan)

Best paperback original: Sharyn McCrumb, *Bimbos of the Death Sun* (TSR)

Best short story: Harlan Ellison, "Soft Monkey" (*Black Lizard Anthology of Crime Fiction*)

Best fact crime: Richard Hammer, *CBS Murders* (Morrow)

Best critical/biographical work: LeRoy Lad Panek, *An Introduction to the Detective Story* (Bowling Green)

Best juvenile novel: Susan Shreve, *Lucy Forever and Miss Rosetree, Shrinks* (Holt)

Best motion picture: *Stakeout,* written by Jim Kouf (Touchstone)

Best telefeature: *Nutcracker: Money, Murder and Madness,* written by William Hanley (NBC-TV)

Best episode in a television series: "The Musgrave Ritual" (*The Return of Sherlock Holmes*), written by Jeremy Paul

Grandmaster: Phyllis A. Whitney

Ellery Queen Award: Ruth Cavin

Robert L. Fish Memorial Award: Eric M. Heideman, "Roger, Mr. Whilkie" (*AHMM*)

Crime Writers Association (London)

Gold Dagger: Barbara Vine, *A Fatal Inversion* (Viking; U.S. edition: Bantam)

Silver Dagger: Scott Turow, *Presumed Innocent* (Bloomsbury; U.S. edition: Farrar, Straus & Giroux)

John Creasey Award: Denis Kilcommons, *Dark Apostle* (Bantam)

Nonfiction Award: Bernard Taylor & Stephen Knight, *Perfect Murder* (Grafton)

Private Eye Writers of America (for 1986)

Best hardcover novel: Jeremiah Healy, *The Staked Goat* (Harper & Row)

Best paperback novel: Rob Kantner, *The Back-Door Man* (Bantam)
Best short story: Rob Kantner, "Fly Away Home" *(Mean Streets)*
Best first novel: J. W. Rider, *Jersey Tomatoes* (Arbor House)
Life Achievement Award: Bill Pronzini

The Anthony Awards (Bouchercon XVIII, for 1986)

Best novel: Sue Grafton, *"C" Is For Corpse* (Holt)
Best paperback original: Robert Campbell, *The Junkyard Dog* (NAL)
Best first novel: Bill Crider, *Too Late To Die* (Walker)
Best short story: Sue Grafton, "The Parker Shotgun" *(Mean Streets)*

The Macavity Awards (Mystery Readers of America, for 1986)

Best novel: P. D. James, *A Taste For Death* (Knopf)
Best first novel (tie): Kaye Kellerman, *The Ritual Bath* (Arbor House); Marilyn Wallace, *A Case of Loyalties* (St. Martin's)
Best short story: Sue Grafton, "The Parker Shotgun" *(Mean Streets)*
Best nonfiction: Bill Pronzini & Marcia Muller, *1001 Midnights* (Arbor House)
Best motion picture screenplay: *The Name of the Rose*
Best telefeature (series episode): "The Final Problem" *(The Adventures of Sherlock Holmes)*
Best telefeature (TV motion picture): *When the Bough Breaks*

Ellery Queen's Mystery Magazine Readers Award

Robert Barnard, "The Woman in the Wardrobe"

NECROLOGY

1. Georges Arnaud (1917–1987). Pseudonym of Henri Georges Girard, French author of three novels of suspense and borderline crime, notably *The Wages of Fear* (1952).
2. Peggy Bacon (1895–1987). Artist and illustrator who published one mystery novel, *The Inward Eye* (1952).
3. Franklin Bandy (1914–1987). Author of paperback mysteries, notably his Edgar-winning *Deceit and Deadly Lies* (1978). Also published three hardcover mysteries as "Eugene Franklin." Served as executive vice president of Mystery Writers of America.
4. Earl F. Bargainnier (?–1987). Professor of English and president of the Popular Culture Association. Authored a study of Agatha Christie, *The Gentle Art of Murder* (1980), and edited *Ten Women of Mystery* (1981), *Twelve Englishmen of Mystery* (1984), and *Cops and Constables* (1986), the latter with George Dove.
5. Josephine Bell (1897–1987). Pen name of the British author Dr. Doris Bell Collier Ball. Published some 65 novels, more than 45 of which were mysteries, notably *Death at Half-Term* (1939).
6. Alfred Bester (1913–1987). Well-known science fiction author of near-future murder novels, notably *The Demolished Man* (1953).
7. Stuart Buchan (1942–1987). Author of short stories and novels including one mystery, *Fleeced* (1975).
8. William Vivian Butler (1927–1987). British author of juvenile books who continued the mystery novels about George Gideon and the Toff following the death of their creator, John Creasey.
9. Terry Carr (1937–1987). Well-known science fiction author and anthologist who published a single mystery short story in the July 1965 issue of *The Saint Magazine*.
10. Vera Caspary (1904–1987). Mystery novelist and screenwriter, best known for the first of her fifteen suspense

novels, *Laura* (1943), from which the classic film was made.

11. Hilda Cushing (?–1987). Short story writer, contributor to *AHMM, Manhunt, Mike Shayne,* etc.

12. Glyn Daniel (1914–1986). British author of *The Cambridge Murders* (1945, originally as by "Dilwyn Rees") and *Welcome Death* (1954).

13. Carolyn Byrd Dawson (1905–1987). Author of two mystery novels, *The Lady Wept Alone* (1940) and *Remind Me to Forget* (1942).

14. Hugh Greene (1910–1987). British broadcasting executive who edited four popular anthologies of Victorian mysteries starting with *The Rivals of Sherlock Holmes* (1970), as well as co-editing two other anthologies, *The Spy's Bedside Book* (1957) and *Victorian Villainies* (1984), with his brother Graham Greene.

15. Sara Henderson Hay (1907?–1987). Award-winning poet who authored a single mystery short story in the November 1954 issue of *EQMM*.

16. Timothy Holme (1928?–1987). British author of novels about Inspector Peroni, starting with *The Neopolitan Streak* (1980).

17. Bernhardt J. Hurwood (1926–1987). Author of paperback novels and nonfiction, active in Mystery Writers of America.

18. Richard Levinson (1934–1987). Author of numerous TV plays and series, plus some early short stories, all in collaboration with William Link, which won them four Edgar awards for television writing.

19. Audrey Erskine Lindrop (1920–1986). British author of numerous novels and screenplays including *I Start Counting* (1966) and nine others in the suspense field.

20. Paul H. Little (1915–1987). Author of some 700 paperback novels under a variety of pseudonyms including "Paula Minton," "Hugo Paul," "A. de Granamour," "Marie de Journlet," "Leigh Franklin James," "Kenneth Harding," and "Sylvia Sharon." More than a dozen were crime-suspense.

21. Alistair MacLean (1923–1987). Best-selling British author of nearly thirty mystery-adventure novels, notably *The*

Guns of Navarone (1957). Published some early novels as "Ian Stuart."

22. George Markstein (1929–1986). British author of seven suspense novels starting with *The Cooler* (1974).

23. Richard Sapir (1936–1987). Co-author, with Warren Murphy, of 68 paperback novels in the Destroyer series. Also published a few suspense novels under his name alone.

24. Ione Sandberg Shriber (1911–1987). Author of eleven mystery novels, 1940–53, including *A Body For Bill* (1942).

25. Hugh Wheeler (1912–1987). Author of 33 mystery novels, 1935–65, under the pseudonyms of "Patrick Quentin," "Q. Patrick," and "Jonathan Stagge," many in collaboration with Richard Wilson Webb and others, notably *A Puzzle For Fools* (1936) under the Quentin name. Later became an award-winning playwright, author of *Sweeney Todd* (1979) and other Broadway hits. Winner of special short story Edgar, 1962.

26. Emlyn Williams (1905–1987). British actor who authored a fact crime book and three suspense dramas, notably *Night Must Fall* (1935).

HONOR ROLL

Abbreviations:
AHMM—*Alfred Hitchcock's Mystery Magazine*
EQMM—*Ellery Queen's Mystery Magazine*
MOC—*A Matter of Crime*
NBM—*The New Black Mask*
(Starred stories are included in this volume. All dates are 1987.)

Adcock, Thomas, "Cracker Jack," *EQMM,* June
Allyn, Doug, "Death of a Poet," *AHMM,* April
———, "Supersport," *AHMM,* Mid-December
Amlaw, Mary, "A Face to Remember, *AHMM,* November
*Asimov, Isaac, "The Stamp," *EQMM,* June
Bankier, William, "Wimbledon Fortnight," *EQMM,* July
Barnard, Robert, "Breakfast Television," *EQMM,* January
———, "Perfect Honeymoon," *EQMM,* August
*———, "The Woman in the Wardrobe," *EQMM,* December
*Baxt, George, "Stroke of Genius," *EQMM,* June
Bayer, Ann, "A Pleasure to Deal With," *EQMM,* November
———, "Two Heads Are Better Than One," *EQMM,* Mid-December
Bendel, John, "Garden Apartment," *EQMM,* September
Collins, Lorraine, "Song of the Open Road," *AHMM,* July
———, "The Hand of God," *EQMM,* November
Collins, Max Allan, "Scrap," *The Black Lizard Anthology of Crime Fiction*
Cross, Amanda, "Once Upon a Time," *EQMM,* August
Davidson, Ray, "Mercy Killing," *AHMM,* October
DeWeese, Gene, "The Joke," *Woman's World,* September 22
Dhami, Narinder, "What Maisie Saw," *Prime Crimes 5*
Dirckx, John H., "When Auntie Dies," *AHMM,* August
DuBois, Brendan, "A Ticket Out," *EQMM,* January
———, "What Friends Do," *AHMM,* April
———, "Still Waters," *EQMM,* September
———, "A Quick Learner," *EQMM,* October
*———, "Final Marks, Final Secrets," *AHMM,* November

*Ellison, Harlan, "Soft Monkey," *The Black Lizard Anthology of Crime Fiction*

Ellroy, James, "Dial Axminster 6-400," *NBM #8*

Estleman, Loren D., "Blackmailers Shoot Second," *MOC #1*

Fidler, Su, "The Ransom of Harry Elbow's Hand," *AHMM,* Mid-December

Fox, George, "Return to Venice," *Murder in Los Angeles*

*Garfield, Brian, "King's X," *Murder California Style*

Gates, David, "China Blue," *MOC #1*

Gilbert, Michael, "Holy Writ," *EQMM,* September

*Gosling, Paula, "Mr. Felix," *EQMM,* July

Graviros, Ruth, "Lies," *EQMM,* September

Hamilton, Nan, "Made For Each Other," *Murder California Style*

Hansen, Joseph, "Death of an Otter," *AHMM,* October

————, "The Olcott Nostrum," *AHMM,* December

*Harrington, Joyce, "The Au Pair Girl," *MOC #1*

*Heideman, Eric M., "Roger, Mr. Whilkie!" *AHMM,* July

Highsmith, Patricia, "Under a Dark Angel's Eye," *EQMM,* February

*Hill, Reginald, "Exit Line," *John Creasey's Crime Collection 1987*

Hills, Rick, "The Quicktrip Church & Grill," *AHMM,* October

Hoch, Edward D., "The Spy and the Short-Order Cipher," *EQMM,* June

*————, "Leopold and the Broken Bride," *EQMM,* July

————, "The Murder in Room 1010," *EQMM,* November

————, "The Problem of the Snowbound Cabin," *EQMM,* December

————, "The Return of the Speckled Band," *New Adventures of Sherlock Holmes*

Keating, H. R. F., "Nil by Mouth, Inspector Ghote," *EQMM,* May

*MacDonald, John D., "Bimini Kill," *The Yacht,* April

————, "Night Ride," *NBM #8*

Martin, Carl, "Retribution," *Woman's World,* October 6

Miller, Martin J., Jr., "Telex," *NBM #8*

Mulder, Michael, "San Diego Dilemma," *MOC #2*

Nielsen, Helen, "Line of Fire," *EQMM,* September

Pachter, Josh, "Eighty Million Noses," *Hardboiled,* Spring

Potts, Jean, "Two on the Isle," *EQMM,* January

Powell, James, "The Tulip Juggernaut," *EQMM,* September
*Pronzini, Bill, "Stacked Deck," *NBM #8*
Romun, Isak, "The Oracle of the Flag," *AHMM,* December
Russell, Ray, "Ding-Dong, the Lizard's Dead," *Murder in Los Angeles*
Schenk, Emmy Lou, "Ice Cave," *AHMM,* August
Sellers, Peter, "Dickerson's Gamble," *Cold Blood*
Slesar, Henry, "Mama's Secret," *Woman's World,* April 14
————, "Harley's Destiny," *EQMM,* November
Smith, William F., "An Almost Perfect Crime," *AHMM,* April
Suter, John F., "That Man's Moccasins Have Holes," *EQMM,* July
Swoboda, Nancy C., "Following His Footsteps," *AHMM,* August
*Symons, Julian, "Has Anybody Here Seen Me?" *EQMM,* September
Turnbull, Peter, "The Surgeon's Daughter," *EQMM,* July
Vachss, Andrew, "It's a Hard World," *MOC #1*
Woodward, Ann F., "The Journey of the Second Man," *AHMM,* May
————, "The Theft of the Fire Pearl," *AHMM,* September
————, "Liftwing's Young Wife," *AHMM,* December

If you have enjoyed this book and would like to receive details of other Walker mystery titles, please write to:

Mystery Editor
Walker and Company
720 Fifth Avenue
New York, NY 10019